Fort Dead

An Undead Ultra Novel

Contents

Prologue: Salesman 1

1 Vilomah 9

2 New Currency 20

3 Trade 28

4 Barbed Wire 37

5 Beachview 45

6 Balance Beam of Death 55

7 Recording 61

8 Sand 69

9 Shelter 74

10 Pink House 80

11 New Regime 88

12 Assholes Live Forever 94

13 Broken Glass 100

14 Smoke 103

15 Precipice 115

16 Tennis Racket 121

17 Truck 124

18 Why 132

19 Rest 136

20 Sprint 141

21 Nails 147

22 Raining Zombies 150

23 Wet Run..155

24 Phone Home...163

25 Zombie Train..168

26 Duct Tape...175

27 Recon..176

28 Red Flower...180

29 Reunion...187

30 Closer..194

31 Prisoners...199

32 Wild Thing..207

33 Endure...214

34 Hallucinations..217

35 Serve..222

36 Assault...227

37 RV..232

38 End...238

39 Angel...240

40 Hope..244

41 The Real Dead..252

42 Strong..255

43 Goodbye, Hello..263

44 Neighbors...268

Epilogue: Right Here, Right Now............................277

Acknowledgments

Prologue
Salesman

SHAUN

Shaun has exactly two goals to accomplish in the next thirty minutes.

The first goal is to save his ex-wife.

He turns to Alvarez, his best friend of the apocalypse. "I know this Kate woman is your friend. I know she'd be here if she could. But she's not. You have to let her go, Alvarez. We have to win this battle on our own."

"I know that." Alvarez throws his shoulder against a wooden pallet stacked with canned food. Sweat glistens on his temples from the exertion. "Give me a hand, will you?"

Shaun joins his friend on the far side of the pallet. The other man is younger by at least a decade. His dark hair is greasy and badly in need of a cut, the ends curling around his ears and along the nape of his neck. Stubble shadows his face, almost as dark as the crescents of fatigue under his eyes.

"On the count of three," Alvarez says. "One, two, three—"

They throw their combined strength at the pallet. It gives way, scraping against the hard-packed earth. A small trap door in the ground is revealed.

"It's not forty-eight to seven," Shaun says.

Alvarez's mouth tightens, but all he says is, "Grab that

1

empty box." He gestures to a weathered cardboard box sitting on top of a stack of canned food they brought in last week.

Shaun passes him the box while Alvarez opens the trap door. Inside is the secret stash of booze he's collected over the last six months. Shaun is one of the few who knows about this hiding place.

Alvarez transfers the bottles from the hidey-hole to the box. Shaun tries to make sense of this act. Surely he doesn't think he can trade a box of booze for Jessica and the other hostages? Rosario wants Fort Ross. She won't settle for a box of liquor.

"It's not forty-eight to seven," Shaun says again. "It's not a simple calculation. We're talking about lives."

His ex-wife's life, to be exact. Jessica's life. Shaun may have broken her spirit, but he's not going to stand by and watch her get executed. Not when he has the power to save her life.

Even if that means manipulating his best friend to do it.

If there's one thing he knows about Alvarez, it's that he cares about every single resident of Fort Ross. Every. Single. One.

This is his greatest strength and his greatest weakness as a leader.

Shaun plans to exploit that weakness. It's a classic, under-handed salesman tactic.

"Twenty-eight minutes," Shaun says. "You have twenty-eight minutes before Rosario executes our people. You don't want the blood of seven people on your hands."

Alvarez says nothing. He sets the box of booze on top of the pallet. Even exhausted and bent under the weight of hard decisions, the younger man is radiant with goodness.

The sight makes Shaun's throat tight with emotion. The two of them had watched one another's back from the start. Their friendship began when Alvarez rescued Shaun and Jessica from a herd of zoms who had them penned inside a station wagon on the side of the road. Shaun, in turn, saved Alvarez on a scavenging run when a zombie crawled out of a doghouse and went for his legs.

"Twenty-seven minutes," Shaun says, hating himself even as he says the words. Jessica would call him out for being an asshole.

Alvarez walks away, leaving the box of booze in plain sight on top of the pallet.

"You're not going to hide these somewhere else?" Shaun asks.

Alvarez doesn't turn around. "I haven't decided yet."

Shaun deduces this has something to do with Rosario. He takes it as a good sign.

He catches up with Alvarez. They weave a brisk path through the compound of Fort Ross. It's a trading outpost built in the early 1800s by Russians.

Alvarez cuts around tents and RVs that fill much of the interior, making his way toward the large double gates on the northern side. The residents of Fort Ross cluster near the gates. They fall back as Alvarez approaches, making room for him. They are tense with anticipation of the unknown.

Alvarez presses an eye to the slit in the wood of the massive wooden gate.

Shaun does the same. His gaze goes straight to Jessica, one of the seven people held prisoner by the squat, rotund woman known as Mr. Rosario.

A burly man with a chest-length beard and beer belly stands behind Jessica, pinning her arms. His ex-wife looks the same as she always does.

Her face is emotionless, but her eyes burn with bright anger. Looking into her eyes sometimes feels like staring into the forge fires of hell. Shaun isn't remotely religious anymore, but if there is a hell on earth, it's in his ex-wife's eyes.

He could say it was the death of their two daughters that broke the once-loving woman with a heart of gold.

Sometimes, if someone asked him about Jessica, that was the lie he spun.

The truth was, the shroud of anger and rage she wore had been in place before zombies took their children. The blame for that lay squarely on his shoulders. He'd never entirely forgiven himself for breaking her heart. In the end, there hadn't been a choice. Not really. That just made it all the worse. He had singlehandedly broken her.

Of all the people who asked about Jessica's silent, pent-up state, it was Alvarez who peppered him with the most questions. He tried to be casual and off-handed about it, but there was something Alvarez didn't know: Shaun had been a top salesman before the world ended. He could read people the way a professional rafter reads a river. And he knew Alvarez had a thing for Jessica.

Alvarez didn't act on it. To start with, there was the age difference. There was also the fact that she was his best friend's ex-wife. But Shaun saw those seeds of admiration plainly in his friend's eyes.

And right now, as the seconds ticked down, he planned to use that little fact to his full advantage. Alvarez didn't know it, but Shaun had donned his salesman hat the minute he realized Jessica had been taken hostage. He was already in a full-court press, using every trick he had in the book.

"There are no scales," Shaun murmurs to Alvarez. "Fort Ross is a community. A family. We don't turn our backs on each other. You are their shepherd, Alvarez. Those seven people out there count on you every bit as much as the forty-eight in here. Don't let them down."

"Twenty-four minutes," someone in the crowd calls out.

Make the customer a hero. It's one of Shaun's favorite sales tactics. Right up there with deploying his *value wedge.*

"Every person in Fort Ross looks up to you." Shaun leans forward to speak in Alvarez's ear, his voice soft and smooth. "There's a reason for that. They know you'll protect them. They count on you to protect them."

Create a space for yes.

This is a crucial step in closing a deal. If you never shut the fuck up, you never give your customer a chance to say *yes* to the deal you're proposing.

It takes all of Shaun's willpower to shut his mouth and wait.

He studies Alvarez's profile. The younger man stares through the slit in the twelve-foot high wooden fence around Fort Ross. The redwood planks are more than four inches thick.

"Twenty-three minutes."

All of Shaun's attention is on Alvarez's profile. His mind works in overtime, prepping counterarguments to every possible argument Alvarez could pose.

When Alvarez continues to stand there in silence, Shaun drops his last card.

"Be their savior, Alvarez. Our people need you." *Jessica needs you.*

Alvarez closes his eyes. Agony etches every line in his face.

For one panicked moment, Shaun thinks he's misread the situation. That he fucked up his one and only chance to save Jessica.

Then Alvarez turns to him. "I don't know the right thing to do," he says softly. "But you're right about one thing. There are no scales. It's not forty-eight to seven. It's fifty-five. The lives of fifty-five people are in my hands. I'm going to do my damnedest to save them all." The fierce determination in his voice nearly makes Shaun sob with relief.

I've got you, Jessie, he thinks. *You're going to live.*

Shaun grabs Alvarez's shoulders in a brief squeeze. "You're doing the right thing."

Alvarez turns to the gathered crowd. "We let them in." His voice is quiet, yet somehow it carries. "We let the enemy in. Tonight, when they eat our food and drink our alcohol, we strike. We'll take them out when they're drunk and bloated on our supplies."

And finally, Shawn understands. The alcohol. The box of booze left in plain sight on top of the pallet of food.

Alvarez has a plan.

"We have twenty minutes," Alvarez says. "Use that time to hide everything that can be used as a weapon. Tools. The cast iron cook ware. Any pieces of wood small enough to be used as a knife. Do *not* hide the obvious weapons. They will expect us to disarm when we open the doors. If they don't see a decent pile of guns and knives, they'll be suspicious. Any questions? No? All right everyone, get to work."

People disperse into the fort, hustling off to follow Alvarez's orders.

"I hope I'm not making a mistake," he says, watching them.

Shaun's heart crumples at the agony in the other man's eyes, but he steels himself for the next phase of his plan.

Time to turn his attention to his second goal. He didn't work his ass off to save Jessica only to lose Alvarez.

He and Alvarez hide three hammers at the bottom of a wood pile. They stash a few screwdrivers under loose floorboards in one of the original fort buildings. They tuck large rocks underneath one of the RVs. All the while, Shaun maps out his next move.

Rosario's shrill voice echoes through a megaphone. "Sixty seconds, assholes."

Alvarez and Shaun rush back to the gate, each of them taking up position on either side of the large redwood beam that holds the doors closed. It takes two of them to heft the giant log out of the wrought iron slots.

The community gathered behind Alvarez shifts, unease running through them.

"Lay down your weapons," Alvarez calls.

In truth, there aren't a lot of weapons to lay down. There's a scattering of firearms among the residents, but with zombies being drawn to sound, collecting them has never been a top priority. Most people are armed with hammers, screwdrivers, and knives. They might have the drug lord's people outnumbered, but she has them outgunned ten to one.

Alvarez draws in a shaky breath, neck and shoulders stiff with tension. He places both palms on the twelve-foot gate, ready to push it open.

Shaun rests a hand on Alvarez's shoulder. He looks into the dark eyes of his friend.

Time to close. Time to wrap up his last deal, the most important pitch of his entire life.

"Let me do it," Shaun says. *Goal number two,* he thinks. If it's one thing he excels at, it's meeting his goals.

Alvarez shakes his head. "Too dangerous."

"Exactly. Our people need you, Alvarez. Don't throw yourself away."

Alvarez purses his lips. He opens his mouth, argument plain in his eyes.

Shaun holds up a palm, silencing him. He plays dirty, going straight for the younger man's heart.

"Let me do this, brother," Shaun says. "For Jessica. Whatever happens, take care of Jessie for me, okay? She needs you more than she knows."

Invoking Jessica—and Alvarez's feelings for her—gives Shaun the opening he needs. Alvarez's mouth falls open, confusion and protest furrowing his brow.

Before he can formulate a response, Shaun shoulders him out of the way. He pushes open the gate, revealing the besiegers who have come to take Fort Ross from them.

He makes damn sure he's the first one to be seen by the enemy.

He makes damn sure he stands in the open gateway like the leader of Fort Ross, hoping to god Rosario and her goons pin a target to his chest and spare Alvarez.

He feels the moment when Rosario's eyes land on him. Her stare pierces through him like a spear.

He's a dead man.
Goals accomplished.

1
Vilomah

JESSICA

The barrel of the gun is warm from contact with my temple. I accept its hard reality and what it means for me.

It's alright, I say silently, willing Alvarez to hear my words. *Let us go. Let us go for Fort Ross.*

I will him to hear me. I will the doors to the fort to remain closed, for the residents inside to be safe from the monsters that have me.

There are six other residents of Fort Ross with me. It's a simple game of numbers. Sacrifice seven souls to keep forty-eight others safe and alive.

Let us go and keep everyone else safe.

How pathetic that life has been reduced to a game of numbers. The thought almost makes me laugh out loud.

I don't mind being a number. Being a number isn't so bad.

It's better than other labels I've worn.

Jilted. Divorcé. Single mom.

Fag hag.

I thought those titles were bad. I thought I'd hit rock bottom when Shaun left me for Richard. I didn't think things could get worse.

I'd been wrong.

Mother of dead children.

Children who lose their parents are called orphans.

Adults who lose a spouse are called widowers.

There is no word for a parent who loses a child. Not a single word in the dictionary. That's how awful it is.

The closest I ever found is the word *vilomah*. It's not officially in the English dictionary, though before the world ended there was a petition to get it added.

Vilomah is a Sanskrit word meaning "against natural order." I can't think of anything more against natural order than a child—*children*—dying before their parents.

That's what I am. A *vilomah*. A grieving parent without children.

I'm ready to die. I'm ready to see Claire and May on the other side. I'm ready to leave this shitty world behind forever. I'm ready to die so my community inside the walls of Fort Ross can live.

I'm ready to die so Shaun can live.

Even after he ripped out my heart and served it to me on a platter with tears and regrets, I still love him. As much as I despise him, I love him. Always both at the same time.

"Time's up, assholes." Rosario's shrill voice grates over my spine. The horrible woman speaks from inside a loose circle of men and women with automatic rifles. What I wouldn't give to reach through them and strangle her.

Zombies, drawn by the noise of Rosario's initial attack, lay dead and scattered around us. The bicycles she and her minions used to get here are lined up in a neat row nearby.

More of her minions are strung across the open ground before the fort. Among them are more guns and ammo than I've ever seen in my entire life.

Half a dozen of Rosario's goons have long poles with wire hoops on the end. Each of these hoops is cinched around a pet zombie. Those leashed zombies scare me more than the guns.

"What's it going to be?" Rosario calls. "Am I going to have to order the execution of these innocent people, or are you going to open your gates?"

I stare straight ahead, gaze unfocused, ready for the bullet. Ready for oblivion. Ready for my reunion with Claire and May, my baby girls who had been stolen from me as surely as Shaun had been.

Then the worst thing imaginable happens.

The gates of Fort Ross squeak.

My eyes snap into focus.

No-no-no!

Slowly, like an unfolding nightmare, they crack open.

And in the center of the opening is Shaun. Not Alvarez, but Shaun.

I still find him beautiful, even after he shredded me. Tall. Shiny blond hair. A natural physique that looks good both in and out of clothes. A Ken doll could not have had a better model.

There was only one thing I ever wanted in life: a family. A husband and children to love and care for.

I thought I'd hit the jackpot when I met Shaun. Gorgeous beyond measure. Charismatic. Kind and funny. A devoted father and thoughtful husband. He made enough money so I could be a stay-at-home mom.

Some women I knew used to scoff at the idea of being a stay-at-home mom. I'd loved every second of it. It made me feel complete.

I had everything I wanted. Two beautiful girls to raise. A husband to love. A happy, bustling household. We'd been talking about having a third child.

Then Richard came along and stole everything.

Even worse, Richard had gotten himself killed trying to defend Claire and May. I hate him and love him for his selflessness. I hate him and love him for making Shaun complete.

Shaun's muscles bunch beneath his shirt as he pushes open the gates to Fort Ross. The morning sun hits him, illuminating his perfect chiseled cheekbones and sharp blue eyes.

My mouth goes dry. *No.*

The gates to Fort Ross are massive twelve-foot structures, each post made of solid redwood back from a time when redwood trees were harvested with abandon. Each post is solid wood, not the cheap pressed wood sold in hardware stores before the world ended. The gates to the fort are double swinging doors, each one weighing several hundred pounds.

Shaun strains against the heavy wood, singlehandedly throwing it open to the enemy.

His feet flex as he pushes against the earth, pressing all his weight against the thick redwood enclosure. His biceps and forearms bunch under the strain. In plain jeans and a T-shirt, he looks as perfect as he did the day I met him at a college frat party.

Close the gate, you stupid idiot! Close the gate!

But Shaun doesn't close the gate. Just like he hadn't closed down his attraction to Richard. He pushes open the gates, forever altering my fate.

"Let them go." His voice, a rich, strong baritone, rings across the distance. "We surrender, Rosario. Let them go."

The power of Shaun's voice booms through the silence. It fills every crevice, extending out to Rosario and her fucking bastards.

"Let them all go," Shaun says. "We surrender." For a brief second, his eyes meet mine.

And in that moment, I know he did this for me.

The only reason those fucking gates are standing open is because he wanted to save me.

Fucking bastard.

I don't know what he said to Alvarez, but I have no doubt he employed his old-world skills to the situation. Shaun is a salesman down to his toenails.

You bastard. I mouth the words. *Shut the fucking gates.*

It's too late.

The gates are open. The residents of Fort Ross are disarmed. Rosario, her goons, and their firepower have been granted access.

It's too late.

Rosario lumbers forward, her gait slow and rolling. The fat woman wears a crinkled cotton tie-dyed dress that's frayed and stained. She has at least three chins—sometimes four, depending on the angle. How this woman manages to embody terror in every sense of the word baffles me, but somehow she does it.

Shaun stands proud and strong in front of the gates. It would be easy to mistake him for the leader of the fort. His stance is fearless and bold. He looks like he's in charge. Hell, with his natural charisma, he probably could have taken over leadership of the fort if he hadn't been solidly behind Alvarez.

Rosario stops in front of Shaun. The fat woman looks him up and down.

"Are you the one in charge?" she asks.

"Let my people go. We surrender." His head turns ever so slightly, looking at me. I know he's trying to convey a message with his eyes.

Fuck if I know what it is. What could he possibly say to me to justify the sacrifice of forty-eight people? The tears that leak out of my eyes make me want to claw off my own face.

"Are you the one in charge?" Rosario asks the question a second time.

"I'm in charge," Shaun says. "Fort Ross is mine. These people are mine."

"Aren't you a pretty one. Too bad." Rosario raises a fat wrist, gesturing to one of her minions. "Jeanie. Come here, please."

A sneering woman steps forward. Her T-shirt reads, *If fat is flavor I'm fucking fantastic.*

In her hands is a long pole with wire on one end. The wire encircles the neck on a zombie. Jeanie guides the thing along like it's a pet dog.

Rosario sweeps her gaze up and down Shaun. "What's your name?"

"Shaun."

"Shaun. That's a nice name. Well, Shaun, this all could have been a lot easier if you'd just opened your gates twenty-four hours ago. Instead you made me wait. In the rain."

Viciousness oozes out of the terrible woman as she looks at Shaun.

Jeanie stops beside her with the leashed zombie. The creature moans, hands scratching at the empty air in front of it.

Shaun stands tall and proud, stoic in the face of the threat.

"Tell me, Shaun." Rosario's voice ripples out from her fat form. "Why the delay? You could have opened the gates hours ago."

"We were hoping you'd change your mind and go back to where you came from." Shaun's voice is unconcerned and mocking. He cocks his head at Rosario, staring her down. "Guess that didn't work out."

"Guess not." Rosario's voice drips with venom. "I would have preferred to sit out the storm *inside* my fort." She flicks her fingers at Jeanie.

The younger woman steps forward, the sneer deepening on her face. Her expression borders on glee.

Two of Rosario's goons descend on Shaun. When they grab his arms and hold him in place, he doesn't fight.

Jeanie advances on him with the leashed zombie.

"Let this be a lesson to you all," Rosario shrills. "Your life can be easy, or it can be hard. The choice is up to you."

The zombie lunges forward. Jeanie leans with the monster, extending its reach.

The creature swipes. Dirty fingers latch onto the front of Shaun's shirt.

Up until this moment, Shaun has been stoic. As the zombie claws at his chest, pulling itself closer, he breaks. He lets up a shout, twisting in an effort to get free. Rosario's minions laugh and hold him in place.

I can only see the profile of the two men restraining Shaun. Gleeful grins split the side of each face like broken half moons.

Shaun groans as the creature sinks its teeth into his clavicle. He doesn't fight. He doesn't try to get away. He remains upright, his captors anchoring him on either side as the zombie tears a bloody chunk of flesh from his shoulder.

Something happens inside me.

I shriek. My cry slices across the horrified silence like a scythe.

It's not the sound of grief or despair or fear. It's the sound of fury.

"You asshole!" I tear free of my captor.

The man, whose attention had been on Shaun and the zombie, stumbles as I rip free. His gun fires behind me as I tear across the open space.

"How could you?" I scream at Shaun. "How could you, you selfish asshole?"

Most of the onlookers likely think I'm screaming at Rosario. But Shaun knows the truth. I see my words hit him like a slap across the face.

I've nearly reached Rosario, a plan to scratch out her eyeballs with my fingernails half formed in my mind. Jeanie steps forward, her pet zombie in hand. Her foot lashes out, delivering a kick to my gut.

I sprawl across the ground, cheek skidding in the dirt.

Jeanie swings the zombie around, holding it over me. "Say the word, boss," she drawls.

I flip over, glaring up at Jeanie and Rosario. Daring them.

Rosario chuckles. "We've got a fighter. I like her, Jeanie."

I turn my glare on Shaun. In less than a second, all the years pass between us—the love, the loss, and everything in between.

Shaun grasps his bleeding shoulder as blood pours

down his chest. "I'm sorry, Jessie." He sways. His captives are the only things keeping him upright.

"You're not supposed to be the one who gets to die," I grit. "It was supposed to be me."

"Life's not fair, honey," Rosario says. "Rufus, Scooby, string him up. Everyone else, let's go."

My captor catches up to me. I don't resist as he twists my arms behind my back.

Shaun is half dragged, half carried into the fort. Rosario follows in her fat, wallowing gait. Her people fan out behind her, their automatic rifles trained on the crowd.

I spot Alvarez near the front of our people. He flicks his hands. His people take their cue, all of them falling back. They cluster in a tight circle, crowding up against the redwood fence that has, until this moment, kept them safe.

Inside the fort are three large buildings that housed the original Russian residents, along with a tiny wooden chapel. In the center of the fort is a large open area of hard-packed dirt and an old well. Surrounding the well are tents and RVs, all homes to various residents of Fort Ross.

Around the well is a scattering of fire pits and laundry lines. The area has become a default gathering center for Fort Ross residents.

Rosario's people tear off the laundry. Clean clothing is ground into the dirt.

The pet zombies are frenzied. They let up long, ululating keens.

Shaun is dragged through the dirt and tied to one of the laundry poles. I have a sick fear that he's going to be burned alive like a Salem would-be witch.

His beautiful face and pale blond hair are stained bright red in places. Blood gushes from the gaping wound on his clavicle. Rosario's people are ruthless as they lash his body in place.

Rosario's rumpled dress drags in the dirt as she crosses the compound and comes to stand before Shaun. She looks him up and down before turning to address the crowd.

"This asshole made me wait outside *my* home for twenty-four fucking hours," she says. "Twenty-four hours and thirteen seconds, to be exact. And for what? Just to be ornery. Just because he *could*." She delivers a stinging slap to Shaun's face. He grunts, chin rolling against his chest. "Your pathetic resistance was for nothing."

As soon as she finishes speaking, a series of thuds ring across the compound. Half a dozen grappling hooks bite into the southern fence of the fort. Seconds later, men and women swarm over the top. They drop another set of rope ladders down the interior side of the wooden wall and descend into the fort. In less than two minutes, another fifteen of Rosario's minions are within our home.

Fifteen assholes we never saw coming.

Rosario had the means and the manpower to take Fort Ross anytime. She only let us *think* we had a choice. This realization takes the breath out of me.

This was all a game. A show of power to put us in our place.

"You see," Rosario drawls, "Fort Ross was pre-ordained to be mine. I let you enjoy the illusion that you could think or fight your way out of your fate. I hope now you see how pointless that would have been. This will be your first and only warning. As for this asshole." Her attention rivets back onto Shaun. "Let him be an example to all of you. Follow orders and you will be kept alive. Cause trouble and I won't hesitate to string you up beside your leader."

Something happens when I take in Shaun's bleeding body tied to the laundry pole. I don't feel grief. I don't feel crippling sadness. These things can't touch me through the ice that has grown around me.

What I feel is a doubling of my outrage. Rage that this man who served my heart up on a platter doesn't have the decency to let me die first.

He's leaving me. Again.

Asshole.

I don't want to rail against the monsters who did this to him. All I want is to pound on the chest of my ex-husband as his life drips out of his body.

A hand comes down on my shoulder. I hadn't even realized I was on my knees in the dirt. I pry my eyes away from Shaun, expecting to find one of the pricks responsible for his death.

The dark eyes of Jorge Alvarez find mine. Shaun, the selfish bastard, had to know what this would cost him. The pain it would cause him. Shaun is one of Alvarez's few confidants and close friends. On top of that, Alvarez carries the life of every person in Fort Ross on his shoulders. He takes every death personally, even when it's not his fault.

I should share Alvarez's grief. I'm too broken and fucked up inside to feel sadness. Every drop of sadness held in my soul drained out of me when the girls died. I don't think I have the capacity to feel sorrow anymore.

"I'm sorry." The word falls from Alvarez in a broken whisper.

I have no words for this man with a heart of gold. This man who gives all of himself to the caretaking of others. He doesn't want to hear my thoughts. He's too good for them. I can barely stand them.

The new monarch always cleans house.

This was something Shaun used to say. In his corporate world of wine sales, there was an ever-revolving door of upper management. Every time a new executive swept in, Shaun would say, *The new monarch is going to clean house.*

"He *knew.*" My words come out low and guttural, like an animal.

The bastard *knew.* He knew what would happen when he threw open the gates.

Somehow, he'd convinced Alvarez to trade places with him.

I can't imagine what he said to convince Alvarez to let him be the one to do it, but somehow, he'd done it. There was a reason he'd been number one in sales for his wine company four years in a row.

There's a reason he'd buried his sexuality. The man could sell anything. Even a lie to himself.

This thought brings another burst of anger bubbling forth. Part of me wants to claw out Shaun's eyes. Or maybe turn a zombie loose on him and let it finish the job.

My gaze shifts to Alvarez, who is once again staring at Shaun with open grief. The man is a bottomless pit of love. I've never met anyone like him. Sometimes I think that if I could bottle up even an ounce of his good will and optimism, I'd be a new person. A whole person, instead of the broken mess I am now.

Anger rolls through me in a hot wave—anger that Rosario has hurt Alvarez by killing Shaun.

Somehow, someway, I'm going to make every one of these fucking bastards pay for hurting him.

For hurting both of them.

Somehow.

2
New Currency

KATE

"I only have two things to say."

Eric greets me and Ben as we jog down the Lost Coast trail. I read tension in his pursed lips and hunched shoulders.

"What is it?" With Ben at my side, I join Eric and the rest of our companions, Caleb, Ash, Reed, and Susan.

"First of all, I just finished my first ultramarathon. That means I'm officially no longer a fat bastard." The grin on Eric's face is huge. You wouldn't know he'd spent the last several hours slogging through the dark on a cold, muddy trail.

"Second of all, there are people up ahead." Eric jerks a thumb to the south, in the direction of Usal Campground. "Live ones. They haven't seen us yet."

The seven of us cluster behind the low-hanging branches of a large cypress tree. I peer down the trail, searching for a campground I've only seen on a map.

Five hundred yards away, I spot the people. There are several vehicles and perhaps a dozen or so people. It's a mix of adult men and women, no children among them.

"Are they wearing wet suits?" I ask, relying on the sharp vision of my younger companions.

"Some of them," Reed confirms. "The rest are in

hunting gear. I see rifles and fishing poles."

"Who would want to swim out there?" Ash shivers, casting a look of loathing at the ocean.

"Maybe they're spearfishing?" Caleb suggests.

"No." I shake my head. "I bet they're diving for abalone." That was a popular sport in Northern California before the apocalypse.

"Hunting, fishing, and abalone." Ben nods in approval. "That's a good way to live."

Eric attempts to clean the mud from his glasses on the sleeve of his shirt. "What should we do? Wait here until they pack up and leave? Try to go around them?"

Ben snorts. "Ever try to sneak around men with hunting rifles? That's a good way to get mistaken for a deer and get your head blown off."

"We're not sneaking around."

I weigh our options. We could wait them out, find a place to rest until they pack up and leave. The problem with that plan is I have no idea how long they plan to be out here. It could be hours.

Alvarez and Fort Ross don't have hours.

On top of that, these people have vehicles. I don't know exactly how far away Fort Ross is, but I do know the Lost Coast has thoroughly kicked all of our asses. If there's any chance of getting a ride in one of those vehicles, even for a short distance, it's worth a shot.

I swallow, making up my mind. "We introduce our-selves. See if we can get a ride south with them."

Six pairs of eyes turn to me in astonishment.

"Did you just say you want to ride in a car?" Reed demands.

"I think I must have a rock lodged in my ear." Eric makes a show of cleaning out his ears. "The words coming out of our mom's mouth aren't making sense."

I huff in exasperation. "You all know how I feel about vehicles. In general, they aren't safe. But it's deserted out here. We haven't seen a single zombie since we crashed on the Lost Coast."

"If it wasn't safe to drive, those guys would already be dead." Ben gives me a curt nod of agreement. "It's a good plan. I don't know about all you assholes, but my feet are killing me."

"I have blisters under eight toenails," Caleb says.

"The lady with the fucked-up ankle votes for Kate's plan." Susan raises her hand into the air.

I lead the way, moving at a brisk walk down the trail. As we near the campground, I wave my arms to get the attention of the people, hoping to convey friendliness.

There's a flurry of activity as they notice us. They fall into a tight group, several of them raising the rifles in our direction.

My stomach flips.

You'd think seeing other humans would be a cause for celebration. After all, this world is sorely short on humanity right now. But nope, these people go straight to suspicious.

I was guilty of the same thing when Leo and his people arrived at Creekside. It's the new norm.

"Don't." I reach out a hand, resting it on Ben's wrist.

He scowls in response, but releases the hold on his Sig.

"You, too, Caleb. Ash. We're trying to hitchhike, remember? We need to appear friendly."

The two younger soldiers also release their firearms. Neither looks happy about it.

As we draw closer to the campground, a ratty brown dog bursts forth. Tail wagging, tongue lolling from his mouth, he streaks up the trail in our direction. He barrels into our group, attempting to sniff everyone's crotch. I push the wet nose away with a hand, not taking my eyes from the people.

A man breaks away from the group, a rifle gripped between his hands as he approaches. He's small and lithe, no more than five-foot-eight. He has bright eyes and a big mustache.

He halts twenty feet away.

"Brando," he says. "Come here, boy."

The ratty brown dog barks, running to his master. He runs in a circle around the man, then lays down at his feet. One ear cocks in our direction as the dog regards us.

"Hello," I call, doing my best to put on a friendly smile. "My name is Kate. We're not here to make trouble. We're just passing through."

"Hello, Kate." The man sounds pleasant enough, even if he is still pointing a gun at me. "My name is John. You'll have to excuse me if I don't buy your story. We're in the middle of fucking nowhere. No one just *passes through* this place."

My people tense. I take another step forward, trying to keep John's attention on me.

"We're from Arcata. We need to get to the highway and go south."

John snorts. "Lady, you aren't anywhere near Arcata. You should look at a map and get a better story."

I shake my head. "We're from Arcata," I repeat. "We took a boat out of Humboldt Bay, but it sank off the Lost Coast. We're headed to Fort Ross."

John looks me up and down, assessing. Every last one of us is rumpled and dirty. We smell like a locker room that's never been cleaned. Our clothes and skin are encrusted with salt and mud.

"What's at Fort Ross?" John says at last.

"Friends. They need our help. Some people are trying to take the fort from them."

"Let me get this straight," John says. "You say you're from Arcata. Your friends in Fort Ross are under attack, so you get in a boat to sail down the coast to help them. On the way, your boat sinks. Then you hike the Lost Coast and show up here."

"We ran it, actually," Reed says from the back of the group. "We ran the Lost Coast. We got caught in one of the impassable zones and almost died. Then our friend got hypothermia and—"

"*Reed.*"

"Sorry, Mama."

I draw in a long breath and force a smile. "We're just trying to get to Fort Ross. We don't want any trouble and we don't plan to cause any trouble. Like I said, we're just passing through."

John continues to study us. "You the one who got hypothermia?" He gestures to Ash with his chin.

She nods.

"The Lost Coast isn't a place for amateurs," John says. "Every year, it kills experienced backpackers."

"Our mom isn't an amateur." This time, it's Eric who speaks up. "She's an ultrarunner."

"All these kids call you mom?" John asks me.

"Yes."

"That's a lot of fucking kids."

"Sometimes, yes."

"What about you?" This question is directed at Ben.

Ben flicks a questioning glance at me. "I'm her . . ."

"They're boyfriend and girlfriend," Reed supplies. The others snicker.

"She's your girlfriend, huh?" John eyes us.

"Yeah."

My belly wriggles with emotion. Whatever runs between me and Ben is admittedly deeper than the adolescent terms of *boyfriend* and *girlfriend*. But I'm not going to debate the finer points of the English language with a stranger who's pointing a rifle at us.

"Will you let us pass?" I ask.

"I'll do one better," John replies. "I'll give you a ride. Not all the way to Fort Ross. But I can give you a ride to Westport. It's the closest town, about twenty miles from here."

Even though this is the very thing I had hoped to secure, the offer comes too fast and too easily. I don't get a warm fuzzy feeling from John. There's something else at play here. I need to figure out what it is before I put the safety of my people in his hands.

"What's the catch?" I look him straight in the eye, a silent warning not to bullshit me.

A feral smile splits his face. "A trade. You give me something interesting out of your packs and I'll give you a ride to the south side of Westport. You go on your merry way from there."

"Cars aren't safe where we come from," I reply, still testing him.

John meets my eye. "Yeah. They're not safe far outside of Westport, either. We cleared the town, the campground, and the road between here and there. My people come here to hunt and fish. We even bagged a seal last week." John shrugs nonchalantly. "I could take your packs and everything in them. We have you outgunned and out-numbered." At his words, his people take a few menacing steps in our direction. "I'm trying to be civil. I'm a fair man. Trade is the new currency of the apocalypse."

My mind races as I think of all the precious firearms we have in the pack on Caleb's back. We need those supplies. There's no way we can help Alvarez if we don't have weapons.

What do I want to offer them? Bear meat? We all have a fair amount of it in our packs.

"I have something." Reed steps forward.

I frown at him as he unclips his pack. He rummages inside and produces a small plastic jar with a black lid. Even though the sticker on the top is ruined from the salt water, I recognize the yellowish substance inside.

"You brought that?" Eric's jaw sags open. "That's one of the last jars she made."

Reed shrugs. "I thought we might need it."

"You could have shared that around the campfire last night," Eric snaps.

"I forgot about it. I sort of had bear on my mind, you know?"

"What is that?" John asks.

"Homemade cannabis salve." Eric snatches the jar out of Reed's hand. "My girlfriend made it." He grips the jar, face contorting with emotion.

"Eric." I rest a hand on his shoulder, giving it a squeeze. That jar is a piece of Lila. I don't want to hurt him, but this is a good trade for us. "I think she'd want to do this for us."

"She's probably yelling at us from the afterlife to make the trade," Susan adds. "That girl loathed the idea of running."

Eric lets out a short, panged bark of laughter. After a beat, he holds the jar out to John. "It's good stuff. My girlfriend spent two years refining this recipe."

John's eyes light up as he takes the jar. He screws off the lid and inhales. The grin he gives us is pleased.

"This will help my mom's arthritis." He slides the jar into his leather jacket. "Trade accepted. Come on. Blue truck. I'll take you to Westport."

At his words, two men peel off from the campground, heading toward a dirty Chevy Colorado. I send a silent thanks to Lila for looking out for us.

Two armed men join John in the cab. My group climbs into the back.

As the truck rolls forward, Ben scoots up beside me. I grip his hand.

I haven't been in a vehicle for six months. Being in one now puts me on edge. Every muscle in my body is tense. My free hand grips my knife as I scan both sides of the one-lane gravel road. I keep expecting zombies to come loping out of the trees.

None do. Either John was telling the truth and this road has been cleared, or we're getting lucky.

"Did you get a good look at their weapons?" Ben asks in a low voice.

I shake my head. "They all look the same to me."

"Those were Barrett M107s and M110 SASS."

"You can't get those at your local Walmart," Caleb adds.

"What are you saying?" I keep my voice low as the truck crunches along the gravel road.

"Home boy was probably a pot farmer before the shit hit the fan," Reed says.

Ben nods. "It's the only industry up here that can afford firearms like that."

My first thought is to leap out of the truck and make a run for it. "Do you think we're safe?"

Ben purses his lips. "I think if he wanted to kill us he would have done it. But I do think it's a good idea to get the hell away from him as soon as possible."

3
Trade

KATE

We exit the narrow gravel road and turn onto a paved, two-lane highway. The Chevy picks up speed, rumbling past towering redwoods interspersed with red alders.

Susan breaks the tense silence hanging over our group. "Once we get to Westport, there's a chance we may be able to keep driving. If we can find a car, I mean."

This statement gets nothing but incredulous stares.

"Think about it," she says, unphased by our skepticism. "Westport, the town they're taking us to, had a population of less than a hundred before the outbreak. All the towns in this area are tiny until you get to Braggs. There might be some legitimately safe sections of road."

"You do know that zombies hear cars coming from miles away?" Eric says.

Susan shrugs. "It's worth a try."

I can't in good conscience rule out using cars if we can do it safely. Anything that will get us to Fort Ross—and to Alvarez—has to be considered.

We pass a green road sign that reads *Highway 1*. This is the road that will take us to Alvarez.

Not only that, my people have already logged a lot of miles on their feet. Every last one of them is sore, chafed, blistered, and exhausted. Myself included. Alternative transportation would give us all a reprieve.

"Let's keep it as an option," I say to Susan.

I chew my bottom lip in thought as we continue to hum along the tree-lined road. I run through a list of possible places to find a car that might still be working. Somehow, I have a feeling John and the people of Westport might have commandeered all nearby working vehicles. Which means we'll have to travel a ways on foot to find one. Or make another trade with John—an idea that does not sit well with me.

I squeeze Ben's hand, drawing strength from his presence. I force myself to shift my focus back to the moment. First things first, I need to get my people to Westport and safely back on the road. We'll figure out the rest as we go, like we always do.

"Is that the town John was telling us about?" Ash shades her eyes as the truck emerges from the tree-lined road.

A few miles away is a tiny little town perched above the ocean. Gray sky looms overhead, threatening more rain. The Pacific Ocean is almost the same gray color as the sky, stretching like a frothing blanket for as far as the eye can see.

"Yes, I think that's Westport," I say, answering Ash.

We watch the hamlet draw near. A half-mile out, a dozen people come into view. They wield hammers, standing in a cluster over a stack of building supplies.

Ben shades his eyes. "Are they building a wall?"

"Either that or a really long house," Reed says.

I squint. Indeed, a line of fence posts with corrugated sheet metal panels surrounds the northern edge of the town. It currently stands seven feet tall and stretches two hundred yards to the east, away from the ocean. It might not be the strongest wall I've ever seen, but it will be effective in keeping out zombies that stray toward the town.

We pass the wall and its construction crew, entering

Westport. Susan had been right when she said there wasn't much to the town. We pass a series of low-roofed homes along the cliffs that overlook the ocean. I spot a bed-and-breakfast with all the front windows boarded up and an honest-to-god blacksmith shop.

"That will come in handy," Ben remarks, taking in the tiny tourist attraction. A man and a woman glance up from their forge as we pass, studying us with suspicion.

Next to the blacksmith shop is a giant statue of a whale. At one time, it had a working spout that sprayed water. It now sits dormant, the trough below the whale filled with water that's turned a murky green.

The rest of the town is nondescript. We pass a few more tiny motels, a few restaurants, and more homes.

Overall, Westport is mostly intact. Other than some windows and doors that have been boarded up, it looks to have weathered the apocalypse well. I can't help but think the clearance of this town and the surrounding area must have been relatively easy.

There are people out and about, more than I've seen in one place since the world ended. They stare at us with the same suspicion we received from the blacksmiths, each and every one of them halting in their tracks to watch as we go by.

Among the townspeople are men and women with automatic weapons. Local security, I suppose. Between them and the beginnings of the town wall, it's obvious to me that John doesn't take his town's remote location for granted.

As we near the southern outskirts of the town, I spot another crew of men and women erecting fence panels. My breath catches at the sight of a telephone pole standing sentry at the very edge of Westport.

Suspended from either side of the telephone pole are giant wooden birdcages.

Except they aren't made for birds. Each cage is the size of a human being.

And inside those cages are people. A man and a woman, both of them slumped over and lifeless. Vultures and crows and seagulls swarm around the cages, pecking at the bodies inside and screeching at one another.

"Holy shit," Reed breathes. "Did that guy say his name is John?"

Ben gives him a sharp look. "Yes. What do you know?"

Reed purses his lips. "There are stories of a marijuana farmer in this area. His nickname is Medieval John."

I look away from the bodies in the cages, feeling queasy.

"Looks like the nice man driving us through his town has a psychotic edge." Ben's face is set, eyes hard. "Let's hope he keeps his word and lets us leave without any trouble."

"Be ready to run." I study the land beyond the hanging cages. To the west are cliffs that drop off into the ocean. To the east are rolling hills and trees.

"Head east if they start shooting," I say. "Get to the tree line and keep moving south."

Everyone nods, expressions tight as the truck pulls to a stop just below the cages. The people working on the wall slow in their labor, studying us.

I don't waste any time. As soon as the truck stops, I leap to the ground. Everyone follows suit. We cluster on the east side of the truck, closest to the line of trees in case we need to make a run for it.

John swings open the driver's side door and hops to the ground.

"Hey, MJ," calls one of the men working on the wall. "We're running out of fence posts."

MJ. Medieval John. The queasiness in my stomach increases.

John shrugs. "We'll put together another foraging run into Kibesillah. There's plenty of wood we can pull from the big barn we found there."

I straighten, standing tall as the man with the floppy

mustache turns in my direction.

"I hope you enjoyed your tour of Westport," he says. "We don't have visitors very often."

"Is that who they are?" I jerk a thumb at the bodies in the wooden cages. "Visitors?" Ben shoots me a hard look. I know I should keep my mouth shut, but I can't help it.

"No." John shakes his head. "Those are thieves. One of Westport's . . . *neighbors* thought it was okay to send some of her people to raid our food supplies." His smile is hard as stone. "I'm a fair man. I don't kill for fun. But I do protect my people and my town. Thieves will not be tolerated."

I swallow, forcing myself to meet his gaze. "Thank you for the ride. We're going now." I gesture to my group, ushering them forward down the highway.

"I was hoping you'd stop by our trading post before you go," John calls, motioning in the direction of a small house twenty yards from the side of the road. "Like I said, we don't get visitors through here very often. We might have supplies you need for your journey. We're always up for trading." He openly eyes our backpacks.

"No thanks," I reply, even though in my head I can tick off half a dozen things we could use for our journey. Top of the list being a car or some bicycles.

John lets his gaze rest a little too long on the large pack Caleb carries. No doubt he's smart enough to guess there are weapons inside. "Look through our offerings. If there's something you need, perhaps we can come to an amicable trade."

I'm about to decline his offer. I want out of this place as quickly as possible and I don't like the idea of negotiating with John.

Before I can speak, Susan steps forward. "How clear is the highway south of town?"

John shrugs. "It's relatively clear up until Braggs. After that . . ." He shrugs. "I couldn't tell you. Braggs is a dead show. None of my people have been within the city limits."

Susan flicks a quick look at me before turning back to John. "Do you have a car?"

John chuckles. "Not one that you could afford." His gaze again strays to Caleb's pack. "Unless you have something compelling in that bag of yours."

Ben snarls, opening his mouth to no doubt say something rude and inflammatory. I rest my hand on his arm, stilling him.

"The contents of that pack are not for trade."

Reed snorts. "We're going to have a hard enough time killing Rosario *with* the contents of that pack."

I elbow him in the ribs. His words are so soft I think I'm the only one who hears him.

Until John's hard stare lands on Reed. "What did you say, young man?"

Reed casts me an uneasy glance. I shove him behind me.

I face John. It's clear from his expression that he doesn't intend to let his question go unanswered. "He said that if we survive Rosario, we'll be back this way. Maybe we can trade at that time."

John's eyes narrow. "What's your business with Rosario?"

My skin prickles. "She attacked our friends at Fort Ross. We're going to help them."

A feral grin spreads across John's face. "Why didn't you say so? Looks like we have a common enemy." John jerks a thumb at the bodies in the cages. "Those are Rosario's thieves. They were sent here to steal supplies. Before those two died, they told me Rosario lost her camp. It was overrun by the undead."

"She had a fence line surrounded by zombies," I say faintly. "She said they were better than guard dogs."

My short time in that camp comes hurtling back. I taste the fear and smell the scent of the earth mixed with the cloying scent of the rotting dead.

Frederico. His wide eyes, full of fear, as the collar of

bells are locked around our necks.

I shake myself free of the memory, re-focusing on John.

He studies me. "Yeah," he says with a curt nod. "You have the look of someone who's met that bitch face to face. She makes me look soft."

I don't respond. John doesn't look soft by any stretch of the imagination. It's not just the bodies in the cage. A person doesn't earn the moniker of "medieval" because he likes swords and Inquisition trivia.

"I want to help you," John says. "Make me an offer on a car. What do you have to trade besides weapons?"

I turn a helpless look to my people. Besides our salt-encrusted clothing and our running packs, what do we have to trade?

"Bear meat?" I ask.

John snorts. "Don't insult my generosity."

"How about a boat mechanic?" Susan asks.

"What?" I whirl on her. "Susan—"

"I saw boats anchored out there." She jerks a thumb in the direction of the ocean. "I used to own and operate a charter boat. I can service all of them for you."

John nods, eyes thoughtful. "They could all use a little work. Our abalone divers could cover more territory if they had trustworthy vessels."

"Susan." I position myself in front of her. "We can't wait around here while you service the boats. We—"

"I'll stay here." Susan gives me a small, determined smile. "Look, Kate, we both know my ankle is messed up. I know you traveled over a hundred miles on a sprained ankle, but I'm not you. The only reason I came on this mission was to drive my boat, which is now at the bottom of the ocean. I can't fight and I don't want to run another step. Let me help in my way. When you're finished in Fort Ross, come back and get me."

There are so many holes in this plan I can't even begin to list them. "No. You're part of our family. You're not a commodity to be traded."

"You don't have a choice," Susan replies. "I'm staying here." She turns to John. "Which car?"

"What if we don't make it back?" The words burst out of me. I detest them as soon as they leave my mouth, but the truth is that we might not survive.

"I'll find a way to get back to Arcata on my own," Susan says softly.

"But it's not safe here." I jab a hand at the dead bodies in the cage, not caring that John can hear me.

"Susan has nothing to fear from me or anyone in Westport," John says. "You have my word that she will be under my protection."

Frustration wells inside me—frustration at the string of disasters that has followed us ever since we left Arcata, frustration that I don't have a good argument to talk Susan out of her plan.

John cocks his head at me. "Once Susan has my boats tuned up, she can stay here, trade free, until you come back. This is a one-time offer, Kate. No one stays in Westport without some sort of trade. I'm throwing you a bone since you're going after the wicked bitch of the north."

"Done." Susan steps forward and shakes his hand.

John fishes a set of keys out of his pocket and tosses them in my direction. Ben snatches them out of the air.

"Silver Ford Escape parked over there." He flicks his fingers at a nearby driveway. "It's been nice doing business with you fine folks."

His words are like a gavel falling. I swallow, my throat tight with shock.

Susan puts her arms around me in a hug. "I'll be fine. Just get to Fort Ross and kick some ass, okay?"

"Don't do this," I reply.

"It's the best decision and we both know it," she whispers back. "Besides, it's already done."

Legs wooden and mouth dry, I force myself to walk to

the silver Ford Escape we traded for our friend.

I close my eyes for a brief moment, trying not to think too hard on the fact that we might never see Susan again.

4
Barbed Wire

KATE

Salty wind blows in from the open car window, carrying with it the sharp scent of impending rain. As John had claimed, the road south of Westport is clear. We haven't seen a single zombie and came across only two abandoned cars we had to drive around.

Ben sits at the wheel, his face a mask as we rumble down Highway 1. I sit with him in the front. In the back are Caleb, Ash, and Reed. Eric sits in the very back where, six months ago, the grocery bags would have gone.

Susan's loss is like an empty chamber in my chest. The fact that she traded herself for a fucking *car* is like barbed wire in my gut. It's so *wrong*.

Her lost boat, her rolled ankle—they can all be traced back to this rescue mission. *My* rescue mission.

A strong hand squeezes my knee. I look over at Ben. He raises an eyebrow at me and gives a small shake of his head.

I let out a long sigh, understanding his silent message. Ben always gets me, especially at times like this when I feel loss. Probably because he's endured his fair share of loss during his years of service in the army.

I need to look forward. I need to stay sharp and keep my people alive so we can get to Fort Ross and help

Alvarez. Dwelling on decisions made in the past will only bog us down.

"What's the plan, Mama Bear?" Caleb asks, breaking the silence.

I turn to the map in my lap, which I've been staring at since we left Westport. "We should be able to drive the SUV for the next fifteen miles to Braggs. We'll leave the car outside the town and make our way on foot. Once we're clear of the town, we can see about finding another car."

In our current shape—exhausted and beat to hell from our tangle with the Lost Coast—I estimate this car is saving us a solid three to four hours of travel on foot, which will put us in Braggs well before noon. We'll have daylight on our side when we push through to the other side of the city.

I have to admit, it's nice to chew up the miles in a car. I wish we could drive all the way to Fort Ross. But I know better than to try and drive through Braggs, and not just because Medieval John warned us against it. It's the largest town out here and straddles Highway 1. I'm not stupid enough to think we can drive through a town that size without getting mobbed by zombies.

"I think food should be on our list of things to do when we get to Braggs," Reed says. "We don't have much bear meat left. I'm so hungry I could eat a fire-roasted zombie."

"That's disgusting." Ash makes a face. "Can we add clean clothes to our to-do list? I'd like to wear something not saturated in dry salt."

I give them the thumbs up. They're not the only ones sick of salt-encrusted clothes and hungry enough to eat a zombie. "Food and clean clothes are officially on the list of things to do in Braggs."

A green road sign comes into view, telling us we're a mile outside of Braggs.

It also tells us Fort Ross is ninety miles away. I try not

to think about what my body will feel like if it goes another ninety miles on foot.

"Pull over," I tell Ben. "We go on foot from here into Braggs." I turn to look at the others. "Daylight is on our side. We take our time and do this right. Everyone gets through Braggs alive." I fold the map and stash it in a pocket of my pack.

Ben pulls over to the side of the road. We pile out of the car, everyone clipping on running packs. Caleb shoulders the largest pack with the bulk of our weapons.

I pick up a small box of grenades resting on the floor of the Escape. This had been a parting gift from Medieval John.

"Blow that bitch to hell," he'd said, grinning like a feral wolf just before we'd driven out of Westport. "If you get the chance, shove one these up her ass for me."

I pass out the grenades, making sure we each have a few of them.

"Let's go," I say. Running on the road will be much faster than running the Lost Coast trail. "We'll alternate between running and walking. Five minutes on, five minutes off."

No one argues. We set off at a brisk jog.

My body groans in protest. The time spent sitting has not done me any favors. My muscles have stiffened. New aches have settled in. I do my best to ignore them.

The highway snakes along the ocean. Dark clouds mass in the sky, promising rain later in the day. Despite the lack of sunshine, the views are stunning.

The dried salt in my clothing burns along the raw patches of chafed skin. The two worst spots are under my sports bra and along the inside of my thighs. Those parts of my body have always been prone to chafing. The pressure on the top of my left toe and back of my right heel tells me I have large blisters in the works.

"Anyone else feel like they've been run over with one of those monster trucks and dragged through mud?" Reed asks, the usual lightheartedness missing from his voice.

The slump to his shoulders tells me how rundown he feels. I know for a fact that everyone else is feeling the same way, possibly worse. If I don't get their heads into the game, we'll never make it to Fort Ross.

"Everyone is hurting," I say, giving them all a nod of acknowledgment. "That doesn't matter. We push through the pain and keep going. Pain isn't a reason to stop. That's a lesson every ultrarunner learns early. If we all quit as soon as something hurts, no one would ever make it to the finish line."

"Seven hours in the boat," Ash mutters. "That's it. It was supposed to take us seven hours by boat to get to Fort Ross. We were never supposed to do any running."

Ultrarunning isn't about being a *runner*," I reply. "It's about sucking it up and pushing on no matter what."

Eric gives me a sidelong glance. "You're good at pep talks. Even if everything you're saying freaks me out."

"It's okay to be freaked out. You just can't let self-doubt worm its way into your psyche. I know I use the ultramarathon analogy a lot, but there's a lot at stake. If you give in to fear or pain, it could get you killed." That's the simple truth. I don't want to scare anyone, but if it keeps their heads in the right space, it's worth it.

As we near the city limits, a sign proclaims *Braggs, Population 39,612.* The land is covered with golden grass and weathered cypress trees that have been sculpted into eastward leaning contortions by the constant barrage of wind over the years.

A scattering of houses dot either side of the road, all of them on large plots of land. The dwellings are small one-story homes, most of them looking like they were built back in the 1950s. More than a few of them boast large piles of what I would have called garbage less than a year ago.

Now, casting my eye over the mounds of discarded lumber, rusted cars, and other assorted things, it looks like a salvage wonderland. I spot tall cabinets that had been pulled from a kitchen. What I wouldn't give to have something like that back at Creekside in our main kitchen. It would make it easier to store and organize food for everyday use.

There are no signs of zombies, though we see evidence of the outbreak. One cluster of houses sits in ashen ruins. Several clusters of wrecked cars sit abandoned on the side of the road.

We also see evidence of life. I spot a chicken pecking at the ground. It flees at the sight of us, head bobbing back and forth as it runs. I even see a front door hastily shut as we approach.

"Survivors," Ben murmurs. "Everyone stay alert."

We run past a rock quarry, an RV storage facility, another scattering of homes, and two hotels that overlook the ocean. One of the hotels is half burned to the ground.

My body has slipped back into the familiar cadence of road running. I don't have to watch every step for fear of falling when I run on the road. I revel in the sensation of my heart pounding, of oxygen expanding my lungs with each breath. My body has loosened up, the aches fading into the recess of my mind. Even though the ocean nearly killed me, I still love the smell of it.

The outskirts of Braggs seem to stretch on and on. We pass another hotel, this one two stories high and perched on a cliff. Another scattering of tiny homes comes and goes.

The ocean disappears, blocked from sight by tall cliffs. A wide river, waters dark and blue, flows along at the base of the cliff and out toward the sea.

That's when I see the bridge.

Or, to be more precise, what's *left* of the bridge.

Suspended above the bridge is a canvas banner that reads *Annual Whale Festival.* Beneath the words is the picture of a whale.

Beneath that are the crumbled remains of the bridge.

"Shit," I murmur.

A dozen or so zombies sniff around the edge of the ruined bridge. It's the first pack we've seen since we left Arcata. They snarl and moan at one another, scratching at the concrete.

I signal a stop. My hand unconsciously strays to the back of my pack, where I have a portable tape player stashed. That tape player, with its recording of an alpha zombie, might be our most valuable possession.

I study the zombies, wondering if one of them is an alpha. The group is centered around a twenty-something zombie. She tilts her head back and lets out a string of garbled sounds. The rest of the zombies straighten, clustering more tightly around her.

Yep, that's an alpha.

That's when I notice the water. The zombies are standing in puddles of water.

But it's not raining. And there isn't standing water anywhere else.

"Shit," I breathe.

"What is it?" Ben gives me a sharp look.

"I think those zombies came out of the river."

The longer I study them in the bleak light, the more I'm convinced of it. Their clothes are wet, many of them still trailing small streams onto the ground. I pull out my map, unfolding it to look for another way over the water.

"You think they came out of the river?" Reed hisses. "That's fucked up."

"What's fucked up is that was the only bridge into town." I study the map, wishing desperately for another way over the water. "That big river is called Pudding Creek. It runs for miles to the east."

"Can we go back to the part about zombies crawling out of the water?" Reed says. "That's really fucking creepy."

I gesture for my people to fall back. I want to get some space between us and the zombies so I can think.

One thing is for sure: Swimming across isn't an option. I may have the alpha zom recording, but there's no way to know how well the recording will work on zombies under water. I won't risk my people in Pudding Creek, especially not knowing how many zoms are in the water.

Going miles out of our way to find a safe way over Pudding Creek isn't a great option, either. That will take hours we don't have—that Fort Ross doesn't have.

I draw the group to a halt when there's a solid quarter mile between us and the zombies. I watch the alpha lead them away from the bridge to sniff around some cars abandoned along Pudding Creek.

Taking a deep breath, I turn in a slow circle and absorb our surroundings. There's a way around this problem. I just have to figure out what it is.

"Hey, Mom?" Eric taps me on the shoulder.

"Yeah?"

"You ran on railroad tracks to get to Arcata, right?"

"Most of the time, yes."

"What does that look like to you?" Caleb raises a hand, pointing to the southern end of the river.

Spanning the river is a bridge. Not a bridge for cars; that much is obvious by its wooden construction. It's old, most likely from the logging era. Even from a distance, I can tell it's structurally unsound. Some of the supports are broken or missing.

"It was probably built to hold a train full of redwood trees," Caleb says. "That's like, what, ten million pounds? I'm pretty sure it can hold us."

Ben snorts. "That thing's got to be almost a hundred years old. A stiff breeze could knock it over."

I shake my head. "We're checking it out. Come on." It's our best option so far.

We backtrack farther up the road. I draw us to a halt outside of a two-story hotel painted a pale green. Just around the northern side of the hotel is the entrance to the railroad bridge.

The hotel looks unoccupied. One of the doors looks like it was hacked down with an axe. A few others swing open on squeaky hinges. I spot two dead bodies under the eaves, both of them so desiccated that not even the carrion birds show interest in them.

"Come on." I draw my knife and lead the way around the hotel, hustling toward the bridge.

It looks even more rickety up close. There are large gaps in the structure where the dark blue of the river is visible. The entire thing seems to sway in the breeze.

The entrance is blocked by a chain-link fence topped with barbed wire. Several friendly signs sit front and center.

NO TRESPASSING.

DANGER. UNSAFE CONDITIONS.

AUTHORIZED PERSONNEL ONLY.

I turn to my people. "Anyone know how to climb over a barbed-wire fence?"

Reed thrusts his arm into the air. "I do! We need something thick, like a leather jacket."

"You want to climb over barbed wire so we can cross a bridge that's made from toothpicks?" Ben lets out an exasperated huff. "This isn't your best idea, Kate."

His words rankle. The worst part is that he isn't wrong.

"There are no good choices," I reply. "This is the best option we have."

"Let's get a comforter from one of those hotel rooms," Reed says. "We can throw it over the barbed wire."

I nod in agreement. "Let's check out the hotel."

5
Beachview

ERIC

I wish Tom could see me.

The thought flashes through my mind. My brother would never believe that, just a short while ago, his loser of a little bother had just completed his first ultramarathon. Hell, wherever he is, he's probably already written me off as zombie food.

That's exactly what I would be if it weren't for Kate.

From my rumbling stomach to my aching legs and blistered toes, I feel like I'm living life to its fullest. It's nothing like the first twenty-one years of my life, where I made it my mission to follow the path of least resistance. I realize now that I'd been living with only my toes in the water. I finally understand why Kate loves ultramarathons. Because when you run ultras, you know you can hack whatever shit life throws at you.

Like right now. I know that if I can run an ultramarathon, I can follow Kate over a barbed-wire fence and across a rickety bridge without dying.

Even if said bridge doesn't look fit for humans.

Even if looking at it makes me want to curl up in a tight ball and cry like a girl.

I follow the others across the parking lot, turning my attention away from the scrotum-shriveling bridge and instead focus on the shitty hotel.

The sign above the two-story hotel reads *Beachview*. It was probably fancy back in the day when it first opened. Years of exposure to the salt air have left the paint peeling and faded. But I shouldn't blame the elements. The owners of this place had probably been tightwads who hadn't bothered to take care of their building.

There are no cars in the lot. Maybe everyone was at the Whale Festival when the outbreak hit. Or maybe they took off when shit got real. Maybe a bunch of those people we saw in Medieval John's town were refugees from the Whale Festival. Maybe—

Stop it, I tell myself. *Focus. We need blankets. How else are we going to get over the barbed wire and cross a bridge that looks like it belongs in a pile at the bottom of the river?*

Dumb fucks. I hear Lila's caustic skepticism in my head. I imagine her projecting it to me all the way from her grave back in Arcata. God, I miss her.

As we move through the parking lot, I draw my knife. No one knows it, but I named the knife Mr. Pokey. I love this knife. Kate got it for me out of a sporting goods store in Arcata and almost burned down half the town in the process. It's taken out plenty of zombies. Plus it was a gift from my surrogate mom. That means more than anything.

"I think we should try the rooms on the bottom floor first," Ben says. The tendons stand out on his neck, hinting at the enormous effort behind his civil tone. He tries so hard to be pleasant when his default is grumpy fucker. He loves Kate, so he tries. I like that about Ben.

"Good idea." Kate flashes him a quick smile. "Let's start with the room on the far left. Caleb and Ben, you go in first. Reed and I will be right behind you. Eric and Ash, you keep watch at the door."

I don't know how things are done in the military, but I like to think we're an efficient unit. Ash and I take up our post without argument, flanking either side of the door.

Ben kicks open the swinging door and Caleb dashes

inside, weapons raised. Ben hurtles after him. Kate and Reed are hard on their heels, weapons also raised.

I wait, tense, Mr. Pokey raised to strike.

"Dude." Reed's voice drifts out of the hotel room. "You gotta see this."

Ash and I exchange glances before hurrying into the room.

The smell is the first thing I register. The world, in general, is rank these days, what with dead people walking around while they rot and the rest of us not having regular access to showers.

The room of the *Beachview* most definitely smells like zombie. The acrid stench of rot is unmistakable.

"Dude," Reed says again.

My mouth goes dry. No matter how much death I see, it seems like there's always more gore lurking around the corner to top my latest living nightmare.

I mean, just two weeks ago I saw a zombie impaled on the broken glass of a window. He'd tripped and landed on two enormous shards. They pierced his body, spilling out intestines and other various organs. Can it really get worse than that?

Yep. Yep, it can always get worse. What I see now tops even that gory mess.

In the middle of the bed, on display like someone had left a birthday gift for a loved one, is a zombie head. Just the head.

And the thing is still undead. White eyes roll as it tracks our sounds. The teeth gnash. Other than the grinding of teeth, it makes no sound. Probably because the vocal cords didn't make the cut. Literally.

"Found the other half." Ben emerges from the bathroom. "It's in the bathtub."

I stay where I am. I don't need to see the other half of the body. I'm sure it's like every other zombie body I've seen, except in a bathtub.

Reed, of course, has to check it out. He pokes his head

around Ben and wrinkles his nose. "Dude, that is fucked up. Who would do something like that?"

Kate gives us all a tight look. "Get the blankets," she orders. "Both of them."

"Even the bloody one?" Reed asks.

"We're not going to waste time going through hotel rooms to find clean blankets," Kate replies.

The last thing I want to do is touch a blanket covered in zombie sludge, but I make it a point not to argue with Kate. I credit her with the fact that I'm alive. I was a stoned fuck-up when she found me. I'm still a fuck-up, but at least I'm not stoned as much anymore.

I grab one end of the bloody blanket and yank. The head tumbles to the floor, thudding softly. Ash whips out her zom bat. Blood droplets spatter in all directions as she caves in the front of the skull, spattering across her face like bits of spray paint.

Armed with quilts, we hustle back to the bridge that is somehow still miraculously standing. I'd secretly been hoping the wind would push it over while we were goggling at zombie head in the hotel room.

The bridge looks like the sort of thing suitable for a cat. Maybe. A really small, nimble cat. Or perhaps just seagulls.

It doesn't look like the sort of thing that can hold—in my case—two hundred pounds of human being.

Before the apocalypse, I'd been thirty pounds heavier. A rationed diet, coupled with the insane amount of running and physical activity required just to survive, ate up all the excess fat I carried around. For the first time in my life, I don't see a fat fuck every time I look at myself in the shower.

Rub it in, loser. Lila's voice plays in my head. *You're the only one who looks better in the apocalypse.*

We fold the blankets in half like giant PB&J sandwiches, the bloody part on the inside. To the credit of *Beachview*, they apparently invested in new bedspreads at some point in time. These at least look like they were manufactured in the last decade. They had been fashionable back in the day. Like, when I'd been in junior high.

When the blankets are thrown over the barbed wire, Reed says, "I'll go first."

At Kate's nod, he leaps onto the fence like a parkour aficionado. It takes him thirty seconds to scramble over the barbed wire and land on the other side. The guy pisses me off. He's good at all this physical stuff.

One by one, we scale the fence. When it's my turn, I silently thank Kate for taking away my fat fuck status. As it stands, I feel like an elephant as I scramble up the chain-link. Getting over the barbed wire requires me to throw my legs in the air while my hands cling to the metal. I'm pretty sure circus acrobats are weathering the zombie apocalypse without any problem.

My dismount sucks. My feet miss the chain-link on the other side and I end up sliding to the ground. I stagger, but at least I don't fall on my ass. Or over the cliff. Both are good things.

I take a moment to straighten my glasses. I wish I'd gotten Lasik surgery before the world ended. Now I'm going to be stuck with glasses for life. What really sucks is when the lenses get splattered with blood. It gets hard to see through blood splatter.

Once we're all inside the fort, Kate rolls up the blankets. "We need to take these with us," she says. "For when we get to the other side."

My eyes stray reluctantly to the bridge. If I didn't have complete faith in Kate, there's no fucking way I'd walk across that thing. Hell, I'm pretty sure a Shanghai acrobat would balk at crossing it. And Kate wants us to do it with those huge blankets?

Now I find myself wishing the owners of *Beachview* had been as cheap with their furnishings as they were with their exterior paint. The blankets would be thinner and threadbare and much easier to carry.

"I'll take one." I hold out my arms before I can talk myself out of it. I'll pretty much do anything for Kate. And someone needs to carry them.

Besides, maybe it will cushion me if I fall off the bridge. Yeah, right.

Kate gives me a grateful smile and passes one of the blankets to me. Ash takes the other. We roll them up as tight as we can, which is to say we manage to make them look like super-sized marshmallows on steroids.

On the outside of our running packs are things Kate calls *shock cords*. They're basically skinny bungee cords made for securing supplies to the back of the pack. Normally they're used for jackets or extra pieces of clothing.

And now Ash and I are trying to jam enormous hotel blankets beneath the shock cords. It's like trying to cram a size-twelve foot into a size-six shoe.

"Dude, move over." Reed elbows me. "You're doing it wrong."

I grunt in annoyance and move over.

Reed somehow manages shock cord ninja moves. The huge blanket gets bungeed into place. It sticks out at odd angles, but it's secure.

When I swing the pack into place, I suppress a grimace. I feel like an un-balanced teeter-totter. Like all the kids in the playground are piled on one end and the midget of the class sits alone on the other.

"You'll have to compensate for the weight," Ben tells me. "Lean forward for counterbalance."

I silence the alarm bells ringing in my head. I can do this. If the whole bridge doesn't collapse under our combined weight, I'll be just fine.

When Reed gets the second blanket strapped to Ash's pack, Kate leads us onto the bridge. The wood creaks loudly as she takes the first few steps onto it.

"If you go down, I'm coming after you," Ben tells her.

Despite the sentiment behind the words, he manages to make it sound like a threat.

"Same goes if you fall," Kate replies.

Who's dumb idea was it to name this huge river *Pudding Creek*? It's like a distant third cousin to a creek that's been fattened up on Twinkies. Or, in this case, zombies.

"Fuck." Ben glares down into Pudding Creek. "There are way too many undead fuckers down there. This is a bad idea." He lets out a string of curse words to emphasize this statement while simultaneously taking his first step onto the bridge. He's never more than two paces behind Kate.

Now would be a good time to remember that I just finished my first ultramarathon. It would also be an ideal time to forget I've never liked heights.

One by one, we file onto the bridge. I find myself between Ash and Caleb.

The railroad ties are rotted. Loose railroad spikes lay everywhere. The beams supporting the ties are in as bad shape as the railroad itself.

The land drops away as we edge forward, a sheer cliff of striated layers of gray, brown, and tan.

There is now nothing but a rotten railroad bridge between me and certain death.

My chest is tight with anxiety. My breaths are short and sharp. It's impossible not to look at the water below. There are too many gaps in the bridge.

The natural flow is east-to-west from the land, but the current from the ocean flows west-to-east. The waters churn in white froth where the two currents meet. Caught in the middle of the aquatic battleground are the bulk of the zombies.

Hundreds? Maybe. At least dozens. Enough that if I fall, I'm destined to be zombie food. If the fall itself doesn't kill me. It must be at least a hundred yards between the bridge and the water.

Shit. What the fuck are we doing? This was a bad fucking idea. Where's a jet pack when you need one?

"It's official," Reed says. "I'm not calling this thing a bridge. Its new name is the Balance Beam of Death."

"Good name." I shift my eyes, doing my best not to focus on the water zombies. The sensible thing to do is to focus on the crumpling wood that is currently keeping me alive.

I take another few steps, steadily inching farther over the water. A piece of wood flakes off under my foot, throwing me off balance. I curse, grabbing one of the upper supports that arch overhead.

"You okay?" Caleb asks.

"Yeah. Fine." I regain my balance and continue inching forward.

I test each foothold as I go, pressing down before shifting all my weight. The third time I do this, an entire chunk of wood breaks free. It spins end over end into the water below.

Moans and keens drift up. The zombies thrash in the current, all of them trying to converge on the spot where the wood landed.

"The water must be shallow if they're standing," Caleb murmurs. "The zoms we encountered back in Humboldt Bay sank to the bottom."

"So if I fall," I reply, "I don't have to worry about getting eaten alive. I'll die on impact."

"Most likely, yeah," Caleb says.

It's somewhat comforting to know exactly how I'll die if I fall. Which shows just how fucked up things are right now.

I gingerly continue to inch my way forward, testing each spot before applying my weight. I move my hand between the support beams, gripping them just in case. If the wood I'm standing on happens to give way, hopefully the beam I'm clinging to won't be rotten, too.

Sometimes I wish I'd worked a little harder at school. I could calculate the probability of both the support beam and the platform plank being rotten at the same time.

Then again, maybe it's a good thing I spent my college days perfecting pot brownies. I don't really need to know ratios that relate to my survival. It's hard enough to sleep as it is on some nights.

"What the hell are you doing?" Ben barks.

"Getting a railroad spike," Kate replies. "They make good weapons."

"Weapons won't help if you're dead at the bottom of the river."

Kate actually sounds contrite when she replies. "Sorry. That was stupid."

Ash picks her way along in front of me. Her skin is still pale from her bout with hypothermia. As far as I'm concerned, she has the best bragging rights out of all of us. We all completed our first ultra on the Lost Coast, but Ash is the only one of us who almost died.

Below, I see a zombie lurch forward, hands clawing in the water. It snatches up a large, wriggling fish. Its head comes down, teeth closing over fish scales.

Several nearby zombies moan, reaching out for the fish as the first zombie gnaws on its prize. It jerks, curling its body around the food as three of its brethren close in.

What ensues next loosely resembles a Kindergarten sandbox brawl. One zombie snatches the fish away, which is still wiggling. The original fish champion lets out a moan of frustration and flails its arms. It smacks the perpetrator on the face, who in turn hisses.

During this brief moment of distraction, a third zombie gets its hands around the fish. Rather than attempting to wrestle it away, the third zombie shoves its head forward and clamps its teeth around the fish. It begins chewing while the other two zombies squabble.

"Yo." Caleb pokes me in the shoulder. "Keep moving."

I pull my gaze away from the water just as a fourth zombie wades into the melee.

Focus, I remind myself. *Ignore them.*

Except that it's really hard to ignore the moaning and keening that drifts up from the water. It makes me wish I had earplugs. I—

A shout goes up in front of me. A human shout.

I raise my eyes just in time to see a beam collapse beneath Ash's feet. She goes down, sliding through the planks toward the water below.

6
Balance Beam of Death

ERIC

I dive forward, leaping for Ash. I grunt as I hit the platform. The metal of the rusted railroad grinds into my ribcage. My arm lands on a half-rotted tie, which crumples upon impact. Splinters stab through my long sleeve shirt.

I barely feel the pain. I reach out with both hands, eyes fixating on Ash's blue backpack and black hair. One hand tangles in the matted ponytail on top of her head. The other digs into the lightweight fabric of the pack.

Ash screams in terror as she dangles above the zombie-infested waters.

The zombies below us go nuts. The water churns and they push and shove at one another. A few of them even manage to climb on top of their brethren. Arms extend skyward, their keens slice the air.

"Help me!" Ash cries.

I form a fist with both hands, throwing every ounce of willpower into holding onto her. I should care that I'm pulling her hair, but I don't give a shit. If I don't hang on, Ash is zombie bait.

"Hold on!" Caleb lunges forward to help me.

Several planks give way, crumbling beneath our combined weight. Caleb goes down, one leg plunging through the opening. He scrabbles, grabbing onto the side of a metal rail to keep from sliding all the way into the hole.

No such luck for me. As I cling to Ash, wood splinters and snaps beneath my ribcage.

"Ash," I shout, "grab the boards! Reach up and grab the boards!"

She's too panicked to make sense of my words. Her feet kick. Her hands flail.

She doesn't do the single thing that might save her life.

"Ash!" My body is sliding.

All I can see is Ash's black hair and blue running pack. All I can hear is her screaming and the manic keening of the zombies below us. All I can feel is the inexorable pull of gravity and the groaning, splitting boards beneath me.

I'm-going-to-die-I'm-going-to-die-I'm-going-to-DIE—

"Got you!" Reed is suddenly above me, both feet braced against the railroad. He hangs onto the enormous bloody hotel blanket strapped to my back, teeth gritted as he struggles with the combined weight of me and Ash.

Ben appears at his side, grabbing another handful of the bloody hotel blanket.

Holy shit. I never thought that nasty thing might save my life.

"Ash!" Kate drops to her stomach in front of Ash, extending both arms into the opening. "Grab my hands."

With a sob, Ash reaches up. Kate grabs her wrists. She tugs, but she doesn't have enough leverage.

Caleb has managed to extract himself from the rotting boards. He darts in, dropping to his knees and reaching for Ash. He yanks, pulling one of Ash's arms into view. The weight of her ponytail slackens in my hand as Kate and Caleb haul her up.

As she's dragged out of my grasp, I'm treated to a front row seat of the river of doom. If possible, the zombies are even more crazed than they were thirty seconds ago. All I see are white eyes, frothing water, outstretched arms, and gnashing teeth.

All that separates me from certain death are Ben, Reed,

and the stupid hotel blanket. Oh, and two rotted planks beneath my chest that I can feel crumbling. It's like feeling death reach for you, splinter by splinter.

At least it will be quick. The thought flashes through my mind. *Die on impact.* That would be the best way to go. *Just get it over with.*

"We got you, dude." Reed's voice is strained.

A ferocious jerk. I find myself sprawled across the tracks, metal rails digging into my hip and forearm. I pant for breath, hardly believing I'm alive. If my brother were here, I'm pretty sure he wouldn't recognize the maniac who just saved a girl from falling off a bridge.

No one speaks. I turn my head, taking stock to make sure we haven't lost anyone.

Ash, Caleb, and Kate are in a bundle, the three of them holding tight to each other. Reed and Ben are sprawled beside me.

With a grunt, I roll over.

My ribs ache from where they'd landed on the track. I hope I didn't crack one. Then again, I'm pretty sure I wouldn't be able to roll over if I'd cracked a rib.

Healthy ribs, I tell myself. The ribs are just fine. No one here is running an ultra with cracked ribs. Right? Is that even possible?

"Damn." I hold up my hand and find a knot of black hair tangled in the fingers of my right hand. "Sorry, Ash. I think I pulled out half your hair."

She rolls a wide-eyed look in my direction. "You can have it," she says flatly.

Ben wheezes. And keeps wheezing. It takes me a minute to realize he's laughing. It's the second time I've heard him laugh in less than twenty-four hours. Kate really is good for him.

"That's a little disturbing," Caleb declares. "I like it better when you're a grumpy, old man."

"God damn." Ben gets to his feet, still chuckling. "I thought we were all zombie food. Fuck me. It feels good to be alive." He flashes a squinty-eyed grin at Kate.

I've seen him do this a few times. Seeing Ben smile is sort of like seeing a tutu on a pineapple. It's just weird. And maybe a little creepy. But whatever.

A slow smile spreads across Kate's face as she locks eyes with Ben. The bond between them is unmistakable, even though it took them forever to get together. I always figured Kate held back because she was worried Ben might die on her. Hell, after losing Lila, I can personally recommend not getting too attached in the apocalypse.

A familiar ache settles into my chest as Lila's dark eyes flash across my memory.

Fuck your stupid pot brownies. They're just making you fat, you fat ass.

I miss her insults. I miss everything about her.

"Fuck your stupid, stinky weed balm," I mutter, doing my best to fight the pinch of despair in my chest. I stare up at the sky, seeing the profile of her face in a puffy gray cloud. The beauty above me is at odds with the keening and moaning below me.

"Everyone okay?" Kate sweeps her eyes across us.

There are times when I wonder how Kate deals with all of us. How she finds it within herself to love us all so much. It's like her heart doesn't have a bottom.

"A-okay, Mama," Reed says.

"Yep, we're all in one piece," Caleb adds.

"Let's get the fuck off this bridge," Ben says. "I don't need a second heart attack today."

He turns his back on us, picking his way down the tracks. Reed pulls me to my feet, slapping me on the shoulder.

"Good thing you have the zombie blanket," he says. "Damn thing got stuck between two boards. I don't think I would have gotten to you in time if not for that."

A chill pebbles my arms. "Thanks, Reed." I meet his eyes so he knows I mean it.

"'Course, dude. You're my brother. I wasn't going to

let you fall into the river of death." He turns, making his way down the bridge. "I hope you're up-to-date on your tetanus shot."

It takes me a second to digest his comment. Then I notice the long tear across the front of my shirt, the skin bloody and abraded. Bits of rust cling to the wound.

Fuck. I wrack my brain as I make my way down the bridge, trying to recall the last time I had shots. I vaguely recall getting a physical in high school for something, but I'd been so stoned the memory is insubstantial.

Ash falls in behind me. "Eric?"

"Yeah?" I don't turn around. After our last close call, I don't intend to take my eyes off the bridge.

"You're a fucking superhero. Thank you."

I can't help the grin that spreads across my lips. *A fucking superhero.* I'll take it. "Anytime. Just don't make it a point of falling through bridges. I'm not sure we'll get so lucky a second time."

"I owe you one." Caleb grips my shoulder. "Next time I score a bottle of booze on a scavenging run, it's yours."

"I'll take you up on that." I pause, studying a gap in the bridge. I inch to the left, picking my way over the narrowest part of the gap.

That's when I catch another glimpse down into the river. If possible, it looks like there are even more zombies in the water.

I pause, squinting through the opening. My eyes follow a snaking line of zombies through the water, all the way back to shore.

My stomach falls into my feet. The line doesn't stop at the shore.

That's when I recall all the noise we made when the bridge broke beneath us. The yelling. The screaming.

We'd announced our presence to every undead in Braggs.

A pack of zombies masses at the edge of the southern bluff that leads down to the river. One by one, the zombies step over the edge, plummeting to the hard ground below.

The fall would kill a human. And it does incapacitate some of the zombies, breaking their legs or their bodies so badly they can't move. But at least half of them stagger to their feet and wade into Pudding Creek, drawn by the keening of their fellows.

The keening isn't isolated to the water. A second chorus of keens goes up, this time in front of us.

Several dozen zombies have massed at the gate on the far end of the bridge. They rattle the cage and gnash their teeth, their ruined bodies straining to reach us.

7

Recording

KATE

I stare at the zombies on the other side of the chain-link fence at the southern end of the bridge. Their pallid, bloody faces and white eyes swamp my vision. Their snapping teeth and high-pitched moans pierce my ears.

The sight of them brings my anger to a boil.

"All I want to do is save my friend from a psychotic drug dealer," I snarl. "Is that so much to ask?"

I take in the scene before me, calculating our odds of fighting our way through the pack.

No way. There are too many of them. And there are more and more zombies coming every second, drawn by the frenzy of their brethren.

The chain-link fence extends a good fifteen feet on either side of the bridge, creating a convenient safety net for the zombies. If not for that, they'd probably walk right over the edge.

As far as I can tell, there are no alphas. None of the zoms has the telltale cluster around them, nor are any of them making those strange clicks and keens that function as zombie language.

"This might be an opportune time to use one of Medieval John's grenades," Reed suggests.

I shake my head. "We can't risk it with the bridge.

Besides, we drew enough zombies with the shouting." I gesture to the large clump of them a quarter mile away. "Any fire power we use will bring the rest of them down on us."

As I stand there, struggling to come up with a plan that won't get us all killed, my gaze once again drifts to the open cliffside no more than a quarter mile away. I watch two zombies walk right over the edge, keening all the way down until they're silenced on the shoreline below.

"If only that fence wasn't there," Ben mutters. "The whole pack would eventually walk right over the edge. We'd just have to wait them out."

"That's it." I spin around to face him, mind racing as a plan forms.

"What's it?" Ben narrows his eyes at me.

"I'm going to drive them over the side." I unclip my pack and pull out the precious tape recorder with the alpha zom recording. It's small, no more than four inches tall and six inches wide. Using my belt, I secure it to my waist.

"Eric, give me your blanket." I strap my running pack back into place and face the fence.

"Kate, what are you doing?" Caleb asks.

"I'm going over. Alone," I add, seeing angry red creep up Ben's neck. "I'll use the alpha zom recording to drive them over the edge of the cliff."

The protest is instantaneous.

"The fuck you are," Ben snaps.

"No way, Mama," Reed says. "You're not going over alone."

"We should go together," Eric adds.

"No." I shake my head. "There's only one alpha zom recording. I'll clear the way and the rest of you can follow."

"There are over three dozen zombies out there." Ash waves both arms at the zoms for emphasis. "You can't take them on by yourself with nothing more than a tape recorder."

"We've tested this," I say. "At Creekside. Remember?

We played it in the megaphone from the roof—"

Ben grinds his teeth. "We haven't tested it in *battle*, Kate. Testing it from the safety of a rooftop isn't the same thing as what you're proposing."

Eric frowns as another three zombies join the growing crowd. "Just stand at the fence and play it. That should do the trick."

"No." I shake my head. "Driving them back from the gate isn't enough. If something goes wrong, there's too many of them. I need to create a safe path for the rest of you."

"This is as crazy as the acid brandy plan," Eric says.

"Yeah, but that worked." Caleb's words silence everyone.

I take advantage of the pause. "Caleb is right. This will work. You guys just have to trust me."

I make it a point not to look at Ben. Out of the corner of my eye, I see his face growing a deeper shade of red. I don't blame him. I'd be pissed if this were his idea. Or if he were the one going out into the horde of zombies.

Ben manages to restrain himself for a full twenty seconds. "Are you listening to yourself?" he bursts out, grabbing my shoulder and spinning me around. "You're going to get yourself killed!"

I look him steadily in the eye. The worry etched into his features touches something deep inside me. I force all emotion from my face. "I got us into this mess. I'm going to get us out."

"We can go back." He flings an arm back in the direction of the hotel. "We'll go the long way around."

I take his hand. "If this doesn't work, we'll go back. Okay?"

Ben fumes, glaring down at me even as his hand squeezes mine. Then he jerks me forward, squashing me against his chest.

"If you get yourself killed, I'm going to fucking kill you. Understand?"

I press my cheek against him. "Deal."

"Dude, that didn't even make sense."

I feel Ben lift one arm and assume he's giving Reed the middle finger.

I break away, rising up on my toes to press a kiss to his cheek. "Just be ready to haul ass over that fence as soon as I clear the way. Okay?"

The skin around his eyes crinkles with worry, but he gives me a tight nod of agreement. He doesn't like the plan, but he'll follow me anywhere.

Everyone else huddles in a tight group, eyes flicking between me and the zombies. They're counting on me to save them. I can't let them down.

I face the zombies and hit the play button. The familiar clicks and keens come out of the speaker.

The three dozen zombies still, heads cocking in eerie synchronicity. Then, one by one, they fall back from the fence. They hiss and growl, white eyes rolling. They hunch over, as though being driven by a whip.

As soon as they begin to clear out, I throw the blanket over the barbed wire and grab the cold metal fence. Making sure the volume on my tape recorder is turned up to full blast, I scale upward as quietly as I can. The zombies let up a collective moan. I freeze, poised on top of the fence. They continue to retreat.

I drop lightly to the ground, heart thudding. Separating me from three dozen zombies is no more than an eight-foot swath.

I edge to the right. The sound from the recorder widens the opening around the zombies. I silently thank Johnny for having the foresight to loop the recording.

In one hand I draw my zom bat, a gift from Jesus. In the other hand, I wield the recorder like a lifeline. The rubber soles of my running shoes are silent on the hard-packed dirt. I advance on the zombies, steadily pushing them in the direction of the cliff.

My breath saws in and out of my lungs. Every bodily

instinct urges me to turn and run. I curl my toes, forcing myself to advance on the zombies. Inch by inch, they stumble away from me, herded ever closer to the cliff that will drop them into Pudding Creek.

Just another few steps . . . the first zombie keens as it steps over the edge and plummets downward. There is a satisfying *thud* as its body hits the ground.

Out of the corner of my eye, I see Ben and the others making their way toward the fence. I keep my focus on the zoms.

Another few steps. Two more zombies go over the side.

By now, I'm close enough to the edge to see when they hit the bottom. One explodes in a bloody mess on a rock outcropping. The other lands in the water, hitting several other zombies as it does. The water froths with blood and body parts.

The mass of zombies beneath the bridge is bigger than ever, their numbers swelling from the large amount of undead who have already walked over the cliff, along with those drawn from farther upstream who had been in the water.

I return my attention to the zombies in front of me, advancing on them with the recording. Three more go over the side. Then another two. Then—

Silence blares out from the tape recorder.

The recording is over.

Shit.

I hit rewind, cold sweat breaking out along my back and neck as the zombies mill around in confusion. A few of them snarl and scent the air.

I wave my free hand at my companions, signaling for them to stop. Ben and Caleb are already over the top of the fence. Eric and Reed freeze in their tracks, clinging to the chain-links.

The rewind button on the tape recorder clicks off. The tiny noise has every zombie snarling, faces turning to home in on me.

Heart pounding, I push play. Ben and Caleb reach me, flanking me on either side with weapons drawn.

The voice of the alpha zom once again washes over the zombies. Their snarls fade into grunts and hisses of confusion. They retreat, hunched over and growling in meek postures.

Reed and Eric continue up and over the fence. I pick up the pace, advancing on the zombies. Another handful goes over the cliff. The sound of them hitting the rocks and the water is satisfying.

I jerk my chin at Ben in a silent order. *Go.*

He glares at me. I repeat the motion. Caleb grabs his arm. The two of them fall back with the rest of the group just as Ash drops down over the fence.

Go! I mouth the word. *Go!*

They go, but not fast enough. They move at a fast walk, every last one of them keeping their eyes on me.

Shit. I want them off and running away from these monsters in case anything goes wrong, but it's clear they don't intend to leave me behind.

Another few steps. Another zom goes over the side.

That's right, I think, pursuing the zombies as they stumble back from me. Over the edge, you fuckers. Another few steps . . .

A long, high-pitched keen slices the air, over-powering the small speaker in my tape player. A chill crawls up my spine.

Out of the mass of zombies farther inland, an alpha emerges from the crowd. It wears muddy jeans and a baggy sweatshirt with a San Francisco Giant's logo on it. Standing there, head cocked in my direction, it lets up another keen.

Fuck. I'm no expert on alpha zom language, but I'm pretty sure that one just said hello to me. I've seen multiple alphas on the move before, functioning as a unit.

Apparently, I've just nabbed the attention of one. And now it's coming my way, a large group of zombies in tow.

I'd wanted to get rid of three dozen zombies. Now I've managed to get the attention of twice that number.

This is what Ben meant by battle testing. The alpha recording is apparently not a get-out-of-jail-free card.

As if things couldn't get worse, the clouds decide to let loose the rain they've been holding onto all morning. Cold droplets pierce my clothes and hit the top of my head.

Shit. My small pack of zombies spins in confusion, heads pinging back and forth between me and the new alpha. A few of them are already straying away in its direction.

I take another few desperate steps forward, driving a few more over the cliff. There's no more than a dozen remaining now.

The new alpha is one-hundred yards away and closing. It continues to keen and click.

A hand closes around my right biceps. It's Ben. The look in his eyes is urgent.

I shake my head, determined to get rid of as many of these zombies as I can. The last thing I want to do is leave them for the new alpha to scoop up. I drag him forward with me, watching another two zombies plummet over the side. Another three zombies stagger off in the direction of the new alpha. The new horde is closing in, no more than seventy-five yards away.

There are only six zombies remaining. I give Ben a look. He nods.

We charge forward just as the tape recorder once again goes silent, the track running out for a second time. *Dammit.* I slam one foot into a zombie, sending it stumbling backward over the cliff.

I swing upward, my zom bat taking a second zombie in the nose. Its face crumples beneath the impact.

Beside me, Ben straightens, yanking his knife free from the zombie at his feet. The last three from my pack have staggered off in the direction of the new alpha.

We turn and run in the direction of our companions.

They stand in a tight cluster a hundred yards up the coastline, waving frantically at us.

Rain pelts down. It's not the persistent drizzle that followed us for almost the entire length of the Lost Coast trail. This is a pounding, relentless torrent that soaks through our clothes in seconds and turns the ground to mud. I hunch over as I run, trying to shield the tape recorder with my body.

"You are so god-damn fucking crazy," Ben huffs. "You're going to make me lose my mind. I'd say you'd better not ever do anything like that again, but you wouldn't listen."

He's right. I'd risk myself all over again to save him and the others. Instead of replying, I grab his free hand and hang onto it as we run.

8
Sand

KATE

I fumble the Ziploc with cold fingers, sliding the tape recorder back inside. What I wouldn't give for a dry bag and a towel. The black shiny plastic is damp, and I have no way to dry it. I can only hope the little droplets won't damage it.

A look over my shoulder shows the alpha zom closing in on the zombies we killed near the bridge.

"We have to move."

No one argues, though I know they're all feeling the pain of having run over thirty miles in such a short time frame. We're exhausted and aching.

We run anyway.

I lead them through the storm, putting distance between us and the horde. We run through the blond coastal grasses that bow under the force of the wind. To our right is the Pacific Ocean. To our left, past the open grass and the line of gnarled cypress trees, is a row of homes lining the frontage road. Zombies wander the open area between the two. We give them a wide berth.

A half mile ahead of us looms a parking lot. A banner hangs limp in the rain, one side having been ripped from the pole that held it up. It ripples in the storm, sporting the image of a whale printed in black ink.

I'd forgotten about the whale festival. I slow, scanning the parking lot through the gray mist. The others cluster around me, studying the obstacle course in front of us.

"Of course, there are zombies," Ash mutters. "We can't catch a break."

Yep. Throughout the hard-packed dirt parking lot are zombies. Lots of them. They wander aimlessly in the rain. If the lot had been any closer to Pudding Creek, no doubt they would have been drawn there by the frenzy.

I see what I suspect is an alpha. A tall zombie woman stands off to one side. It makes no sound, but at least a dozen other zoms make small circles around her.

I make a decision. We're too tired to fight and too tired to manage a prolonged sprint. And my alpha recording will just attract the attention of the alpha.

"We're going around."

Ash lets her shoulders sag, some of the tension and worry sliding away. "Thank God. I wasn't up for another fight." Everyone else exhales in relief.

Except for Ben. He is the only one who doesn't one hundred percent approve of my plan. I can tell by the wrinkle on his brow as he takes in the scene.

"Going around will put us closer to those houses." He jerks a thumb at the row of little cottages that dot the east side of the frontage road. "I'm not sure that's a better option. Lots of zoms wandering around."

"We're not going around on the east side. We're going down there." I point out toward the ocean.

Soft moans pepper the air, and they're not from zombies. I ignore them. There are no good choices in front of us. All I can do is pick the least dangerous of them.

If possible, my people look even more defeated. It's possible none of them will think of the beach in a positive light ever again.

"I don't suppose you'd agree to trying our luck in one of those pretty houses?" Ash asks.

I shake my head. "That alpha and the pack from the

river are too close. I don't want to get boxed between them and those zoms ahead in the parking lot. I promise we'll stop for food and clothing before we leave Braggs, just as soon as we get past these hordes."

I turn, heading toward the tall cliff that overlooks the ocean. Reaching the edge, I pause to look down.

There is no official trail leading down to the water, but the locals have carved their own path. My eyes pick out a haphazard trail in the side of the cliff. It's partially overgrown with coastal succulents. Other parts are covered with slides of earth from heavy rains. Despite that, it's still discernible.

"You want us to go down *that*?" Eric stares at me. "There's no trail."

"There's a trail," I assure him. "We're going to follow the coastline and bypass the town and the festival. Come on."

At that exact moment, the rain decides to double its efforts. Gritting my teeth, I step onto the trail.

I lead them through the slippery ice plant, a succulent that grows all over the Californian coastline. In the summer, large pink and yellow blooms adorn the plants. Today, the rain makes their rubbery leaves slippery.

The ground is saturated. Water pools on the flatter areas of the man-made trail. I don't even try to circumvent them; what would be the point, when my feet are already soaked? I step right through them, pushing ever closer to the beach below.

The wind whips across our bodies, carrying the rain with it. The ocean drums against the shore, an incessant pounding.

I slip on the ice plant, landing hard on my hip. Caleb grabs my elbow and helps me up. His face is set into a determined mask. I give him a nod of thanks before pushing onward.

As we near the bottom of the cliff, the trail disappears into a tangle of boulders heaped along the shoreline. We're forced to scramble over them. Eric slips and skins his knee, but never complains.

At last, finally, we reach the beach. The sand is a mottled blend of light brown and tawny grains interspersed with dark boulders.

Ahead, through the shifting mist are wandering zombies. I can't get a count at this distance, but there can't be more than a dozen. And they're spread out. As long as we stay quiet, we can pick them off.

I draw my knife and club. "Weapons out. Teams of two."

Caleb and Ash fall in together, as do Reed and Eric. Ben joins me at the front of the line. We snake forward with our weapons ready.

Even before the apocalypse, I never liked running in sand. We've had our fair share of it on this trip. Hell, I still have sand in my shoes and clothes from the Lost Coast.

I move at a hard walk, not wanting to burn through precious energy trying to run on a surface that isn't conducive to *running*. The first zombie comes into view. It's a lone man in a faded T-shirt with Teva sandals. I signal to Ash and Caleb. They peel away to dispatch it.

Another fifty yards in front of us is a cluster of three zoms and a decomposing body. They look like they'd been in the middle of a picnic when all hell broke loose. Their blanket is nothing more than a dirty mound on the ground. The picnic basket is on its side, contents strewn across the beach. It's only because they're close to the cliff face that the ocean hasn't managed to pull all the contents out to sea.

I gesture to Ben. This group is ours.

As we approach, we find the remains of two couples. The women had once been nicely outfitted in cute maxi dresses. They're now ripped and stained with blood. Near the picnic basket is a decomposing body of a man in khaki shorts. His head and torso are gone, only his legs remaining. The final man, this one undead, wears loafers and his own pair of khaki shorts. He wanders in small circles with the two women. They stay near the half-eaten body of the person who had once been their friend.

Between the pounding of the rain and the constant hum of the surf, the three never hear us coming. I take out the first of the women with a kill strike to the temple. Ben takes down the second woman before pivoting to kill the man.

We continue this way down the long stretch of coast, breaking apart and killing the zombies we come across. It feels like we hike for hours through the rain and sand. In truth, my watch shows no more than an hour has passed.

A chill wracks my body. I realize how cold I am. My hands, feet, lips, and nose are frozen. Hypothermia. We're all at risk. Again. Ash almost died from it yesterday. The rain shows no sign of letting up. I need to get everyone into a shelter.

We near a curve in the coastline that juts out to sea. I study the line of water, noting the beach ends in less than a quarter mile.

"We've traveled as far as we can," I call. "It's time to climb back up." I can only hope we've covered enough ground to have bypassed the zombie whale watchers.

Dull, tired eyes look at me. My heart squeezes. I have to get them out of the rain. Soon.

I study the cliff, looking for a way out. Through the mist and rain, a set of wooden stairs materializes. I blink and wipe water out of my eyes, wondering if I'm hallucinating. But no, the set of stairs remains.

I hesitate, fear of what might lie at the top of the stairs making me search for another way up. Then I take in the shivering forms of my people. Everyone, including myself, is cold to the bone. We need the fastest way out of here.

"Stay alert," I tell them. "Keep your weapons out. We're taking the stairs."

With any luck, we won't find a seething mass of zombies at the top.

9
Shelter

ERIC

Thunder rolls through the clouds, vibrating the air around me. Lightning splits the sky. Rain hammers the top of my head.

I'm cold. Not normal cold, where you just need to throw on a jacket or a thicker pair of socks. This is bone cold, a chill that has seeped through my skin and lodged in my body like a parasite. This is what Ash must have felt like when she got hypothermia.

When Kate leads us up the wooden steps embedded into the face of the cliff, I don't argue. There might be zombies at the top, but all I can think about is getting warm.

I try to focus on my surroundings, but I keep hearing my brother's voice. Tom.

Why are you wasting time with those toasters?

Two years older than me, Tom was every parent's dream child. Varsity athlete. Salutatorian of his graduating class. He was accepted into the competitive engineering department of Cal Poly right out of high school.

He was everything I wasn't. Hard working. Goal orientated. Good looking.

Despite our differences, we got along. Having Tom as an older brother kept things easy for me. Mom and Dad were always so swept up in his accomplishments they never paid much attention to my lackluster grades. If I wanted to spend the afternoon taking apart toasters from the Salvation Army to see how they worked, they'd been too busy heading off to one of Tom's baseball games to care.

Tom noticed, though.

Why are you wasting time with those toasters? You should sign up for a robotics class.

That was Tom. He had the long view nailed. He had drive.

I wasn't a fan of hard work. It didn't take long for me to locate the smartest kids in my high school. After that, it was only a matter of figuring out what motivated them.

Amy liked shopping at Macy's. I introduced her to one of Tom's friends who worked there. Her name had been Darcy. Darcy had a crush on my big brother. She agreed to pass along her employee discount to Amy. For the next two years, Amy wrote all my term papers.

Jim was consumed with *Gods of War*, but pretty much sucked at video games. He had some sort of disorder that limited his hand-eye coordination. I'd go over to his house and play the game while he watched. In return, he did my math homework.

Stop wasting your time getting everyone to do your work for you, Tom used to say. *Spend that time improving yourself instead.*

I always figured Tom would grow up to be one of those multi-million dollar motivational speakers.

A shiver travels through my body. I swing my arms, trying to work warmth into the limbs. My fingers are numb. My lips are numb.

I watched hypothermia take Ash down yesterday. I have no doubt this is what's happening to me now.

Things are going to get worse before they get better. That was Tom's last text message to me before we lost electricity and my phone died. *You can't rely on someone else to do the work for you this time. If you don't take care of yourself, you're going to die.*

He'd been right, of course. It had taken Kate to help me see that.

I wish I could talk to Tom. I want him to know I've grown up over the last six months. I want him to know I'm not a freeloader anymore.

"Hey." Ash pokes me in the back. "Keep moving, slow poke."

I lurch, realizing I've been standing in place the last twenty seconds. I force myself to move.

I'm less successful at banishing Tom's voice.

You need to work hard at your own shit instead of manipulating everyone to do it for you. You'll get a lot farther in life, Eric.

Overlaying his voice is Lila's. *You're a fucking con, Eric.*

Tom would have liked Lila. He would have told me to listen to her.

I climb the last step as more thunder and lightning rip the sky. We're in another parking lot. I rub a wet sleeve across my glasses trying to get a better look at our surroundings. There are cars in this lot, but it's not packed like the one where the Whale Festival had been.

There are zombies. No more than a dozen, but right now that's way more than I'm comfortable with. But between the thrum of the rain on the metal cars and the roar of the ocean, none detect our entrance into the lot.

"We go around them," Kate murmurs. "Kill any that get too close."

Her face is bleached white, fatigue pinching the edges of her eyes while her teeth chatter. I have no doubt she's twice as exhausted as the rest of us. We only have to worry about ourselves. Kate worries about all of us.

She holds one hand above her eyes, shielding it from the rain. "We're heading toward that row of houses." She points to the line of one-story bungalows on the far side of the road. "We'll find a place to wait out the storm and resupply."

Kate cuts a wide swath around the parking lot, keeping us away from the zombies that moan and sway in the rainstorm. The wild grass that grows all along the coast is bent low from the deluge. We tromp through it in a long line, wending our way to the road.

Warm blankets. Dry clothes. I don't even care about food, even though I feel hungry enough to clean out a Las Vegas buffet.

We reach the road unmolested. Nearby are two abandoned cars, both empty.

"That one." Ben points to a pink house with a sagging porch and weeds that grow up to the windows. "That one looks deserted."

They all look deserted to me, but I don't argue with Ben. The guy's sixth sense is freaky good. We hurry toward the house, dashing across the street in a tight huddle.

Something moves in my periphery. I freeze, turning to look. Water sheets across my glasses, making it difficult to see.

"What is it?" Reed slows next to me.

"I saw something move." I squint into the carport of the pink house. There are piles of crap everywhere. "I can't see very well, but I saw something move."

Ben shoulders up beside me. "Zom?" He squints into the gloom.

"It didn't move like a zom." Besides, if it had been a zombie, it would still be bumping around.

"You three check it out," Kate tells us. "Make sure the yard is clear. The rest of us will clear the inside of the house."

Ben scowls, clearly not wanting to be separated from Kate. Ash, catching the look, steps forward.

"You go with Kate," she says. "I'll go with the *niños*."

"Who you calling *niño*?" Reed asks.

"You, *pequito niño*. Come on."

She pushes past us with her weapons drawn, moving into the carport in a crouch.

Ash is hot. Like, Lara Croft hot. The hotness is only accentuated with the rain plastering clothing to her body.

Will Caleb ever make a move on her? I can't tell if they're into each other or just good friends.

Tom would like Ash. He liked tough girls. In high school, he dated a voluptuous hot chick who got it into her head that she wanted to play varsity football. She'd been meaner and tougher than all the guys combined. Tom said it was her way of asserting gender equality.

Maybe I should run to Cal Poly and find Tom. The idea flits through my mind.

"Dude." Reed elbows me. "Stop zoning out. Pay attention, man."

I shake myself. Why can't I get Tom out of my head?

"Sorry," I mutter. "I keep thinking about my brother."

"I get it. I think about my family a lot, too. But we need your A-game, brother."

The three of us sweep through the carport, picking our way around piles of crap. A rotting sofa. A rusty treadmill. Several plastic tubs stacked high with faded plastic flower pots. An old tricycle with a missing wheel. It's easy for me to take it all in without rain sheeting across my glasses.

"These people were hoarders," Ash says.

"That bodes well for us if they stocked up on food," Reed replies.

"I hope they have Kraft mac n' cheese," I say. That particular dish always makes me think of Lila. "I—" Something scurries over my foot. I jump, my knife clattering to the ground.

"Raccoon." Ash raises her brow at me as the animal disappears under a tarp at the far end of the carport. "Good thing that wasn't a zombie or you'd be dead."

Shit. I need to focus and make sure this carport is clear.

I let out a shaky breath and retrieve my knife. At least now we know what I saw moving around in here. "Any of you guys ever eat raccoon before?"

"Don't even think about it," Ash replies. "You'd have to shoot it to catch it, and that would just bring zombies."

Reed stares at the tarp concealing the raccoon. "Fresh

meat sounds good though, doesn't it?"

"No way, dude." I give his shoulder a shove. "Be content with the bear meat in your pack."

Hunting was yet another thing Tom excelled at. I went along on the trips with our dad because I didn't have a choice, but I never had a lot of interest in creeping around in the forest before dawn. I preferred being in the tent with a thermos of hot chocolate.

What would Tom do, if he were here? Would he try to catch the raccoon? I can just see him sauntering into the pink house with a brace of dead raccoons over one shoulder. Everyone would fawn over him and thank him for the fresh meat.

That was Tom. Always the star without even trying. He never knew how to be anything else.

"Come on." Ash slaps me on the arm. "It's clear in here. There's nothing in the backyard but dead plants and a rusted swing set. And that raccoon. Let's get the hell out of this storm."

As we head back to the pink house, another peel of thunder rolls through the sky. The concussive boom vibrates the hair on my arms. Lightning forks the sky.

And just for a second, I swear I see Tom's silhouette in the gloom.

I blink, staring through the rain, realizing just how wiped out and exhausted I am. My brother isn't here. I'm seeing things. I need to get out of the cold and warm up.

Hunching my shoulder against the downpour, I hurry after Ash and Reed.

10
Pink House

KATE

The pink house is abandoned.

There are no corpses inside, dead or undead. It smells like a regular abandoned house, rank with rotting food and musty from being closed up.

Dirty breakfast dishes are piled in the sink, mold growing on the old food—hence the stink—but there are no signs of a family that left in a panic. All the clothes are neatly folded in the drawers and hanging in the closets. A neat row of shoes sits in a rack by the front door. Based on the various sizes, I can see a family once lived here.

"There's a boys room and a girls room," Reed calls from down the hall.

Ash hustles around Reed, an armload of towels in her arms. She passes them out.

"The water heater is full," she says. "The water won't be hot, but we can at least get clean."

I take the towel she hands me, grateful for a chance to clean up. I kick off my shoes and peel off my wet socks.

The first order of business is to get dry and find a new set of clothes. My salt-encrusted pants, shirt, and sports bra have to go.

The bedroom shared by the parents is only slightly larger than the kid's rooms. I find stretch pants that mostly fit. They're too long, as is the long sleeve shirt, but they'll do. The sports bra I find is a little big, but a safety pin is enough to cinch it smaller.

Once changed, I head to the kitchen. Ben is already there, dressed in jeans and a long-sleeve shirt. The sight stops me in my tracks.

He looks good. The shirt is snug, showing off the contours of his chest and biceps. The jeans hug his hips and . . . I jerk up my eyes, feeling my face heat as I realize where I was looking. At least Ben is too busy piling canned food on the kitchen table to notice.

He glances up at me, pausing to run a hand over the stubble at his chin. When he sees the look on my face, he grimaces. "It's sort of like seeing the clown without his make-up on." He gestures to the jeans and plain green shirt.

He doesn't remotely resemble a clown, but I decide to go with it instead of confessing to what I really think. "I've never seen you out of your fatigues."

His nose wrinkles. "I don't usually admit it when I'm wrong, but I'm going to. Just this once. I am chafed to high hell from the fatigue pants."

It takes all my effort not to laugh at the expression on his face. The situation really isn't funny. "Jeans are the last thing you should be wearing. Your skin needs oxygen flow to heal. I saw a few pairs of men's sweatpants in a drawer." I pluck at the ones that hang from my hips. "They'll probably fit you."

"I'll look for them after we eat." He buries his head in one of the cupboards to look for food.

I test the stove, letting out a yelp of glee when a blue flame licks to life. "We have gas! We can make hot water."

"Gas?" Ben lifts an eyebrow. "That's interesting. Guess no one had a chance to shut it down,"

"Yay for us and hot food," I reply.

We spend the next fifteen minutes bustling around the tiny kitchen, attempting not to bump into one another.

The entire scene feels freakishly domestic. If we weren't in the apocalypse, the two of us could be together in a kitchen somewhere, preparing a meal. Cooking real food, not heating up canned stuff.

I can almost see a life like that with Ben. Almost. It's hard to imagine a normal life ever again, but if I could, Ben would be in it.

I bury these thoughts and sort through a box of tea bags. I opt for chamomile. We could all use something to help us relax, plus it will warm us up.

By the time the others are dry and changed, we have a glorious meal of tea and hot food. There's a mixture of canned peas and carrots in one pot. Another holds ten packages of Top Ramen. Ben found a whole case of chili in the cupboard, which we also heated up.

Everyone grabs cups and bowls and digs in. We eat like the pack of half-starved ultrarunners that we are. We plow through the food in less time than it took to heat it up. After that, everyone falls to rummaging in the cupboards and pantry. Potato chips, boxes of crackers, and jars of peanut butter find their way onto the table.

Thunder rolls overhead, loud and fierce. It's a bona fide summer thunderstorm out there. Just great. I hope for a dry patch to finish our journey to Braggs. The last thing I want is to get everyone dry only to shove them all back out into the rain.

"Time for showers and first aid," I say. I have no doubt we all have our fair share of blisters, chafe marks, and other physical ailments among us. "Then we sleep for two hours and get back on the road." We're four hours past Fort Ross's deadline. If we're going to have any chance of saving Alvarez and his people, we can't afford to rest longer.

I collect needles, bandaids, and all other first aid supplies I can find, then set up a make-shift infirmary in the living room. I lance blisters and wrap the tender spots with bandages. I clean cuts and scrapes gathered out on the trail. I even pick off a few ticks from people. Considering what my people have been through, the wounds aren't that bad.

There's not much to be done for chafe marks besides a hydrogen peroxide wash and a smear of petroleum jelly. Ben refuses to let me see how bad things are when it's his turn, but he does change into sweats when I suggest it a second time. The angry red marks under Ash's sport's bra make me wince, though she never complains.

After I finish treating everyone, I wash and change into clean clothes. By then, most of the others have settled down for our short respite. I look for a place to sleep.

I peer into the girl's room. Ash is on the twin bed under a pink flowered bedspread. Caleb is on the floor wrapped in a thick quilt. Eric has the twin bed in the little boy's room, while Reed lays on the floor wrapped in blankets.

"There's another room with a bed," I tell him. "You don't have to sleep on the floor."

Reed cocks an eyebrow at me. "The big bed is for you, Mama Bear."

"You and the old man," Caleb says from the girl's room.

"You guys are boyfriend and girlfriend now, remember?" Eric snickers.

"That definitely comes with perks." Reed gives me a thumbs up and a big grin.

Oh. Consternation sweeps through me, making my face hot. I feel like I'm on display in the worst way.

I turn on my heel, planning to head to the couch—and run smack into Ben. I hadn't realized he'd been standing behind me.

I stare up at him. There is no doubt in my mind he heard everything that was just said. Even if he wasn't standing two feet behind me, this is a very, very tiny house.

I want him. I want his touch and his kisses as much as I've ever wanted anything.

But something inside holds me back. I might be forty, but I was pregnant and married by the time I was nineteen. I've only been with one man in my life. As much as I want Ben, I'm nervous about it. Especially with four other people in a house with paper-thin walls.

I swallow, hoping I don't make a mess of things. "Ben—"

He rests his hands on my shoulders, silencing me with a look that is surprisingly tender. "I had to kill a bear to get a decent kiss out of you," he says. "I never assumed it would be any easier to get you in bed. I'll sleep on the couch."

I stare at his retreating back, mouth sagging open. His words are gruff. From anyone else, they would have been crass. But I know Ben well enough to understand he's making a genuine effort to be a gentleman.

"Come on, old man," Caleb says from the bedroom. "How much easier do we have to make it for you?"

"Fuck you."

"You could at least *try*," Reed calls from the other room. "I mean, there's a big bed for you guys. When do you think you're going to get a big bed again? All we have back at Creekside are bunk beds."

This brings hoots and laughter from both rooms.

If I stand here any longer, I might die of embarrassment.

I follow Ben into the living room. I hover in the doorway, looking across the room at him.

He looks back at me from his seat on the oversized couch. "I'll keep first watch. I don't sleep much anyway." He raises his voice. "I'll wake one of the little shitheads when it's their turn to keep watch."

"We heard that," Eric says.

"That was the point, shithead."

"Do you guys need an instructional video?" Reed asks. "I bet we could find a porno somewhere around here. We could try the master—"

"*No!*" Ben and I say in unison.

"*Suficiente!*" Ash says. "Shut your mouth, Reed."

I lean against the wall and gather myself. There's no way I can sleep after all this.

Ben is watching me to see what I will do. I don't want things to be weird between us. We're finally at a point where things *aren't* awkward. Making up my mind to keep it that way, I cross the room and sit beside him on the couch.

He looks at the six inches of space that separates us. "I gave you the bed, Kate. The least you can do is give me this." He gestures to the gap.

He's right. I owe it to him. Besides that, I don't want space between us.

I scoot over, closing the gap. Even through the fabric of our clothing, I feel the heat from his body. It sends a shiver through me.

"Ignore the little shitheads." He puts an arm around me and pulls me close.

Tension leaches out of me. My muscles relax. I slide my arms around his waist and rest my head on his shoulder.

"For once, I'm in agreement on the nickname."

"We heard that," Eric calls. "We are *not* shitheads."

"Mind your own goddamn business!" Ben's voice is almost a shout. He manages to choke back the volume just as another round of thunder crashes overhead.

The entire situation is ludicrous. Laughter shakes my shoulders. After a moment, Ben's chest rattles with a silent chuckle.

We sit in comfortable silence. I soak in the warmth of his body, listening to the rain drum on the roof and windows.

"What if it's still raining in two hours?" he asks.

I hold up my watch for him to see. The time reads twenty-eight hours and thirty-six minutes. "That's how long it's been since we last spoke to Alvarez. I'm hoping we can get to Fort Ross in another twenty-four hours. Thirty-six at most."

"So you really are going to march us back out into the rain in a few hours if it doesn't let up?"

"I hope it doesn't come to that, but yes. Lives depend on us. I don't like running in the rain any more than you, but it's manageable."

"Ash almost died of hypothermia." He covers my hand with his. "You're still cold."

"Did I ever tell you about the time I ran the Bear?"

He shakes his head. "Is that one of your crazy ultra races?"

"Yeah. It was a hundred miler that started in Utah and ended in Idaho. I got caught in a snowstorm. My legs had frostbite when I crossed the finish line, but I finished."

He snorts. "No wonder you have such a warped perspective on what the human body can endure."

"I think it's everyone else who has the warped perspective," I reply. "We all had easy lives before the zombies. Most people don't understand how much they're capable of. That's what I'm trying to teach these kids."

He shifts. I sense him looking down at me. I tilt my chin up to meet his gaze.

"I love how crazy you are." His murmur washes over me. I close my eyes as he leans down to kiss me.

Our first kiss was a disaster, a drunken impulse on my part that surprised Ben and ended awkwardly. Our second kiss had been fueled by terror and adrenaline after Ben killed the black bear that attacked our camp on the Lost Coast. Our third kiss under the Candelabra Grove had been pure magic.

This kiss is long, deep, and lingering. I allow the world and all my worries to melt away, if only for a few perfect moments. His arms feel safe. His arms feel *good*.

Ben is the first to break away. He pulls back to look at me. "Sleep here with me on the couch. I'll watch over you."

I like the idea of staying close to him. After kissing him one last time, I curl up on my side with my head on his thigh. He drapes a blanket over me and settles a strong hand on the curve of my waist.

I fall asleep in seconds, feeling warm and safe.

11
New Regime

JESSICA

Shortly after Rosario's takeover, our entire group is locked inside one of the original Fort Ross structures. It's a single-story home known as the Rotchev House. We've been in here for hours.

The Rotchev House isn't large by any stretch of the imagination. It was never designed for fifty-five people. The rooms of the house bleed into each other without any modern sense of organization.

I've taken up position beside one of the windows at the back of the house. The glass is old, the world beyond wavering and uneven when seen through it.

Around me are whispers and murmurs. People have broken up into clumps. Some huddle together on the floor, consoling one another. Others pace, talking in low voices. Planning.

Alvarez has a plan. Apparently, he had people stash weapons all over the fort. There are even a few screwdrivers under loose planks in the kids' room of this house. He left out a big box of booze for Rosario's people to find. When they celebrate their takeover of the fort, we'll strike back.

It's a shaky plan at best. Rosario's people have firepower. A *lot* of firepower. And it's not just fuckheads with guns we have to worry about. They've brought a dozen zombies into the fort, all of them leashed like the one that bit Shaun. What sort of deranged idiot brings zombies *inside* her home? No matter what, we're going to lose people.

I watch Rosario's people scuttle through the grounds, ransacking the buildings, tents, and motorhomes. Two women enter an RV, shrieking with triumph as they deck themselves out in new clothes. They toss things out onto the scrub grass that grows in patches around the fort. An old shoe box spills a dozen books across the ground.

I shift my gaze past the desecration of our home. It cuts to the bleeding figure tied to the laundry pole near the well. The worst part is that Shaun is still alive, suffering and dying slowly. My eyes ache as though I've spent hours sobbing, though in truth I haven't cried since the day my daughters died.

"I'm sorry about Shaun." A teenage girl leans up against the other side of the window across from me, watching the pillaging. She sniffles, scrubbing at the tears that leak down her cheek. "I know you guys aren't married anymore, but still—I'm sorry." She swallows, throat convulsing as she suppresses a sob.

Sometimes it's hard to look at the teenager with dirty blond hair. Stephany is her name. Steph.

She looks nothing like either of my girls. I don't see an older version of Claire and May when I look at her.

It doesn't matter. I still see a girl who survived. It's impossible not to think of Claire and May when I'm around her.

I should respond to Steph, but I don't know how. Bitter words curl on the end of my tongue. I refrain from dumping them on an innocent teenager. I'm not that messed up. Yet.

Steph was in the original group who'd come here with Alvarez in the beginning. I'd heard snippets of the story, of how Alvarez rescued her family from a van stuck on a freeway and surrounded by zombies. It wasn't so different from the story of how Alvarez rescued me and Shaun from an abandoned station wagon north of Fort Ross.

Except both my girls were already dead when he found us. Alvarez never had a chance to save them.

"Hey, guys."

My eyes flick to Bella, who joins me and Steph at the window. She's the only other teenage girl in Fort Ross.

Bella and Steph are bound through age and gender, though as far as I can tell that's the most they have in common. Bella was one of those popular kids when there were still high schools. She reeks of confidence. It's no stretch of the imagination to see her dating the high school quarterback, getting straight As, and running for student body president.

Steph, on the other hand, is more of the shy, study-bug type. She follows Bella around like a puppy. Even more so since the day she'd been kidnapped by one of Rosario's men.

At the time, we hadn't known about Rosario. Two of her scouts had stumbled onto our community and snatched Steph and another woman named Kris from the gardens.

Kris never made it back. She'd been raped and later shot when she tried to escape. Alvarez got there before the men could start in on Steph. Another ten minutes and it might have been too late for her. The experience had tethered Steph even more tightly to Bella. She puts on a good fake smile and pretends everything is okay, but it's all bullshit. That girl isn't okay by a long shot.

Tears trickle down Steph's cheeks as she takes in Shaun's slack, bleeding form on the laundry pole. "I'm so sorry, Jessica." She chokes on a sob as she speaks.

I want to walk away from the girls, but there aren't a lot of other places for me to squeeze into. And as much as I want to scream and beat my fists on Shaun's chest, the idea of not being able to see him makes my heart cramp.

"Are you okay?" Bella asks.

I look away without answering. No, I am not okay. I haven't been okay for a long time.

"He's such a good person," Steph whispers. "I'm so sorry."

Their sympathy makes me want to break something.

I feel Alvarez enter the room before I see him. I can tell by the rustle of activity near the doorway when he's near. I switch my attention to him, glad for the distraction.

I watch him move through the room. His shoulders bend as he pauses to speak and offer words of comfort to each and every person. The people love him. They sit up a little straighter when he's near. I see the way his words transform people. They don't strip away fear, but they do leave everyone with a sliver of hope in their eyes.

I look away when he drifts in my direction. I don't want his comfort.

"You girls doing okay?" Alvarez has a warm smile for Bella and Steph.

"What are we going to do?" Steph asks. She, in particular, idolizes Alvarez for saving her family and getting them to Fort Ross.

"I know things are scary right now, Steph, but I promise you we're going to get through this." The words roll off his tongue like honey, a balm to her fear. "Jessie?" He turns his attention to me.

Besides Shaun, Alvarez is one of the few people who calls me Jessie. It stirs something inside me every time he does it.

I ignore the feeling, giving him a flat stare. I don't need this man to sugar coat anything for me. I know how fucked up our situation is.

"Jessie . . ." His voice trails off as he stares out the window at Shaun. "Jessie, I—"

I hold up a hand to silence him, shaking my head. I know where the blame for this situation lies. It was all Shaun's doing. Besides, rehashing it isn't going to make

Shaun any less dead.

How long is Rosario going to leave him strung up on the laundry pole? Until he turns?

The idea makes my stomach hurt. The time it takes an infected person to turn varies. I've seen it happen in several hours, like it did with my daughters. I've seen it take three to four days on adults.

Shaun could be out there for *days*.

I fist my hands, wishing I could smash them through the glass.

Alvarez's smile stiffens. I admire him for even trying with me. I'm not the nice housewife I used to be, once upon a time in a galaxy far, far away.

"Shaun asked me to look after you," Alvarez murmurs. "I intend to do that."

I don't laugh in his face, though I want to. His words confirm my suspicion that Shaun knew he was sacrificing himself. He wouldn't have extracted that promise otherwise.

"You don't have to look after me. You have all these other people to look after." I don't bother telling him I don't care if I live or die anyway.

Alvarez refuses to be rebuffed by my coldness. His hand comes up to rest on the side of my cheek. The unexpected tenderness freezes me in place.

"I know you're hurting, Jessie. We're going to get through this."

For the barest second, I dare to look at his face. Into his eyes. A woman less fucked up than me could lose herself in those soft black eyes. Is it any wonder half the women in the fort are infatuated with him?

He gives me a gentle smile before moving on.

Steph and Bella fold together, huddling on the ground with their arms around one another.

I stay where I am.

I don't know how long I stand at the window watching the blood drip out of Shaun's body. There will always be a part of me that hates every fiber of him for breaking my heart. The fact that he's leaving me a second time—in a more permanent fashion this time—makes me hate him all the more.

Even so, I'd trade places with him in a heartbeat.

12
Assholes Live Forever

JESSICA

A ripple of commotion runs through the old Rotchev House. At first, I think it's Alvarez once again moving through the rooms to spread his kind smile and words of comfort.

Except it doesn't take long to discern there's a different edge to the ripple. A sharp sting of fear hits me.

"Everyone out!" bellows a shrill woman's voice. Jeanie. I'd recognize her voice anywhere. She's the bitch with the zombie who bit Shaun. "I want every last one of you outside and on the ground in five minutes. I'll shoot someone for every extra minute it takes. The timer starts *now*."

A single second of stunned silence hangs in the air. Then every person surges toward the single exit provided to us.

I position myself just behind Bella and Steph. A worry for them has been growing in my mind.

Steph barely escaped the last time Rosario's goons got their hands on her. What's going to happen to her now? To her and Bella?

I'm not stupid enough to think I can provide any sort of protection against men with guns, but I stick close to them anyway. Once upon a time, my whole world had been built on taking care of Shaun and my girls. If I'm honest

94

with myself, I miss it. Desperately.

I miss making little ham and cheese sandwiches on sliced whole wheat with the crust cut off for Claire. I miss cutting out paper gingerbread men for May's class. I even miss ironing Shaun's shirts. Up until the apocalypse, I'd always assumed my calling in life was to be a housewife.

It had been a great gig.

We rush outside into the open dirt area around the old stone well. Shaun's head lolls to one side, eyes slit as he watches us. Armed men and women form a lopsided circle. Jeanie waves us into the circle with her gun. She has on a new shirt that reads *Assholes Live Forever.*

"Into the circle, assholes," she shouts. "Anyone who tries anything stupid will be shot. No warnings, no questions asked. Everyone on your knees with hands behind your head."

I jostle Steph and Bella toward the center of the circle. Maybe if they're in the thickest part of the group no one will notice them.

"Keep your heads down," I murmur to them. "Don't make eye contact."

I surreptitiously take note of our situation. Four men and three women contain us in the lopsided circle, each of them with a leashed zombie. There are more perched on the rooftops of the surrounding RVs, every last one armed with multiple weapons. More people stroll about, all of them also armed.

"Thirty seconds." Jeanie taps her wrist to emphasize the time, even though she doesn't wear a watch. "Chop, chop."

Fear and terror ripples through our people. I put my hands on the backs of Bella and Steph and push them to the ground. I drop to my knees beside them.

"Nice." Jeanie rests her automatic in the crook of her arm to applaud us. "Twelve seconds to spare. We're going to get along famously if you can keep this up."

In my right periphery is Shaun. His head has lolled to

the other side, but other than that, he hasn't moved or made a sound.

In my left periphery is Alvarez. He's also on his knees, playing the part of the cowed subject. I've spent enough time with him to know he's taking advantage of this moment to size up our situation, to look for anything we could use to our advantage in the future.

It doesn't take a genius to see there's no advantage here. Rosario had us out-gunned and out-smarted from the beginning. Some of us are going to have to die. It's the only way out of this situation. There are no fairy tale endings in the apocalypse.

"Slaves." Rosario stands on top of an RV, staring down at us with her hands on her hips. Her voice cracks through the air like a whip. "You're all familiar with the generic meaning. I'm referring to the pre-Civil War meaning of the word. American slaves. You are the first of a new generation. Get used to it."

Slaves. I taste the truth of that word on my tongue. *Slaves.*

"The only good slave is a useful slave," Rosario continues. The ruffles of her wide cotton dress puff up in the wind. "Anyone who doesn't serve a purpose will be *re*purposed."

The lackeys with the zombies waggle their long poles, causing the zombies to moan and swipe at the empty air in front of them. Our community contracts in response, all of us squishing closer together in the dirt.

"There's only one rule: obedience in all things." Rosario faces us, hands on her hips. "Just in case any of you have any ideas about being a hero. Anyone who defies me or my people will be beaten without question. If you survive that, you'll be required to choose one among your fellow slaves to submit to death by zombie. If you don't survive . . ." She grins as the people shrink further into the ground at her words. "Well, if you don't survive, my girl Jeanie will pick one among you to join your fearless leader on the post."

Shaun.

"I'll leave you with that warning," Rosario says. "You get to decide whether or not I'm bluffing."

She's not bluffing. Anyone can see that. And there isn't a soft face among her followers.

"Now," Rosario continues, "we need able-bodied men and women who can fish. You will be expected to bring in a quota of food every day. Volunteers?"

Eyes dart back and forth. Heads turn.

A hand creeps into the air. Andrew. He's out on the fishing boats almost every day.

A few more hands inch into the air.

"You, you, you." Rosario scans the rest of the hands. "And you. Scooby, round 'em up." Rosario gestures to the man with one of the zombies. "I expect to be dining on fresh fish tonight."

"You heard her," Scooby barks. "Fishermen, with me."

Slowly, hesitantly, Andrew and the others rise to their feet and make their way to Scooby.

"Now," Rosario continues, "you can't have fish without people to cook them. Who among you is a decent cook?"

Bella and Steph immediately raise their hands. Both have spent their fair share of hours in the communal kitchen. Hands of several older men and women also shoot into the air.

Rosario selects four people to cook. They're taken to the communal kitchen, which has been set up in the largest of the RVs.

Bella and Steph are not among them. I notice two men leering in their direction. Sick dread takes root in me.

Rosario continues to tick off her list, dividing us into our new roles. It feels like we're in a Sorting Hat horror movie.

Cleaners. Gardeners. Hard labor. Maintenance.

Scavengers. Group by group, our people are led away.

Alvarez is among those who volunteer to tend our pathetic gardens outside the gates. He tries to get my attention as he raises his hand. No doubt out of his so-called obligation to Shaun to look after me.

We both know I have a black thumb. I ignore him and keep my hand down.

There are any number of roles I could fill. I don't raise my hand for any of them.

Instead, I stay close to Bella and Steph. The two of them have raised their hands multiple times but have yet to be chosen.

And then the role I've been waiting for. The word crashes over my head like a shattering vase.

"Whores." That brings grins to many faces, including some of Rosario's women. "It's a time-honored tradition for slaves to serve their masters in all capacities."

No one raises their hand.

"No volunteers? We'll just have to pick from among those who are left. Darren, pull out a few willing ladies."

Darren, a skinny man with a wicked leer, beelines across the clearing. A sob breaks from Bella's throat. It doesn't take an idiot to know he's heading straight toward her and Steph.

I can't let him take the girls. Even though Alvarez has a plan in motion, I can't risk anything happening to them.

"I'll do it." The hoarse words push themselves past my dry lips. My stomach threatens to empty itself onto my shoes. "I volunteer."

"That's more like it." Rosario beams at me. "Darren, help the woman up."

"But—"

"Get the woman up, Darren. She's volunteered, after all."

"But what about these two?" He jerks a sullen chin at Bella and Steph.

Bella looks like she'd rather be electrocuted on the

spot. Tears of terror streak Steph's face.

"I'll take care of everyone." Fury beats in my chest as I speak the words. I'm doing the right thing. Someone has to do this. I raise my chin to look at Rosario. "I don't care how many. I'll do it."

"She's a nympho," bellows one of the men with an automatic. Chuckles run through our captors.

"No." The single word rises from Shaun's throat. His chin lifts as he looks in my direction.

I ignore him. *There's two of us who can fall on our swords, asshole.*

"She's either a nympho or a martyr," Rosario says. "Guess we'll find out. No other volunteers? Well then. If this pretty lady wants the job, it's hers. If she isn't up to the task, we can always institute the draft at a later time." The threat is clear in her voice. "Darren, take her."

As Darren grabs my arm with a venomous glare, I glance at Steph and Bella. I want to tell the girls these fuckheads can't hurt me. I want them to know there isn't anything worse than what's already been done to me. I want to tell them to find a way to escape and get the hell out of this place.

There's no chance. I'm taken to a smaller RV and thrown inside. Darren leers at me with promise in his eyes before slamming the door.

13
Broken Glass

JESSICA

I stare at the familiar inside of the RV. A postcard is taped there, bits of smeared blood dried on the coastal scene.

How ironic that, of all the places chosen for my prison, it's the tiny motorhome I called home for the last few months.

I pull the postcard off the door, flipping it over to look at the handwriting on the other side. Most of it is obscured by blood, but the most important part is still legible.

Love, May and Claire

Seeing their names, written by them less than a day before they died, almost breaks me. It was a postcard from our camping trip to their grandmother. I sniffle and shove it under the bed cushion. The last thing I want is for one of the dickheads out there to get their hands on the last piece I have of May and Claire.

Dread and fury mix inside me at the thought of what's to come. I refuse to let dread get the better of me. I haven't been asked to do anything I can't do. I might not like it, but it can be done. It *has* to be done.

I couldn't save my daughters. Maybe I can save Bella

and Steph. I resolve to give it my all. Which means I won't curl up in a ball on the floor and cry. I *won't*.

My mind races. Maybe Alvarez's plan will work. Maybe all the dickheads out there will get shit-faced drunk and we'll kill them all while they're passed out. Sort of like a reverse Trojan horse. It's a long shot at best, but not impossible.

I do my best to rage against the fear, but it comes anyway. It makes my entire body shake. I sit down on the narrow bed as tremors rock me. The only saving grace is that no one is around to see me like this.

Well, almost no one. Shaun and his laundry pole are no more than ten feet away. The windows of the RV are open, giving him a clear view of me. He's looking in my direction. The sorrow in his gaze breathes life into the inferno I've carried inside me for months. I hang onto it for dear life.

"You're not the only martyr out there, Shaun," I whisper.

"It's gonna be a party tonight!" calls a voice. A skinny man with bad teeth comes out from between two tents. In his arms, he carries a large cardboard box. Bottles clink inside. "Look what I found!" he trills.

Rosario's people gather around him. They cackle and crow and gloat, snatching bottles out of the box to pass them around and admire them.

My body settles, some of the fear leaching out. Alvarez's plan is already falling into place. Maybe these assholes will start their party right now. Maybe the nightmare will end before full darkness descends.

One woman yanks the topper off a bottle. She's just about to take a swig when Rosario marches over.

"Stop," she commands.

The woman freezes, the bottle halfway to her lips.

Rosarios jerks it from her hand. "Where did you find this?"

"Over by the sleeping quarters," says the man who found the box of booze. His chest swells with importance.

"Right on top of a pallet of canned food."

"Uh-huh. And it just so happened to be sitting out in the open where any idiot could find it?"

The man shrinks under Rosario's wrath.

"Answer me, Ratty."

"Yes." His voice is meek.

"These fuckers have been inside here for a full twenty-four hours and you think they just so happened to leave their stash of booze out in the open for you to find?"

No one answers.

Never taking her eyes off her people, Rosario tips the open bottle sideways. Dark brown liquor sluices out onto the ground.

Everything inside me compresses as I watch the earth drink our one and only plan of escape.

Rosario flings the bottle to the ground. It hits a large rock and shatters. I stare at the shards of glass, feeling like I'm in a million pieces just like that bottle.

"Pour them out," Rosario orders. "Every last one of them. The only reason the slaves left them out is because they wanted us to find them. They're probably laced with poison."

Muttering in malcontent, Rosario's people comply.

I force myself to watch until the last bottle is emptied. I force myself to watch hope disappear. Despair fortifies me.

Maybe it's better this way. No hope is better than false hope.

"Jessie . . ." Shaun's voice carries to my ears. I hate the sorrow I hear.

I flip him off. The act edges out my dread, making it easier to hold onto the fury.

I'm going to need every ounce of it to survive.

14
Smoke

ERIC

Not even the thunder and lightning raging outside of the pink house can keep me awake. I'm asleep within seconds of closing my eyes.

I dream of Lila.

The dream is always the same. It plays over and over like a subroutine.

I see the zombie clamp around her leg. I see the bloody gash in her shin. I see her put the gun to her head and pull the trigger. I see the way the side of her face caves in like a crushed flower.

And every time in the dream, my body is stuck. Paralyzed. No matter how much I want to move, I can't. I'm forced to stand by and watch Lila do the unthinkable to herself. I relive that moment over and over and over again.

It had been like that in real life. When Lila had been bitten, I'd frozen with shock and sorrow. I'd stood there like a spectator while she'd ended her own life.

I hadn't been there for her when it really counted.

She wasn't wrong when she called me a loser.

My eyes fly open. My heart pounds. My eyes are wet. I sit up and scrub them dry. I take in my surroundings, momentarily forgetting where I am and who's with me.

Reed sleeps on the floor of the tiny bedroom, wrapped in thick blankets.

A faint smell tickles my nose. I sit up, trying to figure out what it is. My abdominal muscles groan at the movement, aching and sore from the long run down the Lost Coast.

The pink house is musty and moldy from being shut up for months, but this is a new smell. It takes me a minute to figure out what it is. When it registers, a jolt of unease goes through me.

Smoke.

It trickles through the bedroom, caught in the motes of light that filter through the mini blinds.

I get out of bed, stepping around Reed. The sore muscles of my legs protest every step of the way. I have chafe marks all around my waist from the running shorts. More around the area where my leg meets my groin. I'm so sore, it feels like my body has been pounded with a hammer.

As perverse as it sounds, I kind of like the soreness. It's a reminder of the crazy shit I've survived in the last twenty-four hours. It's a reminder that *I'm* a survivor.

Out in the living room, I find Kate and Ben on the sofa. Kate is asleep with her head on Ben's lap. Ben's head is tipped back, his jaw hanging loose. A soft snore escapes his mouth. Why they chose a sofa over a functional bed is beyond me, but they look happy together.

Around the room is a distinct gray haze. More smoke. It's thicker in here that it had been in the bedrooms.

Something is burning. I do a quick check through the house to determine nothing inside is on fire. That's good, but with this much smoke *in* the house, something nearby is definitely burning.

"Hey." I give Ben's shoulder a shake.

He bolts upright, hand flying automatically to his side. The knife flashes out. I leap back, holding up my arms.

"Woah, dude. It's just me."

Ben inhales, the sleep clearing from his eyes. Then he glances down at Kate.

"I fell asleep," he says, looking astounded. "I *never* fall asleep on watch."

"Something is on fire. See the smoke?" I wave my hand around to take in the smoky haze.

"Shit." Ben gently dislodges Kate from his lap.

"What's going on?" She sits up, rubbing at her eyes.

"Smoke," I explain. "Something outside is burning."

That wakes her up. The three of us file onto the porch. It's late afternoon, a few hours before dusk. The smoke outside is thick, clogging the air with a gray haze. The rain has stopped.

I scan the road, the nearby houses, and the open land across from us, searching for the source of the fire. I don't see any flames, but there's enough smoke to indicate there's a huge fucking fire somewhere.

"The lightning probably caught something on fire," Ben says.

"Where's a fireman when you need them?" I mean it as a joke to lighten the mood, but my companions ignore me.

Kate's lips are set in a hard line. "Wake everyone up. We're moving out."

Even though the land around us is wet from the storm, the idea of an unchecked wildfire sends a chill through me. We had our fair share of those in California before the apocalypse. I don't want to think about the damage a wildfire could do without anyone to fight it.

It takes less than fifteen minutes to assemble everyone in the living room. I snag the windbreaker I found in one of the closets, zipping it up under my chin. I'm sick of being cold and wet. I'm not sure how much this jacket will prevent either from happening, but it's worth a try. I also grab a baseball cap to keep water off my glasses if it rains again.

Outside, Kate leads us down the road at a brisk jog.

My muscles scream in protest. If possible, I'm even more sore now than I was before going to bed last night.

No wonder ultrarunners don't usually stop to sleep during long races. It's too hard to get going again once your body stiffens up.

A survey of my companions tells me everyone is as stiff and sore as I am. Except for Kate, of course. She looks rested and refreshed.

We follow a small frontage road that follows the profile of the ocean. The smoke continues to thicken as we run. A cough spills from my throat. Somewhere nearby, a zombie moans.

"Try not to cough," Kate whispers. "Don't make any sound that will draw attention to us."

She's right, but that's easier said than done. Smoke forces its way down my throat and lungs. I wish I'd thought to ransack the pink house for a handkerchief. I pull the collar of my shirt up to cover my nose.

Ahead of us, the road curves away from the ocean and heads into town. Kate peels off the road, heading into the knee-high grass that grows along the coastline. We set across the open land, continuing south. As we pass the bend in the road, I look east into town.

A mile away is a strip mall with a Starbucks coffee shop and Denny's. My mouth waters at the sight of the Denny's sign. I wasted many hours of my youth in a Denny's restaurant near my home, hanging out with friends and consuming late-night snacks. What I wouldn't give for a plate of onion rings.

Unfortunately, I see staggering forms in the strip mall parking lot. Zombies. Lots of them.

And that's not all. The zombies are illuminated by a distinct yellow light that doesn't come from the sun.

Fear lurches to life in my chest.

"Fuck me." Ben halts, staring in the direction of Denny's. "That grocery store is on fire."

Sure enough, in the same strip mall parking lot is a

Safeway. Large flames gout from the back of the store.

"Keep moving," Kate says.

She picks up the pace, leading us southward at a run. My legs swish through the grass, each step triggering every ache and pain in my body. My right foot, which had a blister the size of a large spider on the bottom, hurts more than anything else.

The grasses, wet from the rain, soon have my legs and shoes soaked. Water sloshes in the bottom of my shoes. My lungs work overtime, coping with the strain of running and the increasing smoke in the air.

It's impossible not to cough. Everyone is coughing. At least we're far enough away from buildings that we don't have to worry about zombies. Or at least, I *hope* there are no zombies out here lurking in the grass.

Fifteen minutes later, Kate throws up her hand and stops us. "Dammit," she growls.

This might be the understatement of the year. In front of us, the land drops off in a sheer cliff. Another river separates us from the land to the south of us. It's at least twice as wide as Pudding Creek. And deeper, from the looks of things. This one doesn't have zombies standing waist deep in its waters.

"Think we can swim across?" Caleb is the best swimmer in our group. "Doesn't look like there are any zombies in that water."

Kate shakes her head. "You may be able to swim it, but not the rest of us. Those waters are frigid and the tide is strong. We're going that way." She points east.

I follow the line of her finger and spot a bridge spanning the water.

"I hate to be a negative Nancy," I say, "but that bridge is missing half its middle." There's a distinct gap between one side of the bridge and the other. Someone must have blown it in an attempt to keep the zombies inside Braggs.

"The gap isn't that big," Kate says. "Maybe four feet. Five at the most."

I'm pretty sure I've never jumped a five-foot gap in my life. I keep my mouth shut only because I don't have a better idea.

We shift back into a run, hugging the coastline and heading toward the bridge.

"Um, guys?" I say. "That fire is getting bigger." The flames are now the size of a large house.

"The strip wall is probably made from old redwood," Ben says. "Couldn't ask for a better accelerant."

Kate picks up her pace, pushing us harder.

Every muscle protests. There's so much pain I can't even pinpoint its origin. I force myself to keep up.

The bridge looms near. A road sign names the water Noyo River.

Unfortunately, the route to the bridge forces us to pass between two hotels. They flank both sides of the road, ready to catch all the tourists that venture into town. The parking lots are jam packed with cars.

They're packed with even more zombies.

The monsters are restless. They moan, many of them walking in tight circles as smoke fills the town of Braggs. A cluster of five get into a shoving match. They don't use their hands so much as ram their chests and shoulders against each other.

The good news is that they're so distracted by the smoke and each other that none notice as we steal past them, all of us running hard up the bridge.

The last bridge we went over was built to hold a train. This bridge was built to hold cars. Lots of them. It's four lanes wide with a margin in the middle.

Cars litter the roadway. Some were abandoned, the doors left open as their owners made a run for it. There are two pileups, each lumps of three to four cars. I squint into the smoke, keeping an eye out for zombies. I grip both of my knives, palms sweaty on the grips.

A loud *whoomp* goes up behind us. I spin around, using my wrist to wipe at the soot on my glasses. A gout of flame shoots into the sky, embers glinting like fireworks.

"That was probably a propane tank," Ben says. "We gotta move. This town could go up like a tinderbox, especially with gas still in the pipelines."

The explosion sends a ripple through the zombies. Moans and keens rise from their midst.

We have to get the hell out of this town. I don't even feel pain anymore. As I race across the bridge spanning the Noyo River, all I feel is panic.

Two zombies lurch into sight around an abandoned car. It's a mom and her teenage daughter. Kate takes the smaller of the two in the face with her knife. Ben, by her side, takes out the larger.

The bodies slump to the ground. I vault over the body of the mother and keep running, pinning my sights on the gap in the bridge.

Who builds a town between two rivers? What happened to building a town on a nice flat piece of land with no large bodies of water to cross? If I were a king, I would definitely pick a piece of land not surrounded on two sides by water. Some people might say this is defensible, but that's not what I call it. I call it boxing yourself in. Fuck that.

I glance over my shoulders at the zombies in the hotel parking lots. They've split into two groups. A large mass of them moves north toward the fire. The other mass peels off, moving away from the flames—coming up the bridge straight toward us. Leading them is a clicking, keening alpha.

"Fuck." Caleb huffs, running beside me with Ash on his other side. "We are so fucked."

"We just have to get over the bridge," I huff back. Once we get over the bridge, we'll be safe. The river will protect us from the zombies and the flames.

The gap in the road looms before us. Caleb picks up speed, charging toward the gap like a Spartan soldier. I swear I'd hate that guy for his good looks and natural athleticism if I didn't like him.

He barrels past Kate and Ben in a sprint that I'm pretty sure would make an Olympian jealous. The rest of us pant and pump our arms like elementary kids in a game of tag, but none of us can touch Caleb.

He pulls ahead, all his focus honed on the break in the freeway. He hits the edge and vaults into the air, flying through the dusky light like a rock fired from the slingshot.

He hits the pavement on the other side and rolls, body blurring across the ground from the force of momentum.

Seconds later, Kate flies over the edge. She gives a wild shout, her leap nowhere as controlled and focused as Caleb's.

As she arcs over the river, I realize she's in jeopardy. Her jump is short.

"Kate!" Ben bellows.

Her torso hits the edge of the concrete with an audible *thud*. Her hands scrabble at the blacktop. Her legs kick wildly over open air.

Two things happen at the same time.

Caleb rolls to a stop and springs to his feet. At the sight of Kate, he sprints back toward her.

At the same time, Ben picks up speed. He charges the gap with the wild determination of an animal. He leaps from the edge, arms windmilling as he flies over the river.

Ben hits the pavement on the other side of the gap. He trips, flying forward to roll across the blacktop. Caleb sprints past him in the opposite direction, hands reaching for Kate.

Kate manages to get one leg slung over the side of the broken bridge. Caleb grabs her arms and hauls her up the rest of the way.

Ben is there a heartbeat later, his shirt and pants torn from the rough landing. Caleb's shirt is torn, too. Ben grabs Kate in a hug while he simultaneously shakes Caleb's hand.

Less than fifty miles ago, those two hated each other.

Now here they are, shaking hands and congratulating each other on a successful jump over the Noyo River.

I skid to a halt on the edge of the overpass, staring down at the frothing river. It's a good two-hundred-foot plummet to the water below. My feet feel like concrete. Fear makes my tongue stick to the roof of my mouth.

"Fuck me." Reed backs away from the gap, shaking his head. "What the fuck? I can't jump over that."

"That's not four feet." I stare at the jagged abyss that yawns before us. It's not even five feet. "That's got to be six or seven feet."

"Kate made it," Ash argues. "If she can make it, we can make it."

She makes it sound like Kate is the limping gazelle at the back of the herd. In truth, Kate is the toughest in our group. The only one who might be tougher is Ben, but that's only because he spent the last thirty years of his life in active military service.

Ash backs up from the gap, halting when she's twenty feet away. Gritting her teeth, she charges forward.

My palms sweat as she sprints past me, running like a bat out of hell. She lets up a shriek and leaps. Black hair streaks out behind her. Her long legs eat up the empty space. Her arms fling out on either side of her like she's a giant bird of prey.

She hits the other side with both feet. The impact sends her tumbling forward, right into Caleb's arms.

It's like a scene from a bad romance movie. The handsome guy catches the hot girl after her death-defying leap over the chasm of death.

"Don't worry, bro." Reed pats my arm. "You can jump into my arms. I'll catch you."

Without another word, he charges the gap like a kamikaze pilot.

Reed is the fastest of us. When he sprints past me, he runs so fast his body blurs. The wind of his passage ripples the hairs on my arm.

His body catapults through the smoky air. He sails through it like a bird. The fucker looks like he was born to do this shit.

To top it all off, he lands lightly on the other side like a ballet dancer. He throws all his momentum into his feet as he races across the blacktop on his tiptoes.

I'm the only one left.

The alpha and its horde of two dozen zombies have made their way up the bridge. They're fifty yards away and closing.

Another *whoosh* goes up behind them, followed by a *boom*. This time, the flames claw a hundred feet into the air. I hear a building collapse. The rumble of falling timber and concrete echoes through the streets.

The zombies on the bridge split up, some of them turning to hustle back into the city. Reed told me about the time Kate set fire to downtown Arcata; he said many zombies walked right into the flames, drawn to the heat and sound of the fire.

In Braggs, I'm not so lucky to have all of them turn around. At least half follow the alpha and continue on their trajectory toward me, moaning and scratching at the air.

I stare at the yawning chasm in the bridge, a lump of fear in my stomach. There is no one to make this jump for me, no bargain to be struck to get me out of the terrifying task. Magnificent pot brownies can't get me through this. I don't even have a flask of booze for a quick shot of liquid courage.

I flash back to a time before the apocalypse. I sat in the high school bleachers with my parents, watching Tom charge the long jump pit. Of course, Tom was an all-star track athlete, too.

He charged the sandy pit as if his life depended on it. That was how Tom did everything. Full speed.

I'd never once cried for my bother since the apocalypse hit. I wonder if I should have. But how can I cry if I don't even know if he's alive or dead? If my loser ass is alive,

Tom must be alive, too. Hell, he's probably rallied the survivors of Cal Poly into a functioning feudal society with proper hygiene. That would be the sort of thing Tom would do.

Has he cried for me? He probably thinks I'm long gone, his loser of a little brother lost in the first wave that devastated most of the country.

I back away from the gap. I'm not sure if it's so I can get a running head start, or if it's so I can run away from the bridge altogether.

Except the pack of zombies is heading straight for me. Even if I can get around them, fire is eating its way through Braggs. And all my friends are on the other side of the Noyo River.

Quit playing small. Tom's voice scrolls in my head. *Make the leap, little brother.*

I don't recall Tom ever calling me *little brother.* Ever. But his voice is clear in my head. So clear it's like he's standing next to me. Which isn't possible, because Tom is kicking ass down at Cal Poly University. While his lame little brother is trying to figure out if he has a better chance against a wildfire and zombies, or whether he can survive a death-defying leap over the water.

Don't be a loser, Eric. This time, it's Lila's voice I hear. She loved calling me that. She would say it if I brought dinner to her room or if I got mad at the Xbox.

But she'd say it when I was being a wuss, too. She called me on my shit. Like the week I peed in old water bottles because I was too scared to help anyone haul water from the creek to fill up the toilet bowl.

Don't be a loser, Eric.

Quit playing small, little brother.

I take one more terrified look over my shoulder at the zombies and the raging fire that storms through the small coastal town of Braggs.

"Eric!" Kate screams. "Eric, jump!"

I turn toward the gap, and I run.

I don't see the crushed Coke can until it's too late. My shoe hits it at just the wrong angle as I jump.

The metal can slips sideways out from under my foot.

15
Precipice

KATE

When Eric's foot slips sideways, I know he's in trouble.

My heart seizes as he jumps. The fire that chews through Braggs casts a halo around Eric's form. His arms windmill. His legs churn on empty air, as if an invisible walkway spans the nothingness beneath his feet.

"Shit, he's not going to make it."

Ben's words crash over me. As soon as he releases the words, I know it's true. Eric's trajectory is too short. He's going to miss the edge.

He's going to fall into the Noya River and die.

"Eric!" I lunge, arms outstretched, even though there's no mathematically possible way for me to catch him.

Ben hurls himself forward, running for the chasm. He slings off the giant backpack of weapons he's been carrying since we left the pink house. He hurls the pack into the open space, bellowing Eric's name.

My first thought is nonsensical. How can a backpack full of weapons save Eric from a two-hundred-foot drop in the river? Does Ben intend for him to use it as a raft? As a cushion to blunt his plummet?

His intent unfurls before me in slow motion. The pack snaps out, floating in empty air for several seconds. Ben's fist closes around one strap, knuckles white in the ever-growing firelight.

"Grab it!" he roars.

Eric's body drops, swooshing down through the air. He collides with the large backpack, wrapping his body around it like a monkey.

The force of his collision yanks Ben to the ground. Eric disappears from sight, eyes wide behind the lenses of his glasses as gravity sucks him downward. The last thing I see are his limbs wrapped around the backpack as he holds on for dear life.

Ben smacks to the ground with a grunt. His body slides across gravel and debris and he's pulled toward the edge by Eric's weight.

I throw myself on the ground, wrapping myself around one of his legs. "Ben!" Panic surges into my throat. Fear of losing two people I love hammers at me. "Eric!"

Caleb throws himself on Ben's other leg, the two of us wrestling with his limbs like they're giant anacondas. His body slides another foot, then grinds to a halt.

"Do you have him?" I cry.

"I've got him." Ben's torso is half swallowed by the gap. "Pull us up!"

I grapple with his leg, winding my fists into the fabric. I struggle into a sitting position, but as soon as I shift his body slides forward another few inches.

Ash and Reed materialize. Reed takes hold of Ben's belt. Ash latches onto the back of his shirt. With Reed and Ash anchoring Ben's body, Caleb and I scramble to our feet and join them. Together, the four of us pull them up.

Ben's shoulders and head appear, dragged up from the abyss. His knuckles haven't slackened on the strap of the backpack.

A third hand appears, latching onto the side of the broken pavement. I break away and rush toward Eric. I snatch his wrist and pull, leaning back and throwing all my weight into a counterbalance. Reed grabs me around the waist to help.

Eric's body rolls across the ground. The backpack tumbles free of his grasp. He flops onto the pavement, sucking in deep, terrified gasps.

"Eric!" I fling myself at him, attempting to lift him up into a hug. He's bigger than I am, but I try anyway.

Reed joins me. Between the two of us, we manage to haul him to his feet. We cluster in a tight embrace. Tears make my cheeks wet.

"I thought we'd lost you." I dig my fingers into Eric's shoulder. "You scared the shit out of me."

Breath saws in and out of his throat. The lenses of his glasses are foggy from the smoke, but I can still see the whites of his eyes.

"Shit," he whispers. "That was close. Good thing I'm not fat anymore."

Reed squeezes both of us. "For a few seconds there, I thought I was going to lose a brother. You scared the shit out of me, dude. Johnny and Carter would kick my ass if I came home without you."

We all laugh, the sound tinged with the residual panic that clings to us.

"I'm getting too old for this shit," someone grumbles behind me. "Next time, some other shithead gets to risk his ribcage with my dumb-shit maneuver."

I break away from Eric and Reed, whirling around to face Ben. The front of his shirt is ripped. The side of his cheek is abraded from the concrete. But he, too, is gloriously intact and alive.

This should make me happy. Ecstatic. Overwhelmed with joy.

I feel none of those things.

I am overtaken by a surge of anger as my mind flashes through the last sixty seconds. I could have lost Ben. He could have been stolen away from me, just like Kyle had been stolen.

Thinking about this is like stepping through a time machine back to the day Kyle died. To the day Carter and

I came home and found him dead on the front walkway of our house.

I haven't thought about that day since I said goodbye to Kyle on the Avenue of the Giants. It all comes rushing back to me now. I recall the way the world fell out from beneath my feet. I recall the way I had lived, directionless, for the next two years. I'd been a shell of myself.

I stalk toward Ben and shove him. Hard. "What the fuck?" I yell. "You almost died!"

He blinks at me, absorbing my anger with a wrinkled brow. "The kid would have died."

I smack him on the shoulder. When he just stares at me, I hit him again. Then I hit him a third time, just because I don't know what else to do.

My anger is irrational. I know this. But I can't turn the giant tidal wave of fear and anger crashing all around me.

"Kate." He tries to reach for me.

I sidestep, turning my back on him. I can't even look at him right now. My tumbling emotions threaten to unravel me right here on this broken bridge.

Tears blur the edges of my vision. I swipe them away with an angry hand.

As I do, the world south of the bridge leaps into focus for the first time. I'd been so intent on seeing everyone safely over the Noya River, I hadn't paid any attention to what was beyond it.

We've all done our share of shouting in the commotion of the last five minutes. It has not gone unnoticed. Stumbling toward us in a mass of rot are a dozen zombies. They raise their arms, moans piercing the smoky air. The light of the growing fire paints their bodies a lurid orange.

"Get your weapons out," I snarl, fists closing on my knives. "These fuckers are going down." I turn a glare on my people, letting it linger on Ben longer than necessary. "And if any of you even *thinks* about getting bitten, I'm going to kick your ass."

Normally, seven against twelve isn't great odds.

Normally, I wouldn't think of pitting us against so many.

But today is different. Our determination is electric. I feel it gathering around our tight-knit group.

Braggs has not been kind to us. We may have left the main part of the city, but we still have several miles of outskirts to make it through. We didn't survive two bridges, a horde of zombies, and a fire just to die now. No fucking way.

"She's scary when she's mad."

It takes me a second to register Ash's voice. I ignore her, focusing on the horde that lurches in our direction. They're thirty feet away and closing. We're killing these assholes and getting the hell out of Braggs.

I sense Ben's presence just behind my left shoulder, hovering at my back. I'm so angry I can't look at him or acknowledge his presence.

I break into a run, charging at the undead.

The first of them dies with my knife buried in its forehead. I yank it free, spinning around to kill the next monster that reaches for me. This one gets a zom bat to the nose.

More of them edge in, closing around me like the petals of a carnivorous plant. I bare my teeth and slash at the next closest one.

"Dammit, Kate." Ben stabs one in the back of the head, flinging it aside. "Watch yourself!"

Eric steps up on his other side, smashing the skull of a zombie in his path.

All my people are there. Smoke from the fire swirls around us as we fight, cutting a bloody path through the undead. Within minutes, we're surrounded by a pile of dead bodies.

We pause, all of us panting from the small battle. I take in the scattering of small shops, restaurants, motels, and low-roofed homes that stretch before us. The road, still four lanes wide, is cluttered with abandoned cars and zombies.

Many of the zombies make their way toward us. I don't know if they're drawn by the fire or if they're attracted to the commotion we made.

It doesn't matter. They're nothing but an obstacle course to overcome.

"We move fast," I say. "We avoid the zombies when possible. If we have to fight our way through, we fight in pairs. Eric and Ben. Ash and Caleb. Me and Reed." I ignore the exasperated scowl Ben throws my way. "We watch one another's backs. We all get out of here alive. Understand?"

I wait until I see everyone nod in understanding. I turn and break into a run.

A *boom* rips through the air.

Another ball of fire leaps into the sky, blooming over the south side of Braggs like a blazing mushroom.

Shit-shit-*shit*. I'd been so worried about the fire on the north side of Braggs that I hadn't paused to consider there might be fire on the south side, too.

"Gas line?" Caleb asks.

"More likely a gas station," Eric replies. "This town is going to burn to the ground."

"Come on," I snarl. "We have to run."

16
Tennis Racket

JESSICA

I lay on my stomach on the bed, my mind drifting as the asshole on top of me grunts and groans.

Instead of focusing on what's happening to my body, I focus on my surroundings. This very bed—this twin-sized piece of foam—is the bed I shared with Shaun. We lived in this tiny trailer together for months, like we were still husband and wife; there wasn't enough room in the fort for people not to double up, and we preferred rooming with each other rather than strangers.

I didn't mind. Not really. Even if we weren't married anymore, Shaun was all I had left. I still loved him. There was something nice about laying down on the mattress with him at the end of a long day. After he left me for Richard, it was something I never thought I'd do again.

In those rare moments of darkness, I liked to pretend we were still married. I'd take the apocalypse any day of the week if it meant I could keep Shaun.

Pieces of Shaun remain in the room. His jacket is wadded up on the far corner of the mattress. A small Girl Scout patch he found on a scavenging run is tacked to the wooden wall. It's a tribute to our lost daughters, who'd been on a Girl Scout camping trip when they died.

Around the Girl Scout patch are over a dozen one-hundred-dollar bills. Shaun collected those, too. He joked that one day, when toilet paper ran out, he was going to use them to wipe his ass.

My eyes travel to the dented tennis racket on my side of the bed. Besides my crushed soul, it's the only thing I brought out of that Girl Scout camping trip.

It had been covered in blood and bits of hair. Wispy, light brown hair with a hint of curls at the end. Claire and May had the perfect combination of my dark brown hair and Shaun's curly blond.

I feel like that tennis racket most days. I'd taken it to the campground with the intention of hitting some balls in the morning while people still slept. We'd been at one of those over-accessorized campgrounds with a swimming pool, miniature golf course, playground, bocce ball courts, and various other activities to entertain kids.

Instead, I used it to put down my own children. To save my ex-husband who had left me for another man. I may have smashed in little Claire's head with the racket, but it may as well have been a knife through my heart.

I don't know why I kept it. It's a memento of my worst nightmare.

It's easy to ignore the sweating monster pounding into me when I see the tennis racket. My mind fogs over, drowning in memories that are so much worse than the ones being made today.

My dead kids don't know it, but in a really fucked up way, they're saving me right now.

*

I let my head roll to one side as the next asshole pounds into me. In the end, it's all simple mechanics. The only thing I have to do is not resist. Biology takes care of the rest.

My eyes settle again on the tennis racket. It had been a gift from Shaun on our eighth wedding anniversary. A

Babolat Pure Strike. I'd cherished that racket more than any other gift he'd given me.

Three days after Shaun gave me the tennis racquet, I'd found the second cell phone he carried to stay in touch with Richard. It had been dumb misfortune to find that phone.

Sometimes I wonder what life would have been like if I'd never found it. Would I have hummed along in blissful ignorance? Or would Shaun still have left me?

Resentment surges inside me. Even after a year and a half of therapy, I hadn't been able to find peace with my new Shaun-less reality. He'd taken away the simple joy I found in making ham and cheese sandwiches and cutting out paper gingerbread men.

Before the apocalypse, I took out my rage on my tennis partners. Bitchy stay-at-home moms from the private school our daughters attended. Their life purpose seemed to be hunting down all the latest small-town gossip and spreading it around like smallpox.

To be honest, I detested them. But I loved tennis more than I loathed them, so I put up with their petty shit.

Still, their friendship wasn't free. I fed them just enough gossip about my divorce to keep them on the tennis court with me. Then I pounded the hell out them with my backspins and drop shots.

So ironic that I used that same tennis racket to save Shaun.

So terrible that I also used it to put down my zombie children.

I close my eyes, letting the pain wash over me.

The asshole on top of me is nothing compared to the things I've suffered with my tennis racket.

17
Truck

KATE

In front of us, the fire rages. The flames whoosh back and forth like banners, the crackling fabric rippling as it moves. Buildings snap, pop, and collapse as the fire devours them.

The noise acts as a zombie magnet. All around, the undead moan and make their way toward the noise. It's so loud most of them don't notice the desperate humans plunging down the road. Our rubber-soled shoes are mere whispers on the ground. Only our breathing is heavy and harsh, but it's swallowed up by the destructive inferno behind us.

The highway through the outskirts of Braggs is still four lanes wide. Despite this, our path is far from clear. Every time a zombie stumbles in front of us or draws too close, we're forced to take it out.

Ben jumps in front of me as two zombies step in my direction with outstretched arms. He moves fast, the knife a blur as it punches first one zombie in the head, then another. Even after how I treated him, he's still looking out for me.

He's barely dispatched them when Caleb confronts another, this one a rotund man with pants that sag around his rotting middle. Caleb swings his zom bat, clocking the fat zombie in the side of the face.

My eyes flick left, right, then left again, scanning our surroundings as we run. The highway is like a giant obstacle course. We swerve around cars and bodies. Anytime a large group of zombies appears, I lead my people in the other direction. We zigzag down the road of death, killing when we have to.

I wish we could use the alpha zom recording. But after the near-miss in Braggs, we can't risk it. I've already seen two alphas in the surrounding chaos, both of them leading large packs away from the fire. I can't risk drawing the attention of one.

My insides twist as I see the horde of zombies stumbling toward us. There's no fighting our way through it. There's no darting around it, either. I could lead my people into one of the side streets and hope for the best, but the undead drift out of every side street in sight.

"Dammit." I pound a fist on my thigh, desperate for a way out. I didn't bring my people all this way to die now. There *has* to be a way.

Fifty yards away, I spot a Toyota Tacoma. It lists to one side, half on the sidewalk, half on the road.

Before the apocalypse, the Tacoma was shiny yellow with chrome rims and over-sized tires. Now, the front grill is covered with undead gore. Blood streaks the sides. One tire is flat.

"Truck," I hiss. "We can hide in the back." I tear toward the truck in a blind run.

A swirling of the undead stand between us and the truck. I count twelve.

We can take them. We *have* to take them.

Ben, who still hasn't budged from my side, seems to understand my plan. He charges the first of the zoms, taking it out with a knife through the eye.

Reed is hard on his heels, the tall young man swinging his zom bat with ruthless efficiency. He bludgeons one zombie on the head, then leaps forward another two steps and takes out another.

Eric sprints past me. I glimpse a profile set in determination. His knives reflect the orange flames that paint the sky.

He cuts around Caleb, stabbing the zombie that stumbles up behind his friend. The monster hasn't even hit the ground before Eric springs away.

He's the first one to reach the truck. He spins around, planting himself in front of the truck like a defender of the Alamo.

Ash is the next person to reach the truck. Eric darts forward, cutting off the zombie that closes in behind her. He kills it, buying Ash a few precious seconds to vault into the bed of the Tacoma.

I cut down a zombie and rush to Eric's side, planting myself beside him. We fight without words as the zombies pour down the street, keeping one side of the Tacoma clear for our friends.

Caleb and Reed vault into the truck. Ben looms out of the chaos with blood spattered all across his face and the front of his clothes.

"In." His word snaps at me like the end of a whip.

There isn't time to argue. The big hoard is drawing near, led at a shambling run by the alpha. I hurl myself over the edge.

Ben is about to rush one of the biggest zombies I've ever seen, a man easily six-foot-five and three hundred pounds. It barrels toward the truck with a keening cry.

Ben recoils, bunching his muscles to spring into action.

Eric beats him to it. He barrels into the zombie, mouth open in a silent scream. He jams both hands hard against the creature's chest.

It stumbles back, snarling in surprise. Eric doesn't let it recover. His knife hand flashes down in rapid succession, breaking through the flesh and bone of the undead monster's face.

Ben doesn't wait. He turns to the truck, flinging

himself inside.

I rush to the far edge, holding out a hand as Eric hauls ass back to the Tacoma. Three zombies pursue him, letting up a fresh set of wails.

Eric jumps through the air like a spider, arms extended.

I latch onto one forearm. Caleb grabs the other. We pull Eric inside, cushioning his fall as the three of us stumble backward onto the hard metal of the truck bed.

The three zombies chasing Eric slam into the tailgate. They hiss and moan, claws digging at the metal and swiping at open air.

Reed advances, jaw set. Ben grabs his arm and shakes his head, motioning for all of us to huddle near the center of the truck.

Sandwiched between Caleb and Eric, I crouch in a sitting position. The rest of my people squish in around me. We are a silent, huddled mass in the center of the Tacoma.

The three zombies at the tailgate continue to scratch and keen. Another dozen zombies surround the truck, led there by their alpha. The alpha—a teenage girl with half her hair torn away from her scalp—keens and clicks, calling more zombies to surround us. The Tacoma rocks back and forth as they moan and claw.

I barely dare to breathe. My hands are sweaty around my knives. Adrenaline courses through my veins, sending tremors through my sweaty hands.

South of us, the fire is gaining momentum. Big flames lick at the sky, belching up black plumes of smoke. If we don't get out of here soon, we might suffocate and burn to death.

If we leave the truck bed, we risk being overrun.

A zombie swipes at the open air above the truck, nails only inches from my face. It takes every shred of willpower not to swipe back, not to bury my knife in its face.

But this is just one of many zoms surrounding the Tacoma. There's no way for us to fight our way free. The truck continues to rock. The zombies continue to hiss and moan.

Eric's nostrils are flared, his muscles tense and ready to spring. Ben looks as fierce as ever, eyes flicking between the zombies and me. Ash and Caleb sit back to back, equal parts scared and determined. Reed crouches on the balls of his feet, looking ready to fling himself over the side of the truck and into the surrounding horde.

The alpha shoulders through the pack. When it bumps up against the truck, it pounds its fists against the metal with a shriek of frustration. The cry is echoed up the road by other zombies.

The alpha hisses, peeling itself away from the truck. The teenage undead pushes through its fellows and lets up a keen, cocking one ear to listen.

Answering keens sound. More zombies turn in the direction of the Tacoma.

Chills inch their way down my back and a dozen more zombies plow into the side of the truck, causing one of the wheels to lift off the ground. I latch onto Reed and dig the soles of my shoes into the floor, struggling to maintain my position.

Reed returns my grasp, the two of us clinging to each other as the zombies plow into the truck a second time. It's shoved several inches across the sidewalk.

Holy shit. My mind races. If they do that another few times, they just might manage to flip the truck onto its side. Should I risk using the recording in my pack before that happens?

A shoe repair shop stands no more than five feet away from the truck. The glass window is shattered. Inside are two corpses, desiccated and rotted from many months left exposed to the elements.

At least fifteen zombies fill the narrow space between the truck and the shop. Could I use the alpha recording to cut a path from the truck to the shop? How we'll hold them off once we're inside the shop is beyond me, but at best we wouldn't be surrounded on all sides.

The Tacoma bucks and slides again. Nails grind against paint. Our little group clings to one another, all of us smashed into the center of the bed.

I study the front of the shoe repair shop, weighing our odds. Another push from the zombies will put us another few inches closer. That, combined with the alpha might—

The truck rocks again, this time struck from the other side. It's pushed back in the other direction, sending several of the street-side zombies sprawling.

Smoke gathers around us, growing thicker by the second. I tip my chin forward and suck from the drinking straw, willing myself not to cough. Sound will rile up the zoms even more.

Eric rubs at his throat, working his jaw. I push the straw toward him, angling my body so he can drink.

The others see what we're doing. They all take drinks from their packs.

A *boom* echoes across the landscape, followed by a blinding flash of light. A rumble rolls through the ground. All around us, zombies are thrown to the ground.

I turn my head just in time to see a mushroom cloud of smoke and fire bloom from the north, coming from the heart of Braggs. Seconds later, fireworks start to explode.

They whine into the sky and burst open, letting loose a show of colorful sparks against the smoky backdrop. Dozens and dozens of fireworks, all of them showering us with a beauty that contrasts the horror around us. The ground trembles with each detonation.

"Fireworks are legal in this county," Eric hisses to me. "I drove down here with some buddies freshmen year to get some and take them back to Arcata."

Something happens. A handful of zombies break away from the truck, stumbling away into the smoke. They make their way toward the fireworks that shred the air with sound.

I hold my breath, not daring to hope.

The alpha hisses, lips peeling back from teeth. It stalks away from the truck, moving in the direction of the fireworks. It clicks as it goes, calling to its horde.

The truck vibrates as the zombies pound and scratch at it in frustration. Then, one after another, the monsters lumber away in clumps. They follow their alpha while showers of light explode in the sky above us.

Finally, the way is clear. The last of the zombies breaks away like an iceberg sloughing off a glacier.

As a unit, we surge to our feet. We leap out of the truck, each of us landing lightly on the ground. The edge of the city is still littered with the undead, but the bulk of them have moved on to the firework show. It's early evening now and the sky is darkening. It makes the flames and fireworks look even brighter.

I lead my people out, heading south. Once again, we zigzag down the highway. The little noise we make is masked by the fireworks. Another *boom* rakes the air, followed by another burst of fire light. Another gas line, no doubt, or something equally flammable.

As I dodge around a cluster of bodies heaped on the side of the road, it occurs to me that I'm exhausted. Physically and mentally exhausted. My body aches. All I want to do is curl up and go to sleep somewhere safe.

Frederico's voice patters in my brain, his words from so long ago rising to the surface.

Don't think about the pain. Think about the finish.

That had been spoken to me at a one-hundred miler in the Arizona desert on a day when temps blistered well above one-hundred degrees. I was tired. I was hot. I was sunburned. Crystals of salt covered my clothes, having leached out of my body during the long hot, toiling day.

How about I just lay down on a cactus? I had asked. *It's a legitimate DNF if I'm covered with cactus quills.*

What did I say about pain? Frederico replied. *Quit thinking about it. Focus on the finish.*

I can practically feel Frederico running by my side. My

friend might be dead, but he isn't gone.

I set my jaw and will myself to see the end of this zombie-infested town. The safety of the open road lies ahead. Just one more mile. One more mile, and we'll be free.

We head into a narrow tunnel of cars. Stray zombies bump around, struggling to find a way toward the fireworks. We cut them down as we run.

Three-quarters of a mile.

We hit a patch of dead bodies. There must be at least three dozen of them. We jump over and around them. When one latches onto Reed's ankle, Eric is there. His knife crunches through the skull, spraying blood across his face.

Half a mile.

I see the pinch point of Highway 1, the four-lane road narrowing to two. Dusk looms large and welcoming, open coastal land rolling out beyond the town.

Quarter mile.

Ash and Caleb cut through three zombies that wander too close to our group. They make no sound as they attack. All I hear is the crunch of bone and the thud of bodies.

The sign reads: *Thanks for Visiting Braggs. Come Back Again Soon!*

And just like that, Braggs ejects us from its depths.

We run into the cool evening, smoke from the fire boiling after us and clinging to our clothes.

We don't speak. In silent consent, we keep running, putting distance between us and the town.

Finish line. We made it. I send a silent *thank you* to Frederico.

Wherever he is, I know he hears me.

18
Why

JESSICA

I have a perfect view of Shaun through the open window. It's nearing dusk. The fence surrounding the fort sends long shadows across the ground.

The team of fishermen and gardeners are just returning to the compound, herded at gunpoint by Rosario's minions. The smell of beans permeates the air, a sign that dinner is being cooked. The idea of Rosario and her pack of leeches eating our food makes my blood boil.

Chill, salty air pebbles my skin with gooseflesh. I don't close the window. I like the cold air. Makes it easier to forget the heat of the skin of the men who have been in here.

And Shaun. The asshole. I know he heard everything. He's the real reason I opened the windows in the first place. No reason for me to suffer alone. I know my fate hurts him every bit as much as it hurts me. Just like his fate is like an open wound in my chest.

We might not be married anymore, but we still love each other. It's not the same kind of love that existed when we first met, when we were two dumb college kids getting wasted at frat and sorority parties on the weekend. It's evolved into something darker and infinitely more complicated. But I still love that man more than I love life itself.

It's too bad the loathing and resentment outweigh the love.

I run through the list of STDs I remember studying in high school. Syphilis. Chlamydia. Hepatitis. Gonorrhea. Herpes. Crabs. I don't even remember what most of that stuff is.

AIDS.

I push that thought away as soon as it creeps into my brain. There's nothing I can do about it.

At least I can't get pregnant. I hang onto this knowledge. I had an IUD put in after Shaun left me. I had vague ideas about trying to meet someone on a dating website. I never got around to creating a profile for myself.

The thought of Bella and Steph getting impregnated by the monsters who have enslaved us makes me want to burn shit down. That's another thing I've saved them from. At least for the moment. I have the men entertained for now, but I'm not stupid enough to think it will last. Sooner or later, they'll turn their eyes to other women in the fort.

They'll turn back to Steph and Bella.

We can't exist in this new state as slaves. It's no way to live. I, for one, would rather die than endure another hour inside this awful motorhome. Alvarez is going to have to make the hard call, and soon. He's going to have to accept that he can't save all of us. We're going to have to fight even if Rosario's minions are stone-cold sober.

"Jessie."

The voice, cracked with thirst and infused with pain, carries to me through the window.

I turn, looking out at Shaun.

"Jessie," he croaks.

I stare at him without responding. His wrecked body is a perfect mirror to my wrecked soul. Combined, we would be the perfect embodiment of ruin and waste. It's the first time in a long time we've been on an even playing field.

"Jessie, I'm—"

"What did you say to him?"

Shaun hangs his head. I didn't think it was possible for his shoulders to sag any lower, but they do. He doesn't ask me what I'm talking about. He understands my question perfectly.

Silence stretches. Somewhere in the distance, I hear crying. Even more distant is the pounding of the ocean waves.

"Fort Ross was going to fall no matter what I did," Shaun says.

"Don't bullshit me. You know what I mean."

Shaun says nothing. When he looks across the ten yards of hard-packed dirt that separates us, I see the truth in his eyes.

Seeing it isn't enough. I want to hear him say it. "What did you say to get him to let you pretend to be the leader?"

Shaun raises his head. The waning light glistens off his open wound. Much of the blood has scabbed over, but parts of the bite wound still seep fresh red.

"I told him to take care of you."

It's the confession I wanted, but the words don't make any sense. I try to grasp them, to study them for better understanding, but the meaning eludes me.

"What are you talking about?"

"You're too angry these days to notice how he looks at you."

I recoil from the screen.

Surely Shaun doesn't mean what I think he means. I must be at least ten years older than Alvarez. Besides, there are plenty of women in the fort who fawn over him and flirt because he's . . . well, he's *Alvarez*. Our leader. Strong. Capable. Caring. Good looking. A perfectly eligible bachelor in every sense of the word. Hell, he would have been a catch *before* the apocalypse. Now that the world's ended, he's the gold standard.

"Jessie, you deserve to have someone. I want you to be

happy."

"*I would have been happy if you'd let me die!*" My words stab across the distance like a striking snake.

Shaun flinches at the force of them but doesn't back down. "You two would be good together. You both like taking care of other people. It's what you do best."

I snort. "I don't take care of anyone anymore."

"Bullshit. You're taking care of Steph and Bella right now. Don't deny it. It's what you *do*, Jessica. You nurture. You love. You protect."

His words ignite a fire inside me, and not in a good way. I'm so angry I feel like hellfire might blast from every pore in my body and raze Fort Ross to the ground. My hands tremble with the force of it.

I slam shut the window and yank the curtain in place. I can't look at Shaun.

I flop onto the bed and cover my head with a pillow, grinding my teeth as my heart races in my chest. My hands shake.

I'm almost relieved when the door to the RV opens and another stinky, rotting man climbs inside. I rise up to face him, refusing to let him see fear or submission.

There's so much fire inside me that I half expect him to burst into flame when we make contact.

He doesn't, of course. Science doesn't work that way.

But he will. All these fuckers are going to pay. Somehow, someway, if I have to burn Fort Ross down myself to make it happen.

19
Rest

KATE

I don't stop until we're a mile out of town.

I pull to a halt beside a green sign with reflective white letters that reads, *Mendocino, 10 miles.*

I've been to this area enough over the years to know that it's mostly unpopulated. There are miles of open land that snake alongside the ocean. There may be the occasional home or ranch interspersed along the highway, but there will be no more big towns to contend with.

Until we get to Mendocino. The town is a fraction of the size of Braggs, but it's a tourist destination. There's no telling how many undead we might encounter within those city limits.

My people stand in a loose circle in the middle of the road, everyone breathing hard from our brush with death. Caleb leans over his thighs, sucking in great gulps of air and wiping sweat from his forehead. Reed crouches on the far side of the road, puking. He's never had a good stomach for running.

Ben stands off to one side, staring back in the direction of Braggs while he catches his breath. Watching him stirs the kernels of fear I felt earlier when he nearly died on the bridge. But the fear is small compared to everything else I feel for him.

I touch his shoulder. "Hey." When he turns around, I step into his warmth. His arms come around me.

"I'm sorry." I knot my hands in the fabric of the sweat jacket he wears and lean my cheek against him.

His arms tighten. He holds onto me like he'll never let me go. It feels so good.

"I told you I wasn't dropping this," he says gruffly into my ear. "A little temper tantrum isn't going to deter me."

I laugh silently into his chest. When I look up at him, the skin around his eyes crinkles. I love the way he looks at me.

"Just don't almost die on me again and we won't have a problem," I say.

"Ditto."

I plant a quick kiss on his lips, trying to shake the fear of losing him. Despite my apology, it still looms large and scary in my mind.

We congregate with the others. They're smudged with soot and look exhausted.

Reed swishes his mouth out with water and spits it to one side. "Dude. That sucked."

"Could be worse." I try to keep my voice light. "I once saw a man at an aid station who'd tripped on a root and snapped a bone in his foot. The bone stuck out of the top of his foot." The story is meant to make everyone feel better, but I can see by the widening of eyes that it's having the opposite effect.

"Let me guess," Ben says. He leans against the road sign, shoulders hunched with fatigue. "The motherfucker still managed to make it to the finish line."

I shake my head. "No. He had to ride a horse out of the canyon where he fell. We were miles away from a road."

No one speaks. The distant keen of zombies fills the air. Where are crickets when you need them?

I want to kick myself. I should have lied. I should have told Ben the guy managed to drag his ass to the finish line with a bone sticking out of his foot.

"Mama," Reed says, "you just ruined our ultrarunner illusion. I thought you guys were supposed to keep going no matter what."

Maybe that hadn't been the best story to tell. I try again. "There's a race through the Colorado mountains called Hardrock. A few years ago, one of the front runners fell and dislocated his shoulder thirteen miles in." That piece of ultrarunner history had left me and Frederico awestruck for days. "Not only did the guy finish the race, but he won it."

"How far is Hardrock?" Caleb asks.

"A hundred miles."

"*Maldita sea*," Ash breathes. "That is some crazy, fucked up shit."

I rake my gaze over the group. "You guys are all ultrarunners. Every single one of you. You all ran thirty-three miles on the Lost Coast. We just ran another five to get through Braggs. You guys are all badasses."

"And we're not even done yet," Ben mutters.

"And we're not even done yet," I agree.

"Does it count since we rode a car from Usal Beach to Braggs?" Caleb asks.

"Hell, yes. It's called a stage run. It means we're running in stages. It's a different kind of ultra."

They look at one another, exchanging slow, pleased grins. Thank God. So long as I can keep their heads in the game, I can get them to the finish line.

"It's another ten miles to Mendocino," I say. "After that, it's a good seventy-five miles to Fort Ross. None of us are going to survive this trek if we don't decide, here and now, that we're going to finish. Understand? It's mind over matter. Every single one of you has to make the decision that you're going to finish. That's all it takes."

No one answers. Ben looks like I just kicked him in the balls. Even Reed, ever upbeat, looks like I deflated his inner tube.

"Can we go back to that part about there being eighty-five miles between us and Fort Ross?" Caleb asks. "Are we going to run the whole way?"

I shake my head. "There are long stretches of open road. If we can find a car that works, we can drive. Or maybe we can find some bikes. But no, I don't think we're going to have to run the whole way."

"Thank fucking God," Ben mutters. The rest of the group lets up a collective sigh of relief.

So much for my pep talk. I had meant to inspire them. Instead, all I'd done was scare the hell out of them.

We take a reprieve to eat, drink, and relieve ourselves. We don headlamps and flick them on. Reed finds a stream that runs from the open grassland out to the ocean, which we use to refill our packs. No one asks if the water is safe. There's no telling if water out of a faucet would be any good, either. All we can do is keep hydrated and hope for the best.

"Um, guys?" Eric pulls off his glasses and cleans them on the hem of his shirt. "Does it look like it's getting smokier out here?"

Seven heads whip in the direction of Braggs. Eric slips his glasses back on and peers north with the rest of us.

The sun has set. The stars are obscured by the smoke that chugs into the sky.

The fire has grown bigger and more ferocious in the five minutes we've rested beside the road sign. In mounting horror, I realize the flames aren't content to eat the town of Braggs. They're chewing their way through the grassland flanking the side of the highway.

"But, it's wet," Ash says. "The grass shouldn't burn."

"The *top* of the grass is wet," Caleb says grimly. "The undercarriage must still be dry enough to burn."

Dammit. Fire isn't even the worst of our problems.

Stumbling along ahead of the flames are zombies. Hundreds and hundreds of zombies. Where a short while ago they had marched toward the flames, they've now reversed direction.

And it's obvious why. At the forefront of the horde are two alphas, clicking and keening instructions.

The alphas were smart enough to realize the flames are deadly. Now they're leading a horde away from Braggs at a frightening pace down Highway 1 in a collision course with us.

20
Sprint

ERIC

If Reed or one of the other guys had asked me five minutes ago if I had another sprint in my body, I would have flipped him off. Our frantic tear through Braggs had left me ready to collapse with exhaustion.

But there's something about a wall of flames and a horde of zombies that inspires a person to action.

We tear off in a frantic pack, Kate in the lead as we sprint south on Highway 1.

I once ran fast when I stole my brother's car keys on the night of his prom. I was pissed that he had a date with a senior girl I'd been crushing on for months. The girl, of course, had never noticed me. I'd been three years younger than her, and nerdy at that.

Tom, of course, had dazzled her, even though he was only a junior.

I got my vengeance. I stole his car and went out to get ice cream. He'd been forced to drive our mom's beat-up Volvo station wagon to prom.

I'd been grounded for a month. The worst part was that I'd felt like shit the whole time, knowing I was being a dickhead to my brother.

Until I met Kate, that was the fastest I'd ever run in my life. It had been a twenty-yard sprint from his upstairs bedroom to the bright red Honda Civic parked on the curb in front of our house.

Then the apocalypse had arrived, and with it, Kate. She made us do sprints around the track. She even made us run up and down the stairwell in Creekside.

It all feels worth it when we'd been forced to tear through those last few miles of Braggs. The training had paid off and saved our lives.

That near-death experience had been kitten's play.

As we streak down Highway 1 with zombies and fire hard on our heels, I finally understand what it means to *sprint.*

Spit flies from my open mouth as I suck in gulps of air. My lungs feel like they're going to explode out the front of my chest. My arms and back ache from the effort of swinging my torso back and forth in a desperate bid to outrun nature.

My feet, already covered with blisters, are blocks of pain. I can barely feel them as they tear over the pavement. They churn, propelling me forward as fast as they can.

Don't be a loser, Eric.

Quit playing small, little brother.

I dig deep and make a silent promise to my brother and my dead girlfriend. I won't give up. I'll run as hard and as fast as I can until my body gives out or the fire catches up with us. I open myself up to the physical pain and embrace it.

The fire gains on us, leaping over the open grassland like demonic gazelles. It smashes through scattered buildings and swallows trees in whole gulps.

The zombies keen and moan. Many are devoured by the flames, but huge swaths of them continue to stagger forward and stay just ahead of the fire.

I do my best to block out the madness behind us, to narrow my focus on my breath, my body, and the road beneath my feet.

You could be faster than any of them if you didn't half-ass it,

Lila once said to me. It had been at the end of a particularly grueling workout in the stairwell. I think Reed had thrown up two times that day.

No more half-assing it. There is one point I'm very clear on: I don't want to die.

Our group streams down the road in a pack. The waves pound against the cliffs to our right in a never-ending surge. I focus on the sound of the water, finding it preferable to the roar of the flames and the keening of the zombies behind us.

How ironic that a little over a day ago, I never wanted to hear the ocean again after nearly drowning in it.

Tom.

I picture my perfect big brother. He's crystal clear in my mind's eye. In his jeans and a tight-fitting tee, he carries a baseball bat. A baseball bat would definitely be his weapon of choice. It was his favorite of all the varsity sports he played. He can swing that thing hard and fast. It would be his perfect zombie weapon.

And he would take out a lot of zombies with it. Sure, some of them would be his fraternity brothers; that was inevitable. But he would save a fair number of them, along with some of the girls from the neighboring sororities.

Now they'd be holed up on their campus, just like I was with the Creekside crew. They would be discovering new ways to survive. Tom would be their leader.

"Don't let up," Kate shouts. She sucks in big gulps of air between words, trying to encourage us even as she struggles to breathe. "Whatever you do, don't let up! This run is for keeps. You have to make it count."

How she can talk at all is beyond me.

My eyes flick across the road before us. To the left is an abandoned barn, half of the roof caved in. In front of the barn is a pick-up truck with faded blue paint.

"Truck," Reed gasps.

"No," Kate snaps. "No time."

She's right. The fire eats its way south, devouring

everything in its path. If we stop to try and get a vehicle, it will be on us.

"Breathe through the pain," Kate says. "Don't let up. Focus on the finish."

A sob rips itself from Ash's throat. She keeps up, but from the look on her face, I can tell she's in as much pain as the rest of us.

Tom.

My brother's face again floats before me. Tom would make it out of this alive. Hell, he *is* alive, somewhere. He's alive, and he's keeping his frat brothers and their sorority sisters alive.

I can do this. My brother was a golden boy, but only because he chose to be a golden boy. I chose to be a half-assed slacker.

From now on, I choose to be a golden boy like Tom. I'm getting out of this alive. Whatever it takes. I don't care how much I hurt. I'm not stopping until it's safe.

We hurtle past two abandoned cars on the side of the road. One of them has a zombie inside. The doors hang open on the other. There's no time to look for keys.

"Five miles." Kate wheezes at us as she glances up from her watch. "We've gone five miles."

Halfway to Mendocino. This news might hearten me if the fire wasn't gaining on us.

If we can just get to Mendocino. If we can just get there, maybe we can find shelter.

I don't know why I think it will be any safer in Mendocino. I've never been there. Kate says it's a small tourist town perched over the ocean. It sounds like a nice place. A safe place. A place where we can wait out of the fire.

But California wildfires are monsters in their own right. This one could burn for hundreds of miles out here. I've seen wildfires devastate thousands of acres, and that's with fire crews fighting to contain them.

The hordes behind us have disappeared, devoured by

the flames. There are a few stragglers, but not enough to worry me. Our true enemy is the flames.

Fear pumps through my veins. It fuels me, pushing me through the pain. It propels me down the road on a headlong run for my life.

"Zombies."

My eyes flick up. The sky is dark. The beam from my headlamp cuts through the smoke that swirls around us.

It illuminates another horde of zombies—this one coming straight for us. They march north on Highway 1, drawn to the sound of the fire as surely as the zombies of Braggs had been before the alphas led them away. This new horde cruising in our direction has no alpha to turn back.

We're going to be sandwiched between fire and two hordes of the undead.

"Kate," I call, panic tearing through my bloodstream. "Kate, what are we going to do?"

She throws me one anguished glance. Her eyes rake over our small contingent, wild with fear for our safety. Then I see her jaw set.

"Ocean," she barks. "Now."

Fuck me.

I don't argue with Mama Bear, even though the idea of going into the ocean makes my legs want to collapse. Not to mention there are sheer cliffs between us and the water.

We stream off the road and toward the precipice that snakes along the coast. We skid to a stop at the edge, staring over a sharp bluff that plunges straight down to the water.

"Over the edge," Kate orders. "Drop down to that ledge."

That ledge she refers to is a good ten-foot drop. *Shit.* My discomfort with heights clogs my throat. First the bridge, then *another* bridge, and now over the edge of a cliff.

"Are you going to be a golden boy, or are you going to be a dead loser?" I mutter to myself.

My muscles scream as I crouch down and lower myself over the side. I dangle there, digging my fingertips into the earth. I kick at the sandstone bluff, trying to find a toehold for my shoes.

The fire rips by overhead, burning the tips of my fingers.

I shriek, sliding down the face of the cliff. My nails snap off as I try desperately to dig them into the hard surface. My feet search for even the smallest toehold.

I'm going to fall. I'm going to fall into the ocean and die.

Thank God Tom is still alive. There's still someone to carry on the family name.

I'll get to see Lila. I never really thought much about what happens after death, but in my gut, I'm sure I'll see Lila again when I die.

Someone grabs the back of my pack and yanks.

I land on a small, uneven ledge, sprawling on my back. Ben leans over me, breathing hard.

"You have a bald spot on your forehead," he remarks. "At least your whole head didn't catch on fire."

I have no words. I remain sprawled on my back, sucking in air and staring at the world above me where fire burns.

21
Nails

JESSICA

I lay on my side, eyes closed, aching from the inside out.

I'm swathed in the tightest clothes I could find in the tiny closet I shared with Shaun. Tight clothes are the hardest to get off. I don't plan to make it easy for the next asshole who comes in here.

With several hours to go before sunrise, I have no doubt there will be another one. Since Rosario poured out all the booze, there isn't much else to entertain our captors. The ones not on watch sit around campfire rings feasting on our hard-won food stores. I listen to them dice and tell exaggerated stories of bravery.

"Jessie?"

I jerk upright at the familiar voice.

"Alvarez?" His face is a dark silhouette in the window screen. "What are you doing here?"

"Are you okay?" He presses a hand against the screen, as though trying to touch me.

I inch up to the screen. "They'll kill you if they catch you." I don't add that they'll kill someone else, too. From inside the RV, I can see the guards patrolling the Rotchev prison. "How did you get out?"

"I crawled out through loose floorboards. I waited

until the patrol passed then slipped over here. Are you okay?"

The pity and anguish in his voice makes me recoil. "I'm fine." I don't want or need his sympathy. "How are Steph and Bella?"

"The girls are okay. They're scared for you."

"Tell them I'm fine. Tell them to take care of themselves. They should make a break for it if they get the chance. Get as far as possible from this place."

"Jessie . . . ?"

I shake my head at his unspoken question. There's no reason to talk about it. "Alvarez, we have to fight. Sooner rather than later. I know we lost the booze, but—"

"I know," he interrupts. "Soon. We'll attack soon. I want you to be ready."

He pushes against the screen. I catch it as it pops free. "Open your hand."

I extend my palm as Alvarez's arm slips inside. He drops a handful of nails into my hand.

"You still have that tennis racket you brought to Fort Ross?" he asks.

"Yes." How does he know about the tennis racket? I haven't pulled it out since the day I took up residence in this RV with Shaun.

"Good. And you still have that duct tape Shaun used to carry with him on missions?"

That fucking duct tape. Shaun took it everywhere with him even before the world ended. He bought it in bulk at Costco and kept a roll in every suitcase, briefcase, and car. He was always on the lookout for it on scavenging runs.

"Yes. I have two rolls."

"Good. Use it to fortify the tennis racket with the nails. Be ready."

I tighten my fist around the nails. "What's your plan?"

"I'm still working out the details. My trip to you was a test run, to see if we could slip out from under the Rotchev House without being seen." His mouth stretches into a thin line. "I just proved it's doable. We can move out under the cover of darkness and recover the weapons we hid."

He has a plan. It's a ballsy plan, but it's not a complete kamikaze mission. "What kind of weapons did you guys hide before Rosario got in here?"

"Lots of metal tools. Hammers. Wrenches. Stuff like that. We have things hidden all over the compound. Everyone is ready to fight."

They have hammers while Rosario's people have guns. I swallow. I might be scared for Alvarez, but that doesn't change the fact that we have to fight. It doesn't change the fact that some of us will have to die to win back our home.

"I'm going back now." Alvarez squeezes my shoulder. "I'll regroup with our people and finalize our plans. With any luck, we'll attack tomorrow night. Just hang on a bit longer. Can you do that?"

I wish they would attack now. It's the middle of the night and many of Rosario's people are sleeping. But he's right. They need time to finalize details of a plan. We'll only have one shot at this. I need to be patient. I don't want to endure another minute in this RV, but I will.

Alvarez looks at me with earnest eyes. I see how much my situation pains him.

"I'll be fine," I tell him. "You're the one who has to be careful."

"We have the element of surprise on our side," he replies. "They'll never see us coming."

"I'll be ready to kill when you give the signal," I whisper.

Something swells between us in the dark. Silence stretches. His dark eyes soak me in.

"You're a warrior, Jessie. A damn fine warrior. Don't let these assholes take that from you."

"These assholes," I grind out in reply, "take *nothing* from me."

He flashes me a grin. "I'll see you soon." He gives my shoulder one last squeeze, then disappears into the dark.

22
Raining Zombies

KATE

The six of us crouch on the rocky outcropping above the Pacific Ocean. I'd call it a ledge if it wasn't so uneven and covered with sharp points. It's ten feet wide at the tips and juts out no more than two feet.

The fire burns above us, pouring heat and smoke over the edge of the cliff. Below us, the ocean pounds away at a rocky shoreline.

There's nothing for us to do but wait it out.

Does this count as a break? I decide to pretend it's an aid station on the most fucked up ultra I've ever run in my life.

We huddle together. I find the closeness comforting, but the truth is that there isn't room to be anything but squashed together. I'm sandwiched between Reed and Ben.

I lean my head back against the cliff face and close my eyes. How the fuck are we going to get off this cliff? Going down isn't an option and the top is at least ten feet above us.

I have a wild vision of us standing on one another's shoulders, Looney-Tunes style, in a desperate bid to escape.

A ball of fire spurts over the cliff side, searing us with

heat. We hunch down, doing our best to protect our faces. I squeeze Reed and Ben's hands, wishing I could do more to protect the two of them. Wishing I could do more to protect *all* of them.

I look down at my watch. Thirty-two hours. We've been on the move for all that time. Alvarez and his people have been at the mercy of Mr. Rosario for eight hours.

My mind replays the series of disasters that have plagued us ever since we left Creekside. Running out of gas in Humboldt Bay. Getting attacked by pirates. Our boat getting destroyed by zombies in the rudder. Our subsequent shipwreck on the Lost Coast. The impassable tidal zone, hypothermia, and bear attack all seem like a really twisted joke.

We haven't had a break since we stepped foot on Highway 1. Between zombies, bridges, and fires, it's done its best to eat us alive.

And now here we are, huddling on a tiny outcropping, held hostage between the sea and the inferno.

A growl sounds above us. I look up just in time to see a zombie totter over the side of the cliff. Flames lick across his shirt.

He falls straight for us.

"Incoming!" Ben bellows. "Look out!"

The zombie crashes down on top of Ash.

Ben and Caleb act fast, the two of them like a well-oiled machine. Caleb stabs the zombie in the face while Ben grabs it by the ankles and flings it over the edge. Ash shrieks, batting at the bits of flame that sprang up on her shoulder. Eric jumps in and smothers it with his backpack.

"Are you okay?" Caleb grabs Ash by her good arm and turns her so he can inspect her shoulder.

"*Sí.*" Her voice is shaky as she bats at the burned fabric. Beneath it is red, blistered flesh.

"Let me see." Ben pulls out a small first aid kit. He cuts away the burned fabric, applies ointment to her wound, and wraps it with a clean bandage.

As he works, another zombie pitches over the cliff. It's twenty feet away, burning from head to toe. It plummets into the ocean below, hissing all the way down.

"Um, guys? There's more." Reed raises a finger, pointing to the line of tottering bodies above us.

There's at least a dozen of them. As we watch, another two fall off the ledge, burning as they fall into the ocean.

"Fuck me." Ben glares up at the clifftop. "Zombie rain."

One by one, they continue to walk over the edge. Most of their falls are silent, accompanied only by the customary growling and snarling. They're smashed to pieces on the rocks below, blood and body parts littering the shoreline. If I had any notions of trying to climb down, the pulverized zombies change my mind.

Luckily, no others land on our tiny little slice of the world, though there isn't one of us who doesn't keep an eye toward the sky.

There's nothing to do except wait out the firestorm. Fire and ash rain down on us. Smoke pours over the side of the cliff in a gray-and-white tumble.

We all cough. I pull my shirt up over my nose to block out the worst of it. The others do the same, a few of them pulling out bandanas.

"Put water on the cloth you're breathing through," Ben says. He takes a drink out of his pack and spits the water out on his bandana.

I squint my eyes in an effort to protect them from the smoke and ash. Of all the things I've encountered on a run, this is the first time I've come up against a wildfire.

We huddle together, waiting out the firestorm. It feels like days. According to my watch, several hours have passed.

We might die out here. Right here, on this ledge over the ocean with fire raging above us. I squeeze Ben's hand and lean into him. He puts his arm around me and holds me tight, resting his forehead against the back of my neck.

I regret not taking advantage of the big bed when I had the chance with him. I'd let my brain get in the way. I make a silent promise not to let that happen again. If I have the chance to be with him—even if it's on some dirty floor in a cold shed—I'm not going to miss out.

"Did you guys feel that?" Ash holds out both hands. "Is that rain?"

I squint into the smoke. A second later, a cold sting hits the top of my head. Another few seconds pass. Three drops hit the narrow space between me and Ben.

"God damn," Ben exclaims. "We may survive after all." He plants a kiss on my lips.

I'm so relieved that I grab him around the neck and kiss him back, just because I can. Because we're both alive.

"Good thing we got chased by zombies and fire," Reed remarks. "If not for near-death experiences, you two would never make out."

Good-natured laughter fills the air. I can't help laughing myself as I squeeze Ben tight with both arms.

The rain begins to fall in cold earnest. Thunder rolls through the sky, sending vibrations through the earth.

Never in my life have I been so happy for rain. I turn my face skyward, letting the fat, cold drops hit my skin. A fork of lightning flashes above us.

The wind picks up, whipping across our bodies. It isn't long before we're all shivering in the rain. I crane my neck, trying to gauge the severity of the fire above us.

The heat of the flames is gone. The ash that falls is sodden. There's still smoke, though most of it has turned into steam.

We have to get off this ledge and find shelter, or we're all going to be hypothermic. It would be nice to have a day where we're not being yo-yoed between hypothermia and burning to death.

I shield my eyes from the ash and study the cliff face. "Any of you expert rock climbers?"

Five pairs of eyes turn in my direction. Everyone

shakes their heads.

"All right," I mutter. "Looney Tunes escape plan it is." I survey our group. "Caleb, Reed." I gesture to the two young men. They're the tallest among us. Reed is the lighter of the two, his build lean while Caleb is the stronger.

"Caleb, you need to boost Reed up to the road. Reed, once you get to the top, you're going to have pull us up, one by one."

They stare at me.

"You're serious, aren't you?" Caleb says.

"Dead serious. Unless one of you knows someone who can pick us up in a helicopter, that's the only way any of us is getting off this ledge."

"I can always count on a big dose of crazy with you." Ben slaps me on the shoulder. To the rest, he barks, "What you waiting for? You heard the woman. Let's get the fuck off this ledge."

23
Wet Run

ERIC

Sooty, scraped, and exhausted, the six of us soon find ourselves back on Highway 1.

The beams of our headlamps reveal road scarred with ash. All the grassland on the east side of the road has been reduced to scorched earth. The wildfire tore through everything in sight, turning the land black. A quarter mile down the road is an abandoned car that's been reduced to a crispy shell. Farther down the road is the remains of a house that still flickers with flame.

Smoke and steam trail into the sky amid the wet sky. Despite the chill that's settled into my body, I feel nothing but whole-hearted love for the rain. I'd rather be cold and drenched than dead.

"Now what?" Ben asks.

"Now?" Kate wipes rainwater out of her eyes. "Now, we run. The town of Mendocino is only a few miles away. We can look for shelter and regroup once we get there."

We slog down the road at a steady lope. Grit and ash rush down the road as rain sloughs down. Water splashes up with every step I take. I'm forced to shorten the angle of my headlamp to better see the road directly in front of me through the rain. The hat I picked up in Braggs keeps my glasses from being a smeary mess.

Zombie corpses are everywhere. Huge piles of them litter the road in charred heaps.

"That's an efficient way to get rid of zoms," Ben says as we veer around a pile of bodies.

"Yeah, if you're not worried about burning your town down," Reed replies.

The rain is miserable. I narrow my focus to the road, concentrating on each step. One foot in front of the next. It's the only thing I can do. It's what Kate taught me to do.

My fingers are the first things to go numb, followed shortly by my toes, then both of my feet. Black water splashes up from the road with every step, soaking me all the way up to my waist. The windbreaker I'd donned in Braggs is plastered to my body.

Lila never would have made it out here.

I hate the thought as soon as it forms. Yes, Lila didn't handle the apocalypse well. Yes, at one point it got so bad she refused to leave Creekside. Yes, there were days when she wouldn't even leave our dorm room.

I wrote her off. I hate myself for that. In my mind, I never saw her surviving more than a year. Two, tops.

Sometimes, it feels like she's still here. Her almond eyes—always alive with fear—follow me around like hunting hounds.

It had been like that when she was alive. Looking at her was like staring fear in the face.

The only exception was when she argued with me. Whenever we bickered, she didn't look afraid. That was part of the reason why I liked riling her up. It was also fun to banter with her, but mostly I liked seeing her not afraid.

Left foot. Right foot. Left foot. Right foot. I focus on the essential rhythm of moving forward.

The road seems to stretch on, and on, and on. It doesn't help that rain clouds have blotted out all the stars. If not for our six headlamps, we'd be in complete darkness.

I think about Fort Ross, about the people counting on us. I might be wet, cold, and tired, but at least I'm not being held at gunpoint. I have it easy in comparison. What's a little physical discomfort in comparison to the hell they're probably enduring right now?

A green road sign leaps out of the darkness, the reflective letters catching the headlight beams.

Mendocino. Population 1,008.

A large house comes into view. It looks like it may have been a bed and breakfast, gauging by the burned sign in front of the two-story gingerbread house. Though the building wasn't completely destroyed by the fire, it doesn't look entirely stable, either.

"Stay alert," Kate calls. "Be on the lookout for anything that looks safe enough to give us some shelter."

The downpour coats my skin with an icy overcoat. My fingers shake with cold. Only running keeps me from succumbing to the chill completely.

My friends don't look any better. They're all as numb and exhausted as I am.

Then I see another green road sign. Even through the rain slurring my glasses, it's impossible to miss.

Fort Ross. 75 miles.

I stop dead, staring at the sign. Everyone halts in the middle of the road, all of us taking in the enormity of that green sign.

Seventy-five miles. I swallow. We've probably already gone over forty on foot.

Do we have another seventy-five miles in us?

The doubt feels like a betrayal of Kate and everything she's done for us. I know better than to let that kind of thinking sneak in. Kate warned us about it many times.

Ultras are finished with the mind, not the body. How many times has Kate said that to us? More times than I can count. If she says we can run another seventy-five miles, that's what we'll do.

"Look." Kate raises a hand, pointing through the damp. She adjusts her headlamp, sending the beam out into the darkness. "Come on," she says. "Let's get out of the rain and regroup."

It takes me a minute to see what she's talking about. I'm looking for a building or a house of some sort, but I don't see any.

Then I spot it. In a roadside turnout is a big blue semi-truck with orange flames on the side. The trailer is scorched black from the wildfire, but the cab is miraculously intact. Not only will it get us out of the rain, it will keep us safe from any stray zombies that might be around.

I pick up the pace, angling toward the semi.

Ben is the first of us to reach it. The side of the driver's door is painted with the words *Wild Thing*. The edges of the letters are highlighted with flames.

He has a knife out when he opens the door. A zombie in a bloody flannel tumbles out, snarling and raking the air with stubby hands. Ben makes short work of it with a knife through its nose. When no other zombies emerge, we clamber inside.

The stench of rot is strong inside the semi, but we're all used to it by now. There's a small bed in the back of the truck cab. I pile onto it with Reed, Caleb, and Ash. Ben and Kate take the front seats.

The first thing I do is take off my shoes and turn them upside down. A stream of water runs out of them. I root around in my running pack. The extra pair of socks I packed are also wet. Oh, well. Not that I really had a chance at having dry feet with that rainstorm outside. At least it's not drumming down on my head anymore.

I peel off my shirt, attempting to wring out the damp. I glance up to see Ben and Kate staring at each other. He's in the sweatpants he picked up in Braggs; she's in a sports bra and stretchy black pants. Both are shivering like the rest of us. From the looks on both their faces, the gap between the two front seats may as well be the English Channel.

"I forgot my *Dating for Dummies* handbook back at

Creekside," Reed says, twisting his shirt between both hands. "But I read that thing cover to cover five times and I know for a fact that on page one-hundred sixty-seven, it says you can hold your woman when you're both half naked and shivering. It's totally legit. Even with all of us around."

Ben flushes and grumbles a string of curse words. Kate wrinkles her nose with embarrassment before sidling out of the driver's seat and into Ben's lap.

These two might be the oldest among us, and they might be apocalypse badasses, but they're worse than teenage virgins. If not for that bear, I'm not sure they'd have ever gotten together.

Kate lets out of small sigh of contentment as Ben's arms wrap around her. In spite of everything, she looks happy. Seeing them together makes me remember how much I miss Lila.

"Here's some towels and dry clothes." Ash pulls out a handful of dry cloth from an overhead compartment.

I grab one of the T-shirts, glad for a chance to dry my skin.

Now what? The unspoken question rests on the tip of my tongue. Do we take a short breather then resume our run through the rain?

Fort Ross. 75 miles.

Up until this point, I've embraced the running. It hasn't always been fun and it sure as shit isn't easy, but there's a quiet satisfaction in knowing I can make it.

For the first time, I find my confidence wavering.

Suck it up, loser. That's what Lila would say. *Don't be a weanie.*

Tom wouldn't roll over and throw in the towel, that's for sure. For the first time in my life, I feel like I'm cut from the same cloth as my big brother. He wouldn't give up. Neither will I. Lives depend on us. If I have to drag my sorry ass another seventy-five miles, that's what I'm going to do.

I dry my glasses and return them to my face. That's when I spot the CB radio.

A jolt goes through my body. Leaving my sodden clothes in a pile on the floor, I shoulder my way into the front. Ben frowns as I wedge myself between the front seats. I'm too excited to explain.

I snatch the CB microphone, my thumb pressing the switch on the side. My other hand reaches out to spin the dial on the display.

"Dude." Reed has seen what I'm doing. He leans forward, his body filling the tiny egress between the front and back part of the semi.

"If we can get it working, we may be able to talk to Creekside." Just saying those words sends a bolt of excitement through me. "If we can contact Carter and the others, they might have an update on Fort Ross. They may even be able to get a message to Alvarez and let him know we're coming. Ben, did you check that zombie truck driver for keys?"

"Do I look like an amateur?" Ben pulls a set of keys from his pocket.

"Wait." Kate grabs the keys out of his hand. "That could bring zombies. Semis aren't exactly quiet."

"I think most of the zombies were burned up in the fire," I reply. "You saw the big piles of them on the road while we were running."

She hesitates, glancing out the dark window.

"I think it's worth the risk," I say. "Any information we can get could help us."

"The kid has a point," Ben says.

Still, Kate hesitates. "It's not just zombies we could attract."

That sobers everyone. I can't speak for anyone else, but I for one am thinking of Mr. Rosario. If any of her people are out here, firing up the semi would be equivalent to shooting off a flare gun.

But that seems like a small risk. Fort Ross is seventy-five miles away. Presumably all of Rosario's people are there. The likelihood of any of them being around here is slim. The chances of reaching Creekside are high if I can get the semi to fire up.

"Okay." Kate nods. "We'll try it. Ben and Ash, you two take up a position on the north side of the truck. Caleb and Reed, you take the south. Protect this truck."

Wordlessly, everyone pulls on wet shoes before climbing out of the truck.

Ben passes out Glocks to everyone. "Just in case," he says. "Knives and zom bats are the first line of defense, but don't hesitate to use the Glocks if shit goes south."

Kate gives a tight-lipped nod of approval. She dislikes guns almost as much as she disapproves of engines. But if you're going to use one, might as well use the other.

The rain is still dumping as Ben, Ash, Reed, and Caleb exit the truck.

Reed flips me a good-natured middle finger. "Next time, I get to mess with the radio."

As soon as the door closes, I count to one hundred, giving everyone a chance to get into position around the truck. Then I slide the key into the ignition.

I step on the break and turn the key. To my delight, the engine groans and turns over—then promptly dies.

I turn the key again and pump the brake. Again the engine protests, snorting and murmuring like a sleepy teenager.

"Come on, boy," I murmur, turning the key a third time. "You can do it. Come on. Lives are depending on you, man."

The engine snorts and roars to life. Blue lights flare to life across the console.

"Yes!" I slap the dashboard, grinning. "That a boy!"

Kate doesn't share my elation. She's too busy staring off into the dark after Ben.

I remember her reaction when he almost died saving my sorry ass. Having lost Lila, I understand her terror and anger.

I want to apologize to her for nearly getting Ben killed. But when I open my mouth and speak, unexpected words tumble forth. "I don't regret loving her."

Kate's head whips in my direction. She doesn't play dumb, but just looks at me. The fear is plain in her eyes.

"It hurts like a motherfucker, but I don't regret it. Not for a second." Lila was, hands down, the most amazing girl I ever met.

A shudder goes through Kate. "I already lost one love in my life. If anything happens to Ben, it will break me."

My throat tightens with emotion. "I'd do it all again, Kate. I'd take the pain all over again just to have one more day with her." Tears press against the back of my eyes, but I hold them back.

Kate looks away, but her hand reaches out and squeezes mine. "Thanks, Eric."

I furtively wipe a hand across the back of my eyes, then focus my attention on the CB radio. Time to phone home.

24
Phone Home

ERIC

"Creekside, this is Mama Bear and Company, over. Creekside, I repeat, this is Mama Bear and Company. Are you there? Over."

"Holy fuck!" The answer explodes out of the microphone, stinging my ears with its intensity. I recognize Johnny's voice immediately. "Mama Bear, is that really you? Over."

Kate's eyes widen. Her voice wavers with emotion as she says, "Wandering Writer? Is that you?"

"Holy fuck. It is you! Where are you guys?" Muffled noise comes out of the CB speaker. "Guys!" Johnny bellows. "Wake the fuck up! It's Mama Bear! She's alive!"

I feel a grin spread across my face. I snatch the microphone from Kate. "Wandering Writer, this is Fat Loser, over. You guys okay?"

"Fat Loser! Oh, my God, man, we've been so worried about you. Where the hell are you guys? Is everyone okay?"

"Mom?" Carter's voice fills the speaker. "Mom, are you okay? Where are you?"

Kate takes the microphone back from me. "I'm okay, baby. We're in Mendocino."

"Mendocino? Are you on your way back from Fort Ross?"

"Negative. We haven't made it there yet. We . . . ran into some obstacles."

Understatement of the year. I snatch back the microphone. "Any word from Fort Ross? Have you guys heard from them?"

"Negative," Johnny says. "I check in with them every two hours, but they've gone radio silent."

A chill runs across my spine. *Just because they haven't answered doesn't mean they're dead,* I remind myself. It could just mean they're in a shit load of trouble.

"How are you communicating with us?" Johnny asks. "You must have found a radio somewhere."

"We're using a CB radio in a semi-truck. Eric figured out how to get it working." Kate flashes me a quick smile. The quiet pride in her eyes is enough to make me feel like I could run another seventy-five miles without breaking a sweat.

"Are you okay, Mom?" Carter asks. "Is everyone else okay?"

It's our turn to be silent. Kate and I look at each other. "Mom?"

"Who's there with you, baby?" Kate asks.

"It's just me, Wandering Writer, and SoCal." SoCal is Jenna's call sign. She adopted it in memory of her family and her former life in Southern California.

Kate draws a long breath. There's no easy way to break the news.

"Leo is gone." Her voice is dry with grief when she speaks. "He was gunned down in Humboldt Bay. Susan is . . . Susan stayed behind in another community farther north. She was injured and couldn't travel anymore. Tell Gary we plan to go back for her. Tell Todd . . ." Kate's voice breaks. Todd is Leo's nephew. She takes a moment to gather herself. "Tell Todd I'm sorry."

Silence.

"We'll let Gary and Todd know." Jenna's even voice fills the speaker. "Everyone knew the risk when they left.

Tell us what's happened to you guys."

Kate looks too upset to speak, so I take over. I give them a quick summary of the series of disasters we've encountered since leaving Creekside.

"Now we're seventy-five miles away from Fort Ross," I say. "It's pouring down rain and we're freezing our tits off."

"You guys plan to keep going?" Johnny asks.

Kate's eyes flare. She snatches the microphone back from me. "Affirmative. We're going to Fort Ross."

"Mom—"

Someone muffles the microphone on the other end. We hear raised voices.

It's easy to imagine what's going on. Carter wants his mom to turn around and come home. Jenna and Johnny are arguing with him.

Johnny returns to the radio. "Gary and I made a . . . *discovery* shortly after you guys left. The alpha recording isn't as bullet-proof as we originally thought."

"Too late," I say. "We used it and almost got ourselves killed."

"Shit," Johnny replies. "Sorry about that. We field tested the alpha recording after you guys left. It did drive the zombies away from us, but—"

"But it also attracted two nearby alphas," Carter says.

"But we have a solution," Johnny says. "We—"

"Man, it's not a solution. You have to quit calling it that. It—"

"Dude, Carter, just shut up for a second. Mama Bear, listen to me. If you can get rid of the alphas—"

"By that, he means shoot them with a paintball gun—"

"Shut up, man. Let me finish. We found a paintball gun and loaded it with some steel ball bearings we found in the maintenance department. They expel the bearings at almost two-hundred miles per hour. That's fast enough to put a hole in a zombie brain. The side benefit is that paintball guns aren't very loud."

"What you're saying," Kate replies, "is that we have to get rid of the alphas in order to use the recordings. And we have to do that without getting ourselves killed in the process."

Pause.

"That's exactly what he's saying, Mom."

Kate exhales. To me, she says, "It was too much to hope for a simple cure-all, wasn't it?"

As though sensing our despair, Johnny pipes up again. "Do you guys still have the recorder? We have two new alpha commands. One brings the alphas toward you. The other one makes them scatter."

Kate's eyes grow distant. It's the look she gets when she's coming up with an idea. Usually the idea is equal parts thrilling and equal parts what-the-fuck.

"Play them for me," Kate says. "I think we can use them."

"Any chance you can FedEx us that paintball gun?" I ask. "Maybe half a dozen of them? We could really use them."

No one laughs.

"Are you guys really going to keep going?" Carter asks.

"Yes," Kate and I say together. "If Fort Ross has fallen, I'll make sure Mr. Rosario falls, too."

"And you're going to use the zombies to do it?"

"Possibly. I'll have to assess the situation when we get there. But I want to have the new recordings just in case."

Carter sighs. "Be careful out there, mom. I already lost dad. I don't want to lose you, too."

Kate's face softens, as it often does when she talks to Carter. "I'll be safe, baby. Promise. You do the same, okay?"

It takes us another few minutes to get the new alpha recordings on Kate's tape player. It's a miracle the small recorder hasn't been crushed, broken, or ruined during our trip. The plastic ZipLoc doesn't look like it's going to hold out much longer, though.

When we're finished, Kate says, "I'll find a way to make contact when we get to Fort Ross. I'm counting on you guys to hold Creekside together until I get back."

"Will do, Mama Bear," Johnny says.

"Be safe, Mom."

"You, too, baby."

As I switch off the CB, I reach for the keys, intending to turn off the semi.

To my surprise, Kate stops me. "Don't turn it off."

I frown. "What? Why?"

"We're driving to Fort Ross."

"Driving? The semi? But that will draw every zom between here and the fort."

Kate's eyes are fierce when she turns to look at me. "That," she says, "is exactly the point."

25
Zombie Train

KATE

I can't believe we're driving.

I can't believe it was my idea.

I sit in the passenger seat of the semi beside Ben, watching the sideview mirror. My running pack sits in my lap; I clench and unclench my hands around the straps, fighting the anxiety that knots in my chest.

"I can't believe we're driving," Reed says, echoing my own incredulity.

"Believe it, kid." Ben doesn't look up as he navigates the semi down the two-lane highway. Somewhere in his thirty years of military service, he'd learned to drive Class 8 vehicles. "It means we'll be at Fort Ross soon. Get your head ready for battle."

The heater is on full blast, filling the cab with glorious warmth. It's the warmest I've been since leaving Creekside. The drive to Fort Ross will give us all a chance to defrost and dry out.

We've left the rain behind. I lean forward, squinting into the sideview mirror. A large moon sits in the sky, illuminating the train of zombies we've picked up over the last fifty miles.

"What are we up to?" Ben asks me.

"A hundred and fifty or so, give or take."

Considering how far we've driven, that isn't a lot of zombies. If we were in an urban area, we'd have thousands of them on all sides of us. The section of road between Mendocino and Fort Ross is mostly open land.

"That's a fair amount to use against the fort. Have you sorted out the details of that plan yet?"

I shake my head. My thoughts drift to Fort Ross, and what we're going to do when we arrive.

It's been years since I visited the fort as a chaperone for Carter's elementary school field trip. I wish I remembered more about the land surrounding it. There are a few trails, but I only explored them once or twice over the years. There was nothing substantial enough to draw me and Frederico there for long training runs.

What will we find when we get there? The Fort is defensible, which presumably is the reason why Mr. Rosario set her sights on it. Thinking of that disgusting, cruel woman gets my hackles up.

My plan is pretty loose at the moment. It's impossible to plan specifics when we don't even know the state of the fort. We'll drop the semi five miles outside of Fort Ross. We'll go the rest of the way on foot, recon the area, and devise a plan from there. If we need the zombies, we'll have them, along with the new alpha recordings from Johnny.

"How do our guns look?" Ben calls.

Spread out on the narrow bed in the back of the cab are all the remaining weapons we have from Creekside. There's also the generous collection of grenades from Medieval John. Caleb and Ash have been meticulously cleaning the firearms.

"Almost finished," Ash says.

"Good," Ben replies. "Start thinking about how we're going to divide everything up and how you're each going to carry them."

"There's only two rifles," Ash says. They're folding AR-15s, which is the only reason Ben had been able to fit them into the weapons pack.

"Eric gets one rifle," Ben says. "He's the best shot out here. I'll take the second. I want everyone to have at least five grenades each. That includes you, Kate."

I don't argue, even though I'd be more comfortable handling a live snake. It would be stupid to walk into this situation without weapons. Mr. Rosario scares me more than five grenades ever will.

"My thighs and waist are chafed raw," Reed announces. "They burn like a motherfucker even when I'm sitting still. I think it was almost better when I was running. At least then everything else hurt, too, so I didn't really notice the chafing."

Caleb shoots him a quick look. "If it makes you feel better, my balls are rubbed raw. I'm pretty sure I'll never have any children."

Reed gives him a lopsided grin. "Apocalyptic birth control, huh?"

"We better get Ben on board." Caleb cracks up at his own joke. "He's the only one of us who's gonna need birth control in the near future."

A rumble of irritation rises from Ben's throat. He leans over the steering wheel, glaring out at the road.

"Enough, guys," I say, exasperated.

The guys snicker in the back seat as we continue to rumble down the road.

"How far back are they?" Ben asks me. His jaw has loosened.

They are the zombies. He's been driving slow, enabling us to gather the zombie train.

"Quarter mile or so."

"We only have another few miles to drive. I'm going to speed up to put some distance between them and us. That will give us a good head start when we get out."

"Good plan," I reply. We don't want to risk getting bitten when we get out of the semi.

I haven't exactly figured out how I'm going to use the

zombies. With any luck, I won't need them at all. But if the situation at the fort is bad enough, having some undead at our command might be enough to tip the scales in our favor. I won't know for certain until we recon Fort Ross.

The engine of the big rig rumbles as Ben downshifts and accelerates. I absorb his profile, trying not to worry about what's ahead of us. Ben has been fighting one war or another his entire adult life. If there's anyone who can survive what's to come, it's him.

So why do I have a sick feeling in my stomach?

He turns off the road into a long driveway, parking the semi behind a thick strand of oleander bushes. "Hard to hide a beast this big. This is the best we can do."

"It's a good spot." I turn to Caleb and Ash. "Weapons ready?"

We spend the next fifteen minutes sorting weapons and stashing them on our bodies. The Glock that Caleb hands me goes onto the belt that holds my knives and zom bat. A spare handgun goes into the back compartment. Two extra magazines go into the large front pockets of my running pack.

Squished between the dashboard and the passenger seat where I sit, Ben fusses over the location of my five grenades. He puts two of them in smaller pockets on the upper straps of the running pack. Two more go into the stretchy cell phone pockets on either side of the leggings I wear. He frowns, searching for a place to stash the last one.

"How about the kangaroo pouch in the back?" I suggest.

"The what?"

"Kangaroo pouch." I flip the pack around. In the lower portion of the back is a compartment held closed with magnets. The magnets make the interior easily accessible without having to take off the pack.

Ben slides the grenade inside, tugging on the fabric to test the strength of the magnets. "That'll do," he says after a solid sixty seconds of frowning. "It's not ideal, but it's better than sticking it in a pouch you can't easily reach. Promise me you'll blow shit up if you have to?"

"I promise." I squeeze his hand, anxiety gnawing at my gut. "How's everyone doing back there?" I ask the rest of the group. They've been oddly quiet.

"We're taking bets on whether or not you two will start making out before we leave," Reed says.

"I told them it's not dangerous enough," Eric adds. "You guys only make out after near-death experiences."

"I told them the old man isn't going to let his lady go into battle without a big wet one." Caleb gives Ben a wicked grin.

"*I* told them they're being children," Ash proclaims.

"You little shitheads make me crazy." Ben throws open the door and jumps down.

I follow him. Cold ocean air slams into my wet clothing.

"I'm stashing the keys here." Ben deposits them on top of the front passenger wheel. "That way we don't risk losing them. They'll be here for whoever needs them."

The others haven't joined us yet. I tug on his hand, pulling him into the shadow of the semi.

"Be careful out there." I press a quick kiss to his lips. "I can't lose you."

"I'm too mean to die." He draws me close. "Keep the crazy shit to minimum, okay? And don't hesitate to use this." He taps the hilt of my gun. "We're not going up against zombies this time. A bullet could be the difference between living and dying."

I nod, hoping I won't have to follow his advice.

"I mean it, Kate. I'll kick your ass if anything happens to you."

"Dude." Reed drops down out of the semi. "Let's go back to the *Dating for Dummies* book. I guarantee that line was nowhere in that book."

Ben turns away from me, growling something unintelligible at Reed.

"Dude, I'm just trying to help."

Ben curses before marching toward the road. I shake my head at Reed, unable to suppress a small smile. Reed is always good at diffusing tension.

"Silence from here on out," I say as the six of us assemble on the asphalt. "We stay together until we see Fort Ross. Then we split into our teams, recon the fort, and meet back at the designated rendezvous to finalize our attack plans. Any questions?"

No one has a joke or a sarcastic comment this time. I take in my small group, savoring this moment with the six of us. There isn't anyone here I wouldn't give my life for.

"All right. Let's go. Everyone be safe and be smart."

I lead them out at an easy run.

We run without headlamps. If Rosario posts a watch—and it would be stupid to think otherwise—the headlamps will expose us from miles away. It's slow going without any decent light, but at least the moon is out. At least it's not raining anymore.

Ben falls into step beside me. It feels good to have him close. Maybe someday, we can go for a real run together. Not a training run. Not a supply run. Not a frantic run for our lives. Just a regular fun run for the sheer joy of running and being together.

I would like a world like that.

We make very little sound as we move down the deserted highway. My eyes constantly roam the area, flicking between the road and the land on either side of us.

Over the years of running, I've developed an innate sense of mileage. I mentally count down the miles as we run. Five. Four.

The eastern sky turns from black to charcoal gray. Sunrise is near. I pick up the pace, knowing we'll have to get off the road before sunrise or risk being spotted.

Three miles. Two miles. One.

The land drops away into a cove. And suddenly, there it is. Perched in the innermost curve of the cove, is Fort

Ross. The great wooden fortress from a time long ago is once again made relevant in the apocalypse.

We draw to a halt, stepping off the road into a cluster of trees. The sky is a dark gray. The moon edges into the horizon, withdrawing its light.

The old Russian fort was impressive before the apocalypse. In this new landscape, it seems too good to be true. Towering wooden walls of redwood rise twelve feet high, surrounding the fort in a perfect square. Each fence post is topped with a wooden spike. The walls are six inches thick, built oh-so-long ago to hold off Native American attacks.

Inside the fort are five large structures. Like the fences, they are constructed of thick redwood plants. A lookout tower stands at the southwest and northeast corners, both of them slotted with openings for cannons. I recall the fort having real cannons inside the walls.

Besides the original wooden structures, inside the walls are also motorhomes and a scattering of tents. All in all, it's a great set-up. I can see why Rosario wanted the compound for her people. With the gardens, grazing land for cattle, and proximity to the sea for fishing, it's an ideal location.

"Time to split up. The mile eighty-six marker will be our rendezvous point." I point back up the road to the small green-and-white road sign sticking out of the dirt. There are a lot of trees and shrubs there for cover. "Meet there in two hours."

Five heads nod. I gather everyone close for one last group hug. Not even Ben complains about this. I grip his hand hard, hoping to convey all my feelings for him in that single touch.

Then we break into two pre-designated groups. Ben, Eric, and Ash sweep southeast. Reed and Caleb are with me. We sweep southwest toward the ocean as the sky brightens with the dawn.

26
Duct Tape

JESSICA

I sit in the pale light of dawn on the floor of the RV. All the curtains are drawn, but the windows are wide open so I can hear if anyone approaches.

In my lap is the tennis racket from Shaun. On the floor next to my knee is the pile of nails from Alvarez. I slide the nails through the slots in the top of the racket, securing them in place with duct tape.

I imagine Shaun's expression if he knew what I was up to. He'd love to see me making use of his duct tape, most especially because I'm making a weapon. Among other things, Shaun had been known to fix ballet slippers, a loose exhaust pipe, and a broken suitcase handle with duct tape.

When I finish, I hold up the racket and admire it. The dozen fat, rusty nails fan around the curve of the tennis racket like a mohawk. Looking at the weapon makes my blood sing. I am going to kill people today.

I slide the racket between the bed and the wall, making sure it's completely concealed.

There's nothing to do now but wait.

27
Recon

ERIC

Ben leads us off the road into the tall meadow grass covering the land. We run in a crouch, doing our best to stay out of sight. We skim over the ground, passing the official Fort Ross visitor's center. The entrance to the property is blocked by two cars, both of them with their tires deflated.

My back aches and my quads burn from the hunched position. The coastal breeze whips across my back, chilling my damp clothes. I grip my rifle with two hands, holding onto it like a lifeline.

Just past the visitor's center, Ben leads us into a shallow ditch that runs along the highway. I breathe heavily, gripping my sore thighs as I kneel in the mud. Dampness soaks through my pants. I shift the rifle, positioning it across my back to keep it from getting wet.

I take in the enormity of Fort Ross. If I ever imagined a fort from a western movie, this would be it. It looks like someone magically transported the massive structure through a time machine. The thick timber walls are topped with spikes. The guard towers have cannon slots.

A loud creaking sound echoes up to the road. The giant gate swings open. A dozen people, surrounded by well-armed men, are herded out into the dawn. The guards are each armed with a leashed zombie. The monsters are secured around the neck with leashes that are attached to long poles carried by the guards.

The Fort Ross residents are escorted toward a large enclosure surrounded by a tall deer fence. I adjust the binoculars and pick out tilled earth dotted with green shoots. That must be the community garden.

Once inside the enclosure, the men and women gather up tools: hoes, shovels, and buckets. Around the perimeter of the garden are large plastic trash cans. Those with buckets dip them into the cans. They come up dripping with water.

Rain basins, I realize. There are some benefits to living in Northern California. There's always plenty of rainwater to go around.

"We need to scout the south side of the fort," Ben whispers. "Follow me. Stay alert."

He army crawls through the ditch. Ash follows behind him and I bring up the rear.

The earth is muddy from yesterday's rainstorm. My elbows and knees dig into chilly muck. Tom wouldn't recognize the person crawling through a trench with guns and grenades.

Ben draws to a halt when we reach the south side of the fort. It looks much the same as the north side; a long wooden wall with zombies chained to it.

Another group of people exits the fort, this one headed toward the ocean. The Fort Ross people carry fishing poles, nets, buckets, and tackle boxes. Like the first group we saw, the guards have leashed zombies. They laugh as they herd the fisherman toward the path leading down to the water, passing a cigarette amongst themselves.

"I think it's safe to say Fort Ross has fallen," Ben murmurs. "Security is low. They have the zombies, but there are only two guard towers. We have to assume they have watchmen in both of them. As far as I can tell, there are no other watch points around the wall."

I peer through the grass, studying the fort. Ben is right. We have the high ground on the fort. I can see enough to know there are no guards stationed on top of any of the motorhomes inside. There is no scaffolding along the interior fence for other watch stations.

"She's relying on the zombies," Ash says.

"Lazy, but somewhat effective," Ben replies. "It gives us a loop hole to work with. We've seen enough. Let's get back to the rendezvous."

We turn around in the ditch. This time, I lead the way as we army crawl back through the mud. The morning sun above us streaks the sky with pale blue and yellow. I keep my head down as I crawl, not wanting to be spotted by any of the guards in the garden enclosure.

Then I hear the laughter. It's a cruel sound that carries across the open grassland.

Before I can think better of it, I raise my head just enough to peer through the grass.

Bile rises in my throat at what I see. The guards are using the zombies to taunt the garden workers. They push the monsters close to the people, laughing as people dodge out of the way as they desperately continue to work.

"*Hijos de puta,*" Ash growls.

I can't peel my eyes from the scene.

A guard pushes a zombie in the direction of a teenage girl. She leaps out of the way. He laughs, pursuing her with dark glee down a row of tomato bushes. She scrambles backward.

The guards chortle. The rest of the people look on in horror, all of them too afraid to speak.

The man with the zombie chases the girl to the far side of the garden—straight into the hands of another guard. He flips her onto the ground, passing his zombie pole off to his friend.

That's when the screaming starts. One guard stands over the scene with two zombies, laughing as his friend tears at the girl's clothing.

My stomach churns. All the aches and pains and fear I've endured over the last two days fall away, seeming insubstantial to what this girl is experiencing.

You're such a con, Eric.

I grit my teeth. Lila was right. I had been a con. I had been content to let the world pass me by without any discernible effort to participate in it.

Not anymore. That was the old Eric.

Before I can think better of it, I swing my rifle around. I reposition my body, leaning up against the side of the drainage ditch. I'm the best shot in Creekside. Everyone says so. Time for me to put that skill to use.

I prop my elbows in the mud and raise the scope to my eye, sighting on the bastard terrorizing the girl.

Ben pushes aside the muzzle of my gun. "Not now, Eric."

"But—!"

"Don't be short sighted." Ben leans forward. "I get it, Eric. I understand where you're coming from. But trust me when I say that saving that girl right now will cost a lot more lives in the long run. We can't go off half-cocked. We need to find Kate and come up with a solid plan."

A low, long cry ripples through the air. The terror and anguish in that sound is a gut punch.

Ben rests a hand on my shoulder. When he looks at me, I see something in his eyes I've never seen before.

Compassion. Understanding.

"We'll get those fuckers, Eric. I promise.

My throat tight, I nod. Turning away is the hardest thing I've ever done.

Ash leads us north, crawling through the ditch in the lead. Ben is right behind her. I follow in the back, the rifle heavy across my shoulders.

And then I hear it again. That long, low cry.

Something in me snaps.

Pivoting on my knees, I bring the rifle around.

28
Red Flower

ERIC

I narrow my focus, throwing everything through the AR-15 and down the scope. I line up the crosshairs on the man who stands with the two pet zombies, bent double with laughter as his friend continues to tear at the girl's clothing. She puts up a ferocious fight, but the man is bigger and stronger.

The crashing of the ocean fades to nothingness. All physical sensation disappears, sucked away as I hone in on the asshole with the zombie pets.

You've got this, Eric. Lila's voice rings through my mind, so clear and vehement that my skin shivers.

I exhale and pull the trigger.

The rifle cracks, kicking hard against my shoulder.

The first guard falls. The rapist leaps to his feet, dick hanging out of his pants.

The AR-15 automatically kicks another round into the chamber.

Exhale. Fire.

Another kick from the rifle. Another asshole drops. A thrill shoots through my bloodstream.

"Eric!" Ben hisses. "What the fuck? You're going to bring holy hell down on our heads!"

I ignore him.

The teenage girl turns, scrambling away from the fallen guards.

She isn't fast enough.

One of the pet zombies, no longer restrained, pounces on her. Her screams tear into me as the zombie tears into her.

No.

No-no-no-no.

This wasn't supposed to happen. I was supposed to save that girl.

Her screams rake at me as a zombie sinks its teeth into her abdomen. An echo of a scream from the past blasts through me: Lila.

Instinct takes over. I raise the rifle and sight down it. This is what I should have done for Lila.

Sight. Exhale. Fire.

The girl falls. Her face turns into a red flower.

I drop the rifle, hands shaking. The trembling spreads up my arms like a wildfire.

Chaos envelopes the garden. The workers turn upon their captives. It's mayhem. Shots are fired. More screams erupt. I can't see anything beyond the mass of churning bodies. The shaking in my arms travels up my neck, making my teeth chatter.

I close my eyes, trying to block it all out. All I see is the girl as my bullet turns her face into a flower of death.

I killed her.

No, I amend, thinking of Lila. I released her.

I should have released Lila. She shouldn't have had to do it to herself. I did the right thing for that girl.

"Dammit, kid," Ben says. "Time to go." His voice cracks like a whip as he jerks me to my feet.

Ben breaks into a sprint, tearing out of the ditch and back onto the road. I sling the rifle over my back and sprint after him, grateful to be moving.

Bloody red flowers bloom all around me. I see Lila and Tom in my periphery, the two of them pumping their arms as they sprint beside me.

Run, Eric.

Don't let up, little brother.

You did the right thing, Eric.

Justice was served, little brother.

I'm fucking losing it. That's all there is to it. I'm hearing and seeing my brother and my dead girlfriend.

Hallucinations. Kate told us a horned rabbit visits her on long runs. Her imaginary friend.

That must be what's happening to me. I'm hallucinating. I'm a real ultrarunner.

I'm also a failure. I tried to save that girl and I got her killed. And I've given up our location and revealed us to Rosario.

Maybe there's always some part of me that will be a con.

Just as we reach the entrance kiosk, the fort gates are thrown open. Men and women on dirt bikes pedal out, riding two to a bike. The ones on the back fire guns while the people on the front of the bikes pedal. I count six bikes.

The zombies around the fort go ballistic. They keen, howl, and scratch at the open air, yanking against the chains restraining them.

Shouts of warning erupt from the garden. People scream, stampeding toward the gate. The zombies and the guards are left lying on the ground, their bodies unmoving.

Shots ring out from the bikes. Several people in the garden drop, felled by bullets.

"Fuck." Ben drops to his knees, bringing his rifle up to take aim. "You guys get the hell out of here. I've got this."

"Fuck that." Ash brings up her Glock. "I might not be as good a shot as Eric, but I can still take down assholes."

"This is my fault. I'm not leaving, either." No way am I going to leave those people to be slaughtered. Not when I can do something about it.

"For what it's worth, Eric, I'm glad you tried." Ash's grip is rock steady on her gun. "It was the humane thing to do."

I set my stance and raise my AR-15. We're much closer than we were before, no more than two hundred yards from the guards who advance on them. I stare down the scope, zeroing in on the first of the dirt bikes. My shaking hands miraculously still.

I've never had to take out a target moving at high speed. Sweat breaks out along my forehead and upper lip. With the bikes shooting across the open landscape, there's no time to set up the shot. Dammit.

I fire. The shot goes wide, sending up a puff of soil as the bike races forward.

Cracks ring out on either side of me as Ash and Ben open fire. One of the bikes flips over as the tire is shot. Five others keep coming.

The prisoners are in a tight group. One man yells at them, herding them along. He falls in at the back of the group, shouting at them as they head for the trees growing in a thick clump along the north side of the meadow.

That's where Kate and her team will be. With any luck, she'll find them and get them to safety. All we have to do is buy them enough time to escape.

This is no leisurely target practice. I don't have time to sight, exhale, and fire. I have to act right fucking now, or those bikes are going to overtake those innocent people.

I zero in on one bike, the one at the foremost of the pack. I open fire, cranking off round after round. I pepper the site with bullets, hoping to God one of them finds its way into the assholes riding it. Ben and Ash do the same, bullets leaping from their guns.

My bike veers without warning, going straight for the cliff overlooking the ocean. Before it reaches the edge, it crashes onto its side and skids through the dirt. One wheel spins, the other hangs broken on its axis.

I wait, finger poised on the trigger.

The two people on it struggle to extract themselves from the bike. I don't give them a chance to get up. A woman takes a bullet through the head. The man riding behind her takes two in the chest.

Ash and Ben have disabled another two of the bikes. The remaining two have veered away from the prisoners and are instead riding in our direction. They open fire on us. Good. If they're focused on us, the Fort Ross people will have a better chance to escape.

Ben lobs a grenade. His throw is short, but the explosion sends the bike into a spin. I hit the stem of the remaining bike. The handlebars snap off. The front tire hits a divot in the land and tips over, wheel spinning.

All the bikes are down. I have no time to congratulate myself. There are still enemies out there. Three of them race across the open field on foot, chasing down the prisoners who have disappeared into the cypress trees.

Another four head our way, opening fire as they charge at us. Another half a dozen sprint out of Fort Ross on foot, also storming in our direction.

"Down!" Ben yells.

I throw myself to the ground. Rosario's people charge at us, guns blazing. Ben and Ash throw more grenades. Bodies fly up into the air. I dig in and continue to fire my rifle.

Ash screams, rolling sideways. At the same moment, another grenade goes off. Another body flies across the ground.

I'm aware of Ash panting on the ground beside me, squashing her hand over a wound in her shoulder. I'm aware of Ben on the other side of her, lying in the grass like a lion awaiting its prey.

Mostly, my focus is on the remaining enemies sprinting straight at us. I raise my rifle and train it on the man closest to me. This motherfucker is toast.

I pull the trigger.

The rifle clicks empty.

"Fuck!"

I yank out the magazine, checking for bullets. Empty.

My brain stops working. "Fuck. Ben, I'm out!"

"Grenades," Ben yells.

I fumble at the elastic pull cord on the front of my running pack. I'm so frantic I can barely hold onto the tie. The whole point of sticking them in the front pockets was to keep them secure. I hadn't considered I'd be pinch hitting.

I hear another click. Another empty cartridge.

"Motherfucker!" Ben leaps to his feet, lips pulled back in a snarl of rage. He snatches Ash's gun off the ground. Two more shots rip through the air before that gun clicks empty, too. Another two enemies fall, but there are still more coming at us.

I at last fumble open my front pocket. My hand closes around the grenade—

"Freeze, motherfuckers."

One of Rosario's women stops fifty feet away from us, pointing a shotgun in our direction. Flanking her are two more men, each of them also armed with shotguns.

The woman smiles cruelly at us. Her dirty blond dreadlocks are held back by a handkerchief. She wears a shirt that reads *There's no cure for being a cunt.*

"I still have three rounds," she calls. "One for each of you dickheads. Caesar? Timo?How many rounds do you guys have?"

"Two," says a man with a shaved head and a full beard.

"I have three," says the other man.

"How about that?" The woman's smile broadens. "There are three of you and eight unspent shotgun shells." Hard eyes take us in. "All we need to do is aim in your general direction. Lay down your weapons and come with us, or die. You have until the count of three to make your decision. I really don't give a fuck what you choose. One."

I grit my teeth, hand tightening around the grenade still in my front pocket. Fuck this shit. I'm ready to risk it all. Maybe I can get one of them before I'm taken down. If Ben can get the others—

"Two."

"Stand down," Ben barks. He throws his gun to the ground.

His words stun me. The command in his voice makes my fingers loosen around the grenade.

In a softer voice, Ben says, "You'll never get the pin out before they gun you down, son. Stand down. Now."

I release the grenade and raise my hands in a sign of surrender.

The woman's face curls into a full, nasty smile. "That's what I thought. Get on your knees, dickheads. You're about to meet Mr. Rosario."

This statement is followed by laughter from the two lackeys. It sends a spear of dread down my spine. It makes me think that, right about now, I might be better off dead.

29
Reunion

KATE

Gunfire. Screaming.

Hot dread fires in my veins. I break into a run, tearing through the cypress grove on the northwest side of the fort.

"Kate," Caleb hisses. "Kate, wait!"

I ignore him. Panic mounts within me. *Ben. Eric. Ash.* Without a doubt, I know they're caught up in whatever is going on. The trees are obscuring my view. I race through them.

Before I realize what I'm doing, I find my gun gripped in both hands. I raise it, finger poised over the trigger.

More gunfire. More screaming.

Ben. Eric. Ash.

What's happening?

I hear voices. Pounding feet.

I drop behind a tree for cover. I widen my stance, putting one foot slightly behind the other for extra support. Just like Ben taught me. The gun balances in front of me, pointed in the direction of the noise.

Caleb and Reed catch up to me. They take cover behind two trees of their own.

We wait. Voices and footsteps hurtle toward us.

The first person I see is a short woman in clothes that

had probably once been tight on her. They now hang on her shoulders, revealing a thin frame. She can't be much older than me.

One look at her eyes tells me she's terrified. She doesn't have the look of Rosario's people. Still, I'm not willing to risk my life—or the lives of my people—on an assumption.

"Stop." My voice cracks through the trees.

The woman grinds to a halt, looking around with wide eyes. Another half dozen people rush into view, all of them right on her heels.

"Stop right there," I command.

More people appear, almost a dozen in all. There are no children, only men and women between the ages of twenty and forty. A few of them are armed. They halt as they catch sight of me, Caleb, and Reed. All three of us have our weapons drawn.

"Who are you?" I demand.

A man with dark hair pushes to the front of the pack, both hands wrapped around the handle of a gun. My finger tenses on the trigger of my gun.

The man gives me a hard look, showing no sign of backing down. He's joined on either side by two women, both of whom are also armed.

"We don't want any trouble," he says. "There are people after us. Let us through and we'll be on our way."

My mouth falls open. I know that voice. I recognize it from months and months of speaking to him over the ham radio.

What I don't recognize is the authoritative young man who stands before me. Dark skin, handsome face, black stubble. By the way those around him look at him, it's clear they turn to him for guidance.

"Let us pass," he says. "There's no need for trouble."

"Alvarez." His name falls from my lips. I step out from behind the tree, lowering my weapon. "Alvarez." My voice shakes with emotion. "It's me."

Our eyes meet. His mouth falls open. "Mama Bear," he breathes. "You came."

A shot rings out. A person at the back of the cluster falls to the ground with a cry.

Four people with guns burst into view. I immediately recognize them as Rosario's people. The mismatched clothing, the unkempt hair, and the feral eyes are all a dead giveaway.

"Down!" I shout, raising my gun.

Alvarez and his people don't have to be told twice. They throw themselves to the ground as Caleb, Reed, and I open fire.

I was never a great shot, but I am decent at close range.

Rosario's people have handguns, but they don't have the protection of a cypress. Their shots *thunk* into the trees as our guns crack through the clearing.

I've killed people before. Sometimes I wake up in the middle of the night, sick with the knowledge of what I did to Johnson and his people.

I expect to feel the same cold dread I felt when I set the zombies loose on him and his people.

It's different this time. This time, all I feel is hot rage. These people tried to hurt me and Frederico. Since taking over the fort, who knows what ungodly things they've done to Alvarez and his people.

I pull the trigger again, and again, and again. Rage pumps through my fingertips and propels each bullet from the chamber.

In less than thirty seconds, it's over. Silence fills the clearing. Rosario's people lay dead. Ben would be proud.

Somewhere nearby is more shouting and gunfire.

Reed, Caleb, and I rush to the edge of the tree line for a better look, taking cover so we can't be seen. The north side of Fort Ross comes into view. The gates are open. Scattered across the grassland are half a dozen bikes, all of them overturned or laying on their sides like dead animals. Dead people are scattered across the meadow—Rosario's people, and people from Fort Ross.

Six figures move in the direction of the fort. Two of them walk with their hands clasped behind their heads. A third person walks hunched over, clasping an arm against her chest.

My lungs stop working. I can't move. I can't breathe. All I can do is stare at the figures of Ben, Eric, and Ash. The three of them are herded like cattle at gunpoint.

I'm sucked back to that moment in Braggs when I thought for sure Ben was lost to me. Panic and despair rise up and threaten to suffocate me. The pain of losing Kyle hits me all over again.

I fight against the darkness. It won't help Ben. I have to be strong.

I bury the remembered pain, throwing all my focus into the present. Ben isn't dead. He hasn't left me. I need to bring my A-game if I want to figure out a way to keep him alive.

I wish I had a rifle. I'm too far away for my gun to be any use. I finger one of my grenades, studying the foremost of those harassing my friends.

I get a good look at her. Dirty blond dreadlocks. A sneering profile.

Jeanie. I'd recognize that bitch anywhere.

That woman had captured me and Frederico and taken us to Mr. Rosario.

And now she has Ben. Rage bubbles up.

"Mama." Reed nudges me with his elbow. "No grenade."

"They have Ben," I snap.

"And Ash and Eric." Caleb's eyes are alight with fury.

"It's too far," Reed says. "All you'll do is alert them to our presence."

"They have Ben," I repeat.

Alvarez and his people creep through the trees, coming to stand near us in a scattered ring. From the protection of the trees, they watch my people being taken into the fort.

"They don't know about us," Reed says. "We have to get Alvarez and his people away. We jeopardize their chances if we draw attention to ourselves."

I straighten. "Fuck that."

Reed's brow furrows. "Mama?"

"We can't run," I say. "Not now. That will only give Rosario a chance to circle the wagons. We need to strike now while she's off-balance."

Alvarez regards me, mouth tight. "I don't suppose you guys brought any weapons?"

Caleb pulls two grenades from his running pack and hands them to the bony woman in baggy clothes. I can see from the look on his face that he's as desperate to get to Ash as I am to get to Ben. He'll do anything to get to her.

"We brought weapons," I say. "We have to attack, and we have to attack now. The element of surprise is still on our side." I pass an extra Glock and spare cartridge to Alvarez. He takes the gun and ammo from me with a look of reverence, a grim smile stretching across his face.

"We also have a semi and zombies," I tell him. "You take your people and circle around to the south side of the fort with our grenades. When you see me coming from the north, I want you to blow the south wall. We'll take them from two sides."

Alvarez stares at me like he's seeing me for the first time. "That's insane. We can't destroy the walls of the fort. We can't bring zombies here."

"We can, and we will. We have to strike hard and fast." I'll rain holy hell down on Fort Ross to save Ben and the others. "The longer we wait, the more people are going to die."

Alvarez stares at me. I see the calculations whirling behind his dark eyes. Our attack will jeopardize the home he's worked so hard to build.

"You'll lose the fort completely if you don't do this," I say softly.

"We can't bring zombies here," Alvarez says. "We've

worked hard to clear this area. We—"

I shake my head, cutting him off. "Rosario has us outgunned. A surprise attack won't be enough on its own. The only thing that will tip the balance in our favor is the zombies. They'll cause confusion and give us a chance to gain the upper hand."

"If you bring zombies to Fort Ross, innocent people will die," says a man from Alvarez's group.

"What do you think will happen if we run and hide?" Caleb's jaw ripples with tension. "Rosario will want retribution for what's just happened. She won't stop at killing our people. She'll punish yours, too."

Alvarez's eyes grow distant. In that split instant, I know he has someone back in the fort he cares for.

"We have a secret weapon," I say. "A way to control the zombies with alpha language. There isn't time to fill you in on all the details. I need you to trust me, Alvarez."

"If you knew the shit we went through to get here, you'd know how badly we want to save your asses," Reed adds.

Alvarez's black eyes settle on my face. In the last ten seconds, they've hardened with conviction. He nods at me. "Okay. We'll follow your plan. My people have weapons stashed around the fort. This counter attack is sooner than they expected, but they're ready to fight. There's a small beach just north of here accessible by a trail. It's hard to find if you don't know it's there. Rosario's people haven't found it yet. I keep a row boat stashed there. Steve, I need you to take our people around the cove and come up from the back. Will you do that?"

"Yeah." A lean, muscular man steps to the front of the crowd. "You can count on me."

Alvarez scans his people. "I need volunteers to go with Steve. You can leave if you want to. I won't force anyone to stay and fight."

No one budges. His people are scared—who isn't?—but I see resolve in their faces.

"That's what I'm talking about." Caleb swings off his pack and unzips it. "I have three more grenades and two extra guns. Who wants weapons?"

Alvarez's face flashes pride as his people crowd in. Reed and I join Caleb, handing out grenades and extra weapons. By the time I'm finished, all I have is my knife, zom bat, and Glock.

I hang onto the gun for Ben. He'd want me to have it.

Steve leads his group toward the cliffside beach where the boat is hidden. To my surprise, Alvarez stays behind.

"I'm coming with you," Alvarez says. "If I'm going to allow zombies into Fort Ross, I need to be the one to bring them here. We're playing for keeps here, Mama Bear."

"I don't intend to lose." I look north, back toward Highway 1. "I hope you're ready to run your ass off."

"You're fucking crazy, do you know that?"

"I've been told that once or twice."

Alvarez flashes me a grin. I see a trace of the young soldier I met at the beginning of the outbreak. My heart swells with affection.

He wraps me in a bear hug. "Thanks for coming, Kate."

I hug him back. "We have to look out for each other. It's the only way we're going to survive."

Reed bounces on his toes, something he often does when he's getting ready to run. "I'm ready to sow seeds of death and destruction," he says cheerfully.

Caleb cracks his knuckles, nostrils flaring as he stares in the direction of the fort. "I'm ready to blow some shit up."

"You'll get a chance to do both," I assure them. "But first, we have to get the semi. And the zombies."

We set out together, the four of us running hard. The cypress grove conceals us from anyone who might be watching from the fort.

I'm coming, Ben. Just hold on until I get there.

30
Closer

JESSICA

Twenty-four hours.

It's only been twenty-four hours since Rosario has taken over Fort Ross. Twenty hours feels like twenty-four years when you're living in hell.

I'm alone at the moment, locked inside the dinky RV. The only company left to me are my thoughts, my dying ex-husband staked outside to a laundry pole, and the monsters who come to visit me.

My body hurts in new and awful ways. I do my best to ignore it, grateful for my IUD. At least I won't get pregnant. There's no telling what else might happen to my body, but at least I won't bring a child into this nightmare.

I count them off on my fingers in the morning light.

Crooked Dick. Homer Simpson. Shit Stain. Joe Dirt. Limp Dick. Chimney Sweep.

Six. Six assholes and I've named every one. I stare at the memory of their faces on my closed eyelids, focusing on them. Forcing myself to remember the awful details.

Focus on the prospect. That's what Shaun used to say when he went calling on a new account. *Focus on the prospect and visualize closing the sale. That's what it's all about. Visualizing the close.*

There was a reason Shaun made six figures at his job.

The man could close any deal. Sometimes that meant getting shit faced and partying with a prospect until three in the morning. Sometimes that meant getting someone a pair of baseball tickets to a Giant's game. Sometimes it meant patronizing a restaurant and leaving your calling card—for three years.

Shaun was never one to be put off by rejection or obstacles. He was the closer.

It's time for me to take a page out of his book. It's time for me to close. Fuck the obstacles. If Shaun could sell wine in a dry Kentucky county, I can figure out a way to obliterate each of the men who have come and gone from the RV.

I already have the weapon. My tennis racket. My last gift from Shaun, enhanced with the gift from Alvarez. It's just a matter of waiting for Alvarez to make his move. Then I intend to use my racket for maximum destruction.

"Jessie." My name slurs softly from my ex-husband's mouth.

I look in Shaun's direction. It's sickening that he's still alive, suffering and dying slowly tied to the laundry pole. The morning sheds light on pallid skin slick with sweat. Flies have gathered on his body in a dark mass, writhing on the bloodstains on his shirt and pants. More encrust the wound on his shoulder. He's too far away for me to see if there are any maggots in the open sores, but I wouldn't be surprised if there are.

He sees me watching him. "I don't regret marrying you and having a family." The words spill slowly from his mouth, thick like syrup. "I wouldn't trade my memories of Claire and May for anything. The only thing I regret is . . . is hurting you."

My mouth tightens. I look away, but I don't close the window.

"I'm so sorry, Jessie."

"You've said that before."

"I know. It never seems like enough."

"It isn't." Nothing he says can make up for what he did. Even if he says it when he's dying on a laundry pole from a zombie bite.

Gunfire rips through the air. I leap to my feet, heart racing. I sweep my gaze along all the open windows of the motorhome, searching for the source of the sound.

The interior of the fort bursts into activity. Rosario's people boil forth from buildings and motorhomes, every last one of them armed. Several of them herd a cluster of our people back into the Rotchev House, locking them inside. Bella is among them.

For once, Steph isn't with her. She left the fort at sunrise with Alvarez and the rest of the garden crew.

More gunfire. This time, I discern its direction. North. Outside the fort. Someone is shooting outside the fort.

Alvarez. Steph.

They're on the north side of the fort. That's where the gardens are.

Alvarez. Steph.

I slam my hand into the back of the driver's seat in fear and frustration.

"What's going on?" Shaun slurs.

"Someone is shooting on the north side of the fort."

Shaun groans. "Alvarez."

Fear beats inside me. The attack was scheduled for tonight inside the fort. If there's fighting outside now, that means something has gone wrong.

Rosario's people jump onto dirt bikes and ride out of the fort. The rest race around in disorganized confusion. There's no sign of Rosario.

Now, I think. Now is the perfect time to attack. Their attention is diverted. If we were united, we could rush them.

Except we aren't united. One workforce is outside in the garden. Another is down in the water fishing. The strongest of our people are in both of those groups.

Those of us left inside include kids, a few elderly, and

those less able-bodied. There are no leaders inside, no one to lead an exodus from the Rotchev House.

My gaze narrows on the Rotchev House. It's roughly fifty yards from where I stand. There are half a dozen guards surrounding it. Another contingent of Rosario's people has been sent out of the gates to confront whatever trouble is brewing out there.

Is it Alvarez? Is he fighting back? Did he hatch a new plan since we spoke last night?

I can't just stand around and stare out the window like an idiot. No one is watching me and Alvarez might need my help. I have to do something.

It's time to be a closer.

Licking my lips, I crawl onto the bed and kick out the window screen at the very back of the motorhome.

"Jessie," Shaun whispers.

I ignore him as I slip out the window to the ground. I crouch behind the RV. The escalation of gunfire makes my skin crawl.

There. A pile of firewood lies no more than ten feet away. Alvarez kept it stocked at all times near the community fire pits.

Tucked at the bottom of the pile is a small wooden box—an old jewelry box repurposed for the apocalypse—that contains matches and lighters. Our community knows it's there, but Rosario's people haven't found it yet.

My eyes dart left and right. No one looks in my direction. I sprint from the safety of the RV straight toward the wood stack. I skid into the dirt behind the logs, fingers scrabbling in the dirt as I fumble out the box.

I crouch there, box cradled against my chest.

A fire. A fire could be just the thing. A distraction for Alvarez and the others fighting outside.

The gates are opened. Someone runs inside, shouting for Rosario.

"We got them," a man crows. "We got the fuckers who attacked us!"

My heart stills. Dread pools in my belly. I peek out from behind the wood pile.

Rosario descends from her RV as three prisoners are prodded into view.

I experience momentary confusion. I expect to see Alvarez or others from Fort Ross, but I don't recognize any of the prisoners.

There's a middle-aged man with gray stubble; a young man with glasses who doesn't look old enough to drink; and a dark-haired woman with a bleeding shoulder.

Could these be Alvarez's friends from up north? Could that be the legendary Kate I've heard so much about?

Whoever they are, they're in trouble. Rosario looks like she could breathe hellfire.

And then a wheelbarrow comes into the fort, pushed along by one of Rosario's minions.

Inside the wheelbarrow are bodies.

I recognize them instantly. I see the blue denim shirt of George. The purple socks of Chloe. The red cable knit sweater of Barb.

And on top of the wheelbarrow is the body of a teenage girl. Her face is an unrecognizable bloody mess, but I'd know it anywhere.

It's Steph.

Steph.

And she's dead.

Something snaps inside me. Up until this moment, I thought I'd been carrying around enough rage to incinerate half of Canada. I didn't think it was possible to hold another drop.

I was wrong. The fury inside me now is like a frothing demon. These assholes are going to *pay* for hurting Steph.

Clutching the box of matches and lighters, I race back to the RV and climb inside.

One thing is for certain: Fort Ross is going to burn.

31
Prisoners

ERIC

I don't know if I'm going to live or die. Whatever is about to happen, I know it's going to be bad.

As we're herded at gunpoint inside the looming walls of Fort Ross, my stomach turns. I'm so scared I think I might throw up all over my shoes.

The walls are imposing, the ring of zombies terrifying. The monsters are worked up after the short battle. They moan and keen, jerking against their chains as they attempt to reach us.

"You'll be lucky if Mr. Rosario throws your asses to the dead." The woman with dirty blond dreadlocks jerks a thumb at the zombies as we pass them. Her lips curve into a cruel smile. "Something tells me you aren't going to be lucky."

A crowd has assembled at the open gate, all of them armed with rifles and handguns. They have the same faded, grungy appearance as our captors. Bushy beards, long hair, and dreadlocks are a common theme.

At the front of the crowd stands a large woman with tanned skin. Her gray hair is shorn short. She wears a flowing dark green cotton dress. Birkenstocks cover her feet.

At first glance, she looks like a stale housewife who's

given up on life. Except there's a pocket of space surrounding the woman that bespeaks of deference. And the angry set of her jaw and the fire in her eyes doesn't belong to a depressed housewife.

Without a doubt, I know I'm looking at Mr. Rosario.

A wheelbarrow rolls up beside us. Inside are the bodies of Alvarez's people. On top is the body of the young woman I'd tried to save. I avert my eyes, unable to look at her.

"Jeanie." Mr. Rosario gestures to the dirty-blond woman escorting us. "What have you brought me?"

"Dead slaves." Jeanie jerks a thumb at the wheelbarrow full of bodies. "And these rats killed Jake, Bruce, Twila, Two-Bit, Dave, and Susie." Jeanie delivers a sharp kick to my lower back.

I pitch forward onto the ground, getting a mouthful of dirt in the process. I stay where I am, pretty sure attempting to stand will only earn me another kick.

"Nearly a dozen slaves escaped from the garden." Jeanie plants a boot in Ben's backside, sending him to the ground beside me.

Our eyes meet as we lie in the dirt. I see gritty determination in the older man's face. Good. At least one of us isn't scared shitless.

"And half the fence around the garden is torn down. The deer are gonna get everything." Jeanie kicks Ash into the dirt. She delivers a second kick to Ash's ribs before planting a foot on the back of her head and grinding her face into the dirt.

Ash doesn't cry out or fight. When Jeanie removes her foot, she turns her head to the side, panting for breath. Dirt is smeared all over her face. Her shoulder is soaked in blood.

"The three of you have caused me a lot of trouble," Mr. Rosario says. "Tell me, who sent you?"

Ben speaks up before either Ash or I can attempt to answer. "Medieval John."

As soon as Ben says the name, every drop of sound is squeezed out of the crowd. Not that they'd been loud or raucous to begin with. Even the zombies are subdued.

Medieval John? My mind races. Why did Ben just say that?

"What did you say?" Mr. Rosario's voice is flat.

"Medieval John sent us," Ben replies. "He's taken over the town of Westport."

"Is that so?" Mr. Rosario's eyes narrow. "You're saying you work for him?"

"He sent us to recon Fort Ross."

"Mmm. And you figured you'd shoot up my people in the process?"

"He told us to send you a message. Wanted you to know you're not the only game in town."

Rosario barks out a laugh. "He would. Tell me, what is Medieval John up to these days?"

"He's fortified Westport," I say, afraid to let Ben do all the talking. "He's leading a group of survivors."

Mr. Rosario snorts. "Medieval John doesn't lead. He dictates." She studies the three of us lying in the dirt. "Since he was so kind to send me a message, I'll send him a reply." She jerks a thumb at us. "Get them up."

The crowd around Rosario surges forward. Hands grip my body and haul me into the air. Ben and Ash are likewise lifted.

Wooden buildings of a lost era rise on either side of my periphery, at odds with the motorhomes parked inside. The crowd weaves through the vehicles, carrying us into the heart of the fort.

I fix my gaze on the clear sky overhead. I count the seconds, knowing they might be the last ones I ever experience that are pain free.

I'm hurtled through the air. I bite back a yelp as the hard-packed earth rushes up to meet me.

I hit the ground near an old stone well. I roll, sharp rocks biting into my skin. My glasses fly off. The world around me instantly goes blurry.

Even so, I can see well enough to make out the shapes of Ash and Ben as they, too, are hurtled onto the ground next to me.

Something crunches off to my right. The sound is followed by jeers. I don't have to be able to see to know that my glasses have just been smashed.

You always looked hotter without those things anyway.

For a bare instant, I see Lila. Unlike the rest of the world, her figure is sharp and clear. She gives me a sweet smile, the one she only gave me when we were alone, and very rarely at that.

I swallow, fixing my gaze on her. I know she's a hallucination. I don't care. It's nice to see Lila. I smile back at her.

Something sharp connects with my ribcage. Lila puffs away into nothingness as a rock thumps to the ground. More rocks are hurled at us.

I crowd close to Ben and Ash, covering my head. Rosario's people pelt us with stones, laughing and insulting us as they do.

Are we going to be stoned to death? Is this what's in store for us? How long does it take to die from stoning?

"Enough," Rosario purrs. The rocks instantly cease their pelting.

"I'm going to tell you a story." Rosario comes to stand before us. Her voice booms over the crowd. "It's a story about a man who once went by the name of Donald Rosario. Donald could charm any man, woman, or child. I gave my heart and soul to Donald. I helped him build a booming business. No one came close to rivaling us.

"Then the asshole thought he'd go have himself a little fun. Thought he'd collect himself a few pets to play with on the side. Four of them, to be exact.

"I confronted Donald. I asked him to get rid of the pets and make amends. I was a loving wife. I was willing to forgive and make amends. You know what he did?"

No one utters a word. All I can hear is the constant pounding of the ocean and the distant moans of the zombies.

I think of Kate, Caleb, and Reed. I hope they're safe. I hope they found the people who escaped from the garden and got them to safety. Thinking of them being safe and alive sustains me.

"Donald Rosario laughed in my face. Told me that if I didn't like his pets, I could get the fuck out. Can you believe that? After twenty years of marriage and a booming business, that fucker turned his back on me. And for what? Some lousy teenage cunts?

"So I told Donald to go enjoy his cunts. Then you know what I did?" I can't see Rosario's face, but the tone of her voice sends a shiver across my shoulder blades.

"I put Donald and all his little cunts into a cage. I cut off his balls. Then I left all of them in that cage without food and water. They pissed and shit all over each other for days before they finally died."

Mr. Rosario turns away, leaving us with her story. I'd heard that tale from Reed, though his version had been less graphic.

"Get the slaves," Rosario orders. "Let them all see what happens to people who defy Mr. Rosario."

A contingent of people peels away to carry out orders.

I stay close to Ash and Ben, feeling sick to my stomach. A tiny part of my brain tells me it would be better if we'd died outside of Fort Ross. Death was better than whatever Rosario has in store for us.

"They're pulling Alvarez's people out of a fort building." Ben words are slurred, probably from being punched in the face. "There are more guards with zombie pets on poles. They're herding the people this way."

I squint, though I can't make out anything more than shifting colors and blurred shapes.

The shapes and colors draw near. They're pushed in a tight circle around us. Rosario's people spread out around them. I hear the clacking of teeth and the moaning of the zombie pets.

Now that they're closer, I can better discern the shapes of people. I see men, women, and children. And though I can't make out their individual faces, I recognize postures of abject fear. The cowering forms and hunched backs. The littler forms that cling to the legs of adults.

Mr. Rosario climbs onto a stool to address the people. "These idiots were sent by my enemy to deliver a message to me. They thought it was okay to kill some of my people. It's time for me to send a message back to my enemy."

The air is hushed with anticipation. Rosario flicks her fingers.

Six men advance on us. They're big, muscly men. My mouth goes dry.

"Be strong," Ben whispers to us. "Remember what Kate told us. You are more than your pain. You—"

Whatever else he was going to say is lost in an explosion of pain against the side of my head.

I've never been hit before. Oh sure, Tom and I used to wrestle and knock each other around. Sometimes we were even mad when we did it.

But I've never been punched like the high school dweeb. That's how it feels when the first blow lands. Like I'm the nerd caught by the bullies.

It makes the previous stoning seem like kitten's play.

Blows rain down on me. My head. My stomach. My back. My legs. Everywhere.

I try to go inside myself. I try to remember all the tidbits of pain management Kate taught me.

I can't summon a single one of them.

I curl myself into a ball, wrapping my arms around my head in a feeble effort to protect it.

How long does the torment go on? Ten minutes? Ten hours? I'm not sure.

When it abruptly stops, all I can do is lie panting on the ground.

I thought I was sore after my first day of training with Kate. I thought I was sore after running the Lost Coast. I thought I'd endured the pinnacle of pain when we ran from the fire outside of Braggs.

I was wrong. Until today, I never knew the true meaning of pain.

"Let this be a lesson to all of you." Rosario's voice washes over us. "This is the fate that awaits anyone who crosses me. When we find the other rats who escaped, they'll endure the same fate."

We are hauled to our feet and lashed against large wooden poles staked to the ground near an old stone well. For the first time, I notice another man staked to a nearby pole. He's so still that I can't tell if he's alive or not.

I shift my blurry gaze to my friends. Ash looks like death warmed over. The blood from her shoulder wound saturates the front of her shirt. Ben's face is bloody and bruised. To my eyes, it's a fuzzy array of bright red blood and dark red.

"These three who stand before you are sentenced to death by zombie," Rosario says. "Take a good, long look at them. If any of you fuckers so much as *looks* like you're thinking of rebelling or trying to escape, you'll join them."

The words hang in the air like a hammer.

Death by zombie.

I see the blurry outlines of the pet zombies attached to their leashes. She's going to set the monsters loose on us.

I wish I was dead.

"But first." Rosario holds up a finger. "Let's give the pets an appetizer."

The wheelbarrow is brought forth. Cries of despair go up from the prisoners as the dead are dumped in a pile before them.

"You are dogs," Rosario says. "You live like dogs, and you die like dogs. Jeanie, it's time to feed our pets."

Jeanie and two other lackeys advance with leashed zombies. The monsters go berserk as their questing hands find the bodies of the freshly dead. I force myself not to look away as they tear into the deceased. My only consolation is that they aren't alive to feel the agony.

"Enjoy the show," Rosario tells us. "You three are the main course."

Chuckles rise from Rosario's people. A few of them jeer as one of the dead crunches loudly on finger bones.

"What are you laughing at?" Rosario's voice unexpectedly cracks like a whip.

This time, it's not the Fort Ross residents who cower. It's her own people who back up as she advances on them with a wrath that can only be described as inexorable.

"A dozen of my slaves are missing. More are dead. Some of you are responsible for this. I know who you are. *You* know who you are. Let me be very clear: I want my slaves back." She marches into the crowd of Fort Ross residents and grabs someone. Based on the long hair and thin body, I guess it to be a teenage girl.

The man tied to a pole lifts his head and groans. "No," he croaks. "Not Bella."

"Whoever brings back my slaves can have this bitch for breakfast," Rosario says. "Come back empty handed and I'll stake you up to die like Medieval John's lackeys."

32
Wild Thing

KATE

Reed, Caleb, Alvarez, and I sprint north on Highway 1, racing back toward the semi. The only sounds I can hear are the rasping of my own breath and the pounding of the ocean.

"I have to pee," Caleb gasps.

"Let it out," I say. "Whatever you do, don't stop."

"Did you just tell him to pee his pants?" Reed asks.

"I did." Peeing en route is occasionally done among ultrarunners, especially the men.

Beside me, Caleb lets out of soft moan of relief without ever slowing. "God damn. That feels good."

I glance over and see a trail of urine cut through grime on his legs and ankles.

"Dude," Reed wheezes beside me, also relieving himself. "I just pissed myself. On purpose.

"This is a good reminder of why I don't want to be an ultrarunner," Alvarez wheezes. "You guys are fucking disgusting."

Even though my chest is cramped from harsh breathing, I bark a laugh. The guys join me, their amusement brief and sharp.

"Hopefully we'll live to tell the story to the guys back at Creekside," Reed says.

That sobers the moment. Worry for Ben, Eric, and Ash crashes back in. I lean into the sprint, pushing as hard as I can. The boys keep pace with me.

Thirty minutes later, *Wild Thing* looms into view. The pack of zombies we led here are massed around the semi.

"That's going to be an issue," Alvarez says. "How are we supposed to get to the semi?"

"Just wait," Reed says. "Mama Bear has a surprise."

"Does this have to do with the alpha language you alluded to?" Alvarez asks.

"Yeah. Remember how I told you we were studying alpha zoms? Watch this." I pull out the recorder, unwrapping it from the plastic baggie. "I'll take care of the zombies. As soon as there's an opening, get to the semi and open the trailer. Get the ramp in place."

Alvarez shakes his head at me in disbelief. "Aye, aye, Mama Bear. This had better work or we're all zombie meat."

I hit play. The clicks and keens of the alpha roll out of the speaker.

The reaction of the zombies in instantaneous. They snap around in eerie unison, pivoting in my direction. They totter toward me, moaning and scratching at the air as they unwind from around the semi like a spool.

"Holy fucking shit," Alvarez mutters. He dashes away, following Caleb and Reed as they circle wide around the semi. They head for the newly formed opening.

I grit my teeth, never taking my eyes from the horde advancing on me. I draw them away from *Wild Thing*.

The recording comes to an end. My fingers dance over the buttons, hitting rewind, stop, and play in rapid succession. The clicks and keens play a second time, drawing the zombies farther away from the semi.

A single zombie lurches sideways, away from the rest of the horde. It cocks its head in my direction before letting out a long string of clicks.

Shit. Another alpha. I could use Johnny and his air gun

right now.

Rewind, stop, play.

The horde never stops advancing. Over their heads, I see Caleb, Reed, and Alvarez make a dash for the semi. Caleb snatches the keys stashed on the front wheel. The three young men haul ass to the back of the trailer, unlocking the door and getting the ramp in place.

Many of the zombies twitch at the noise made by the boys, but the alpha recording overrides their instinct to move toward noise. As soon as the ramp is in place, Caleb hauls ass back to the cab and jumps inside. Reed and Alvarez scramble first onto the hood of the cab, and then onto the top of the trailer.

The alpha comes in my direction, still clicking. I keep my eyes on it, hoping it won't choose to issue a conflicting order. Reed and Alvarez pull out their guns, looking to me for permission. I shake my head. The alpha hasn't yet done anything to jeopardize the mission. I don't want to rile up the horde with gunfire if I don't have to.

The alpha continues to move in my direction, head cocked and listening. It looks eerily self-aware.

I make a hard left, putting several dozen regular zoms between me and the alpha. It's comforting to know Reed and Alvarez can shoot if necessary.

Rewind, stop, play.

"Come to Mama Bear," I whisper.

Rewind, stop, play.

The alpha suddenly lets up a long ululating keen, followed by a string of clicks. The sound sends cold shivers across my shoulder blades. The zombies begin to rotate away from me and in the direction of the real alpha. The alpha has turned toward the semi, nose lifted and scenting the air. Shit. Can it smell Reed and Alvarez?

I can't risk it. Johnny said that getting rid of the alphas was the best way to maintain control of the herd. The monster is on the very edge of the horde. I make a hard left, sprinting straight at the alpha. I raise my knife.

I see the moment when the alpha registers the threat. It lets out a long hiss, pivoting to face me.

I spring forward and strike. Hands encrusted with dried blood reach for me, pawing at my clothes.

My knife punches through its skull. The alpha lets out one last hiss before dropping at my feet in a puddle.

Just as it falls, two more zombies close in and reach for me. I stumble back.

Gunfire cracks. The two zombies fall. Shit. I'd hoped to dispatch the alpha silently.

The gunfire acts like a fire accelerant. The zoms instantly switch into feral mode. Growls and hisses run through their ranks as they turn back in the direction of the semi.

"Move, Kate," Alvarez calls. He and Reed keep their weapons trained on the zoms.

I don't need to be told twice. I cut an arc around the zombies and sprint for the semi. Instead of getting inside the cab with Caleb, I climb onto the trailer with Reed and Alvarez.

"Are we going to Pied Piper the zoms all the way to Fort Ross?" Alvarez asks.

I shake my head. "That will take too long. We get as many as we can into the back of the semi. Then we ram the shit out of Fort Ross and set them loose."

"This doesn't feel right." Alvarez's face is somber as he joins me in the back of the semi. "I agree we don't have a better plan, but . . ."

I squeeze his hand. "We'll use the zombies just long enough to overwhelm Rosario's people. Once we have them subdued, I'll drive them out of the fort with the alpha recording."

The plan is loose at best. We all know it. But with nothing else at our disposal, it's our only option.

Drawn by the earlier gunshots, the zombies have already started back in the direction of the semi. I pull out the recorder and position myself over the open trailer door.

Reed grimaces at me. "We're about to load up with passengers from hell."

I hit play. The alpha recording rolls across the road. It may not project like an old-fashioned boom box, but it's enough to get the attention of the zombies.

The reaction is instantaneous. Moans ripple among the ranks. Many of them begin loping toward the semi.

"Holy fuck," Alvarez breathes. "I'm glad we're on top of a semi." He raises his gun, watching the approaching mass.

When the recording ends, the zombies slow, many of them turning in small circles as though searching for their leader.

Rewind, stop, play.

As soon as the recording begins playing again, they resume their forward lope.

In less than three minutes, the first zom reaches the semi. A dozen of them totter up the metal ramp into the truck bed. Another half dozen miss the ramp completely and bump up against the side of the trailer.

"No one ever said rounding up zombies was an exact science," I mutter.

Rewind, stop, play.

I continue to lure the zombies into the trailer. Impatience thrums in my chest. No one ever said a zombie round up could be accomplished in thirty seconds, either.

"There's another alpha." Alvarez takes aim at a middle-aged zombie in a green jacket.

Sure enough, the zom clicks and keens its way down the road. It hadn't been with the main pack a few minutes ago. It must have been somewhere nearby and come when it heard the commotion. A thick knot of zombies follows in its wake.

Alvarez takes his time, waiting until the alpha is fifty yards away. His shot echoes in my eardrums.

The alpha falls. The zombies clustered around it

scratch at the air in confusion.

"Come on," I murmur. "You have a new alpha now."

Their heads cock. Slowly, they turn in my direction.

"That's right," I say. "Come on, assholes."

Another group of zoms reaches us. Another dozen of them ambles into the semi-trailer. Another half dozen scratch at the outside of the truck in confusion, trying to figure out how to get inside.

Play, stop, rewind.

Play, stop, rewind.

In twenty minutes, we have at least fifty zombies inside the semi-trailer. We haven't seen another alpha.

"Time to go," I say. Fifty zoms are more than enough for our purposes.

"I hope you have a plan for getting the door closed from up here," Reed says. "I'm not going down there." He waves his gun in a downward direction, taking in the large group of zoms that's clustered outside of the semi-trailer.

"We aren't shutting the doors," I reply. "We can't waste time getting them back open when we hit Fort Ross. We need instant pandemonium."

I gauge Alvarez's reaction to this. He shakes his head but doesn't argue with me. I can tell from his clenched jaw that he knows my plan is as good as it's going to get.

Reed wrinkles his brow at me. "You're cooking up one scary recipe, Mama."

"I know. Come on."

We hurry back to the cab. Half a dozen zombies have surrounded it. Their broken nails scratch against the paint. I don't want to risk any of them getting caught in the wheels when we drive away from here.

I slide over the windshield, drawing my zom bat. "Come here, assholes," I call.

The small contingent of them growls at the sound of my voice, moving in my direction.

Reed and Alvarez slide down beside me, also armed with knives.

"Here, zombie-zombie-zombie," Reed chants.

"Come and get it," Alvarez growls.

We quickly dispatch them, then climb into the cab with Caleb.

"Fire it up," I tell him.

"But the doors in the back are still open," Caleb protests. "And the ramp is still down."

I shrug. "We're not risking our lives to go back there and button everything up. Drive."

"But—"

"Do you know how to drive this thing or not?" I ask.

Caleb grimaces. "Sort of." He turns the key, letting the big rig hum to life.

Sort of. Well, that's more than I can say. My mouth tightens as I look down the road to Fort Ross. I slide the tape player into the back kangaroo pocket of my pack where it can be easily accessed.

"Get us the hell out of here, Caleb."

The semi lurches down the road. I glance in the sideview mirror and see a few zombies tumble out. The metal ramp shrieks loudly as it's dragged over the pavement. Then unattached at the back, it falls to the ground with a *bang*.

"Instant pandemonium, here we come," Reed says.

"God help us," Alvarez says.

33
Endure

JESSICA

Steph.

A wail of grief breaks out of me as I watch a zombie sink its teeth into the immobile flesh of her arm.

Steph.

What happened to her? Someone shot her, yes, but that's not what grabs my attention.

Her clothes have been ripped. Her jeans are down around her knees.

Someone tried to rape her. I know this instantly. One of Rosario's fucking assholes tried to rape her. My compliance hadn't been enough to protect her.

And now they intend to hurt Bella. I watch as she's dragged into a nearby RV and thrown inside.

No. Fucking. Way.

No man is going to lay a finger on that girl.

And the rest of those assholes are not going to hunt Alvarez down like an animal. Not on my watch. I don't care who I have to kill to save him.

Time for Fort Ross to burn.

I have no plan beyond fire. It's my primary weapon and I have every intention of using it.

Fingers shaking, I dump the contents of the fire-starting box onto the passenger seat. It's covered with a dirty lambskin seat cover. It should go up like a torch.

I fumble with the matches. My hands shake with fury and I drop half of them in my haste.

The door to the RV rattles. What the fuck? Don't they have enough entertainment?

I have just enough time to shove the box under the front seat when Joe Dirt climbs inside.

"It's your lucky day, girlie. I helped capture those prisoners out there. Mr. Rosario has given me some time off. I have *all day*."

The way he drawls those last two words is a promise of slow torture. I resist the urge to back away like a cornered animal.

Alvarez. Steph. Bella. I repeat their names in my head like a mantra. They anchor my feet in place and help me hang onto my sanity. My timing has to be perfect. I'm only going to have one chance at this.

My door opens a second time. Another man steps inside. I name him Bad Teeth. This one hasn't been to see me yet. He scowls at Joe Dirt.

"What the fuck? You had your turn yesterday."

"So what?" Joe Dirt shoots back. "I got here first."

"Well, hurry the fuck up. One of those bitches in the kitchen found some enchilada sauce. She's making stewed chicken."

"I'll take my sweet time and you can wait your fucking turn."

I resist the urge to attack both these assholes with my bare hands. I want to scratch off their faces and rip out their hearts. Adrenaline beats so hard in my temples that I'm half convinced I can do it.

But two against one has never been good odds, even if I do have righteous fury on my side. I have one shot to scorch every last fucker in this place to ash. I can't risk that chance by acting preemptively.

Joe Dirt and Bad Teeth argue for another thirty seconds. I ease close to the window over the sink. Both men turn as the window slides shut. I give them both a flat stare as I pull the curtain closed.

"Come back when I'm finished." Joe Dirt plants his foot in Bad Teeth's stomach and kicks him backward. The other man yelps as he tumbles backward onto the ground.

I turn my back to Joe Dirt as he closes the door and locks it from the inside. He chuckles as I work my way around the RV, systematically closing each window and drawing the curtains.

The rattle of his belt buckle makes my teeth grind. The clump of his shoes makes me want to stab something. The soft crumpling of his pants as they hit the floor makes me wish I had fangs.

He grabs me around the waist as I close the last window. His mouth latches onto the back of my neck.

"Looking for a little privacy with me, hmmm?" His teeth nip at my nape. Each bite feels like poison.

I spin around to face him. I don't smile. I don't pretend. I glare at him with every shred of fury contained in my body.

He chuckles softly and palms my breast. "I like feisty women. You can fight me if you want."

My nostrils flare. I can't fuck this up. One chance. One chance is all I have.

I let him crab walk me back onto the mattress. The cheap springs creak as he pushes me onto it.

34
Hallucinations

ERIC

Mama Bear will come for us.

This is the thought that sustains me as I watch the zombies tear into the flesh of the people who had been massacred in the garden. The jeers of Rosario's people weave with the sound of snapping bones and tearing flesh. Underpinning that are the sobs and whimpers from Alvarez's people as they're forced to watch the bodies of their friends be devoured by zombies.

Mama bear will come for us. Kate always looks out for us, no matter what.

I can't look away from the body of the girl I tried to rescue. Sometimes it's a blessing to be nearly blind. I recognize her by the dark hair and the color of her clothing. I'm grateful I can't see the details of her head and face.

"I'm sorry, guys. I messed up."

"You fucked up." Ben wheezes and spits out a wad of blood. "But your heart was in the right place."

Pain makes my head heavy. The ropes cut into my torso, making it difficult to breathe.

"Have you ever seen those spy movies where the bad guy has a fake tooth in his mouth filled with poison?" I ask. "I want one of those."

"Stay alert," Ben replies. "Be ready for Kate's offensive." Ben's voice is rock-hard with certainty. "She's always at her best when those she loves are threatened."

"She'll come." Ash's voice is a croak, but I'm surprised to hear steel in it. "Kate always comes."

Apparently, I'm not the only one pinning my salvation on Kate. This makes me feel marginally better.

The man staked to the pole beside us stirs. "K . . . Kate?" he slurs. "That . . . that Alvarez's frieeeeend?"

The poor bastard is half dead.

"Yes," Ben tells him. "We're Kate's people."

The man makes another string of garbled sounds. I can't understand anything he says.

"Poor fucker has been bitten," Ben says. "He's turning."

Damn. Bitten by a zom, then strung up on a pole to turn. Rosario's cruelty knows no bounds.

Speaking of which . . . my blurry gaze drifts back to the zombies and their "appetizers." How much longer before Rosario turns them on us?

"Why did you tell Rosario we were sent by Medieval John?" Ash asks.

"She was going to beat an answer out of us," Ben replies. "I gave her an answer I'd hoped would satisfy her."

Well, it *did* satisfy her. But we were beaten anyway. Just not for information.

"I have a confession to make," I tell my friends. "I'm having hallucinations." I glance across the small, hard-packed clearing to where Tom and Lila stand at the front of the crowd.

"Jackalope hallucinations?" Ben asks.

"Sort of. It's Lila and my brother, Tom."

At the mention of her name, Lila rolls her eyes. Tom flashes his frat boy smile and waves.

"My brother is waving to me right now."

"Either of them have a knife?" Ben asks. "We could use one right now."

"Tell the old man I'll leave the killing to the rest of you," Lila says. "But he already knows that."

"I lost my pocket knife weeks ago," Tom says. "It got stuck in a zombie eye socket. There wasn't time for me to get it back. We were overrun."

I don't relay their message. The fact that I'm having coherent conversations with them tells me just how messed up I am right now.

I lean my head to one side and close my eyes, wondering if I can fall asleep. At least if I'm asleep, I won't feel all the pain. If I'm asleep, I don't have to count down the minutes to our execution. If I'm asleep, I don't have to watch the body of the teenage girl I killed get eaten like lunch meat.

"I thought it was bad with Johnson." Ash's bitterness tugs my eyelids back open. "He used to grab me and fondle me whenever Caleb wasn't around." Her throat clogs with anger. "I think life here for these people is ten times worse."

I search for words, but they fail me completely.

"If I don't make it, and one of you do, tell Caleb . . ." Ash's voice trails off, another sob breaking free. "Tell Caleb I love him."

"Finally," Lila says. "Caleb has been, like, waiting *forever* for Ash to let him in." She stabs a finger at me. "You tell her Lila says that."

What the hell? "Lila says to tell you that Caleb has been waiting forever to hear you say that."

Ash half laughs, half cries. "Lila," she says, "I don't know if Eric's fucking *loco* or if you're really out there. If you're out there, I miss your cooking."

Ben wheezes. The sound is part laugh, part gasp of pain. "You're full of shit. You never said a damn nice thing about anything she made."

"I know. But I still miss it. Lila, I miss you. Even if you did make hard pasta."

"It's called *al dente*, Ash," Lila replies.

Oh, my God. It almost feels like we're all back in Creekside, our core group still intact and alive. I can almost imagine away the long miles that have stolen friends and landed me beaten and tied to a stake awaiting execution by zombie.

"What did she say?" Ash asks. "She had to have a comeback. Lila always had a comeback."

"She says hard pasta is called *al dente*."

"*Al dente*, my ass," Ash says. "I've had *al dente* pasta, and let me tell you, those noodles she made were not *al dente*. They were hard and crunchy like crackers."

"Like I said, *al dente*," Lila replies.

"Looks like you found yourself some good friends," Tom says. "I'm glad. I worried about you a lot."

"I never worried about you," I reply. "You've always been at the top of every game. Straight As. Varsity sports in your freshman year. I was always glad mom and dad had you."

"They loved us both."

"I know, but I was glad they had one perfect son. Took the pressure off me, you know?"

Tom shakes his head, a wistful smile on his face. "I saw what you did today, little brother. Believe me, Mom and Dad are proud of you. If there's anyone living in a shadow, it's me."

"Which hallucination are you talking to now?" Ben asks.

"My brother. He was the perfect big brother."

"I had a perfect brother. Guy was an ass hat."

Tom straightens indignantly. "Tell your friend I'm not an ass hat."

"Tom says he's not an ass hat. It's true. He's a good person." I miss him. I miss my brother.

"Even if I die, I'm not going to let those fuckers take my pride," Ash whispers. "It doesn't matter what they do to me. I'm going to die with my head held high."

"No one is dying," Ben growls. "Kate's coming."

There's nothing else to say about that. Lila and Tom try to prod me into talking, but I'm too beaten down to carry on anymore conversation.

There's nothing to do but wait for Kate while the sound of tearing flesh fills the air.

35
Serve

JESSICA

I endure.

For Bella. For Steph. For Alvarez. I endure for them.

Hell, I even endure for Shaun.

I bite my lip so hard it bleeds.

I watch Joe Dirt's face, waiting for the moment. I wait for the orgasm to build in him, for his nasty eyes to roll back into his head.

My hand closes around the tennis racket I slid between the wall and the mattress.

One strike. I have to do this in one strike.

I grip the handle of the racket like it's my last lifeline.

Joe Dirt groans with pleasure. His eyes flutter shut.

I seize the instant.

The racket leaps free of its confines. I bring it down with such force, the nails meet no resistance. They puncture his forehead and the top of his skull.

All those years of playing tennis with those bitchy moms tumbles to bloody fruition. Blood sprays everywhere. Big goopy clumps spill down the front of Joe Dirt's skull.

Satisfaction floods me. I always had a *killer* serve.

I pull up my feet and shove the body away from me. The tennis racket goes with Joe Dirt, lodged in his skull. I yank on my pants and drop to my knees, crawling toward the front of the RV.

It's the only part of the vehicle that doesn't have curtains. I crouch low so no one will see me. My hands shake as I once again fumble with the matches.

A fist pounding on the door makes me jump.

"You done yet?" Bad Teeth calls.

"Wait your fucking turn," I screech.

"Damn," he replies. "You better save some of that for me, honey."

Honey. I grind the word to dust between my teeth. The only thing this honey is going to do is bash in his fucking head.

A single match flares to life. I toss it onto the sheepskin cover and immediately light another.

I light match after match. A small fire licks upward, curling the ends of the sheepskin. I grab another two matchbooks and throw them on.

In less than thirty seconds, the inside of the RV is filled with smoke. I back away from the flames, turning my attention to the tennis racket. Joe Dirt does not get to keep the last gift my ex-husband gave me.

I plant one foot on his chest and grasp the racket with both hands.

"God dammit," I hiss. The damn thing is wedged tight.

"Hey, what's going on in there?" Bad Teeth pounds on the door. "Mitch, you okay? I see fire in the front seat." The door rattles.

In a crackling rush, the entire passenger seat goes up in flames. Another finger of flame races across the ceiling.

The door vibrates as Bad Teeth begins to kick it. "Mitch!" he yells. "Mitch! Guys, something's—"

A huge *boom* rips through the fort. The floor beneath my feet shakes from the force.

Alvarez. He's come back for his people. I know without a doubt.

The heat of the fire crackles over my head as it

continues to spider across the ceiling. I let loose an animalistic scream, my knuckles white around the handle of the tennis racket. It comes free with a sucking sound. Bits of bone and brain matter fly loose. I stumble back a few steps.

The nails in the tennis racket scrape loudly against the ceiling. I maintain my iron grip on the handle. Flames leap onto the dry strings. I don't let go.

The door bursts open, kicked off its cheap alloy hinges. Bad Teeth leaps in.

A half second passes as his eyes meet mine. Confusion clouds his expression as he struggles to absorb in his dead friend and the crazy bitch standing over him with a burning tennis racket.

A half second is all he gets before my racket delivers a raging serve to his face. The nails rake across his skin and tear off half of his nose. He grunts at the impact, stunned. His hands come up out of sheer instinct.

Screaming, I bring the racket down on his head over and over again. I don't stop until it's a pulpy mess.

I stand over both bodies, heart pounding. I raise my tennis racket and scream. And scream, and scream, and scream.

I scream for May. I scream for Claire. I scream for Steph and Bella. I scream for Shaun. I scream for the marriage we lost. I scream for the end of the world and all the people who have died. I scream. The suffering of the world pours out of my lungs while the tiny motorhome burns all around me.

"Jess . . . Jessie!" A weak voice cuts through my incoherence.

Shaun. Reality crashes in around me. I realize my hand is burning. I don't even feel the pain.

I should put out the flame on the racket. But then I see Limp Dick's hulking body rush past the RV.

Another fucking monster who has to die.

A shock of adrenaline courses through me. I leap out

of the motorhome and zero in on Limp Dick.

Part of the south fort wall is in pieces. Someone blew a hole in it. Fire crackles along the edges, illuminating Limp Dick's silhouette.

I close the twenty yards between us in a full-throttle sprint. My burning tennis racket connects with the back of his skull. He drops.

I pounce. The racket comes down with a vengeance, spraying flames in every direction. Nearby patches of dried grass and weeds ignite.

Pain registers as the bulky body of Limp Dick stills on the ground. I drop the racket and smother my burning fingers in the dirt.

The pain is excruciating, but it's only physical pain. It's not even a pinch compared to the hell I've endured in the last twenty-four hours, let alone the last two years. I snatch it back up and sprint toward the RV where Bella is held captive.

The fire is spreading. I see it on the ground eating at small patches of grass. I see it on two other motorhomes. I see it rushing along the two-hundred-year-old redwood timber.

I'm peripherally aware of shouting, running, and general chaos. I barely see any of it. My eyes are locked on the big man who drags Bella out of their motorhome by gunpoint.

He never sees me coming. With a shriek, I swing my nail-studded racket at the back of his head. Just like Limp Dick, he drops. I yank out the racket and deliver another blow to his temple, just to make sure he stays dead.

"Jessica?" Bella gapes at me.

And then a huge semi-truck crashes into the north wall of the fort. The force is like a bomb going off. Chunks of timber fly everywhere. One of the motorhomes is hit, the fiberglass frame crumpling under the impact.

People are screaming and shouting. Guns are firing. My people are being gunned down like cattle.

And then zombies flood the compound.

36
Assault

KATE

"Hold on!" Caleb bellows. "Five seconds to impact. Four."

I brace my feet against the floor as we charge the wall of Fort Ross like a bat out of hell. The semi bounces across the grassland surrounding the fort.

"Three.

In the sideview mirror, I see zombies pitched out of the back. No problem. They'll find their way to the fort.

Two."

I'm coming, Ben.

"One!"

The semi explodes through the north wall of Fort Ross. Timber flies in every direction. Big beams of it smash across the front of the semi. The seatbelt locks, pinning me in place.

The front of the semi plows into a motorhome, smashing right through it. Caleb slams the breaks. Bullets hit the front windshield.

"Everybody out!" I fling open the door and leap to the ground, gun and zom bat in hand. Reed lands beside me.

The compound is consumed by chaos. Fire rages along the south wall, started by the grenades from Alvarez. The old timber is going up like a matchbook. Some of the zombies have already made it past the flames. They stagger through the confusion, swiping at the air as they track down prey.

"People of Fort Ross!" Alvarez bellows. "Fight! Take back your home!" He disappears into the melee, gun blazing, but I still hear his voice. "Fight for Fort Ross!"

Gunshots ring all around us. Smoke boils through the air, illuminated by the flames. I see people rally to Alvarez's war cry. They snatch weapons from their hiding places, taking up everything from frying pans to screwdrivers.

A woman wielding a smoldering tennis racket streaks past us. She's a lithe figure in dark clothing with long hair.

The scream she lets loose it otherworldly. It echoes with the pain of the world. She charges a large man who drags a teenage girl by the hair.

She delivers a wicked, sideways forehand to the back the man's head. The side of her tennis racket connects with his skull. The man drops, releasing the teenager.

The tennis player pounces. Her racket comes down again, caving in his temple. She never stops screaming. Are those nails embedded around the edge of the racket?

"Damn," Reed breathes. "That's one badass woman."

A shriek goes behind us.

"Zombies!" someone bellows. "They've brought zombies!"

"Come on." I grab Reed's arm. "Let's find our people."

The two of us race deeper into the fort. My eyes flick left and right, searching. Where would Ben and the others be? Would Rosario lock them up somewhere? Or would she string them up in a cage like Medieval John?

Fear claws at me. If I lose Ben, it will ruin me. He has to be alive. He *has* to be.

We burst around the side of an RV—and there they are. Ben, Ash, and Eric, all three of them in the center of the fort. They're tied to wooden stakes around an old-fashioned stone well, struggling to free themselves as the battle rages around us.

A zombie canters out of the smoke, white eyes rolling.

I act on instinct. My zom bat comes up, smashing through the forehead with one succinct blow.

Two more zombies appear, hissing as they lunge for me and Reed. I swing my club, smashing in the face of the first. Reed takes out the second one with a knife through the nose.

"Kate! Kate, behind you!" Ben's voice breaks through the confusion. "*Kate!*"

I spin around just in time to see a familiar face appear out of the gloom. A sneering mouth, dirty blond dreadlocks, and a shirt that says *There's no cure for being a cunt.*

Jeanie. Rage ignites in my bloodstream.

She has a gun in her hand, but she doesn't notice me through the shifting smoke. This is the bitch who took me and Frederico captive for no good reason. She attacked Alvarez and Fort Ross. Now the bitch has my boyfriend. She has to die.

I dive straight for her legs, swinging the zom bat. There is a satisfying crunch of bone as my weapon connects.

Jeanie cries out, her leg crumpling under the blow. Her gun goes off, but the shot goes high. I take a second swing with my zom bat and knock the weapon from her hand.

If life were a movie, we'd engage in some sort of verbal repartee. I'd remind her of who I was, she would insult my family, and I'd toss back another well-timed insult.

Frankly, I don't have time for that shit. I don't care if Jeanie remembers me or not. I don't need to have the last word. I just need the bitch to die.

As soon as she hits the ground, I strike again.

I whack her ruthlessly across the face. The crack of bone registers in my senses. I hit her again. Blood sprays everywhere. I hit her a third time, just to make sure the job is finished once and for all.

"Jeanie!"

Another familiar voice hits me just as a bullet grazes my left arm. Pain shoots through me, sucking all the breath from my lungs. The shock loosens the fingers around my gun. It clunks to the ground.

"*Kate!*" Ben's bellow cuts through the pain. A glance in his direction shows me his eyes wide with fear.

I swing back around in time to see Mr. Rosario hustling in my direction. Her large hips roll, her long cotton dress ruffling with her gait.

"You hurt my Jeanie!" Spittle flies from her mouth as she charges me.

I jump to my feet, tightening my grip on the zom bat. My left arm throbs, but I ignore it.

I glare at Rosario. She's next to die, even if she doesn't know it yet. I don't care if I have to die to get the job done. I'm not leaving her on this planet one second longer than necessary.

She levels the gun in my direction as she runs. "You killed my Jeanie!"

My hand tightens around the zom bat that still drips with Jeanie's blood. "Good riddance." I lunge for my fallen gun, trying to get to it before Rosario fires again.

Several things happen at the same time.

Caleb barrels into me, sending me in a tumble across the ground just as Rosario fires her gun.

Caleb lands heavily on top of me. He springs to his feet and hauls me up.

A second shot goes off.

By the time I regain my feet, Rosario is dead. Alvarez stands over her, eyes blazing with retribution. As I watch, he fires his gun once more into her head. Then he turns to Jeanie's body and does the same thing.

Our eyes meet across the carnage. He nods, then turns and disappears back into the melee.

A battle between the two factions has solidified. Alvarez's people fight with the weapons they hid before the takeover—chunks of wood, wrenches, hammers, and rocks. I see one man jam a long metal pipe into the face of his attacker. Some of Alvarez's people have even managed to get their hands on firearms.

Rosario's people fight back, but they're outnumbered. Zombies are everywhere, keeping everyone off balance. Even with superior fire powers, it's impossible for Rosario's people to get the upper hand.

"Get our people," Reed shouts, running forward to head off two zombies who come in our direction.

Caleb and I don't need to be told twice. We race to where our people are staked to poles like Salem witches.

I rush toward Ben. His face looks terrible. It's swollen, bruised, and covered with dried blood.

"You're the hottest fucking thing I've ever seen," he says by way of greeting.

I pull out my knife to slice away his ropes. "You scared the shit out of me."

He shrugs out of the ropes. When he steps in my direction, I notice him favoring his right leg.

"You scared the shit out of me," I repeat, straightening my spine as he bears down on me.

"I'm sorry." He grabs me in a fierce hug, strong arms lifting me off the ground as he kisses me.

Relief floods my body. I wrap my arms around his neck and kiss him back, barely noticing the pain left by the bullet. Ben is alive and in one piece. I cling to him. I don't care if we're both covered with dirt and blood. I'll never let him go.

37
RV

ERIC

There's a battle raging in Fort Ross. The walls are burning, zombies are everywhere, and Rosario's and Alvarez's people are engaged in what I'm pretty sure is a good old-fashioned brawl.

And in the middle of all this is a kiss fest. Ben and Kate on the right, Ash and Caleb on the left.

"Hello? Guys?" I say. "Is anyone going to cut me free?"

The two couples break apart. Kate cuts me free, gathering me and Ash in a quick hug.

"Got your back, bro." Reed produces a pair of glasses. "Lucky for you, some undead out there had a pair. He said you could borrow them."

"Thanks." I slide them on. The world leaps into focus. The prescription is stronger than mine, but all things considered, that's a small concern.

A woman with a nail-studded tennis racket races past us. She and a teenage girl charge after a man with scraggly hair and a wispy goatee. The woman swings her racket like a bat, connecting with the side of the man's head. He drops with the cry as nails puncture his temple.

The teenage girl darts in with a chunk of wood. She raises it over her head and brings it down. The woman with the tennis racket joins her. Together, they make short work of Rosario's man before darting off in search of their next prey.

Damn. Alvarez has some badass ladies around here.

Reed slaps me on the back. Pain ripples across my shoulder.

"Ouch. Careful, dude."

Reed ignores me, wrapping me in a quick bear hug. "Thanks for not dying, dude. Nice to have you not dead."

Ignoring the physical discomfort, I return Reed's back slap and glance past him to the battle raging around us. "Come on. We have to help."

I glance at the nearly dead man still tied to the pole. I want to cut him down, but he looks close to turning.

"Sorry, bro. I'll come back and check on you when all this shit is over."

"Leave me," he slurs. "I'm dead anyway."

Kate, Caleb, Ash, and Ben are already heading into the fray. Reed and I rush after them. The knot of battle is concentrated right inside the gates, a mash of humans and zombies.

Thanks to the new glasses, I can make out the details of the fight. People fight with guns, knives, rocks, screwdrivers, and bare hands.

What I zero in on is the contingent of zombies pouring through the open shattered fort wall. There are already at least thirty of the monsters inside, but there's a huge swell of them racing straight toward the fort.

"Shit," Reed says. "Kate's zombie train. They followed us here. We have to block them from getting inside."

"Motorhome. Come on."

We veer right, heading toward the nearest motorhome. It's an older model, tan with the dark brown W on the side. It looks like a relic from the seventies.

My body protests with every step I take. I lock away the pain like Kate taught me to do. I can focus on it later. When Rosario and all her fuckheads are dead.

Reed pulls out his gun, pausing just outside the door. He hands me one of his knives.

I take his blade and grip the door handle. I yank it open.

Nothing.

I peer around the door—and come face to face with an armed man.

I jump back as a shot is fired. The heat of it sears over my head.

"Right side," I yell at Reed. "He's on the right!"

Another shot is fired. I crouch. Reed sticks his gun into the camper and fires until the gun clicks empty.

"Dammit," he mutters. "I wanted to save a few bullets."

"Didn't Ben teach you to count your rounds?"

"I forgot! It's hard to remember everything, you know?"

We peer around the door, ready to leap back at any sign of life from Rosario's man.

He's dead on the floor, a widening pool of blood spreading across the faded linoleum.

"Good shot, dude."

"What can I say?" Reed replies. "I'm a fucking badass. Come on."

I slam the door behind us and lock it, just in case one of Rosario's men tries to get in. My feet squelch in the fresh blood. I grab onto the kitchen table to keep from sliding.

The inside of the RV is as retro as the outside. It has the same décor it was built with fifty years ago. Wood paneled floor and walls. Orange-and-pea-green plaid upholstery. There's even a macramé wall hanging over the kitchen table.

"Knife," Reed says. "Give it to me."

I knife the dead guy in the temple, then pass the bloody blade to Reed. He wipes it on his pants and plops into the driver's seat. Before I think to ask what he's doing, he rams the blade into the ignition.

"Dude! What the hell?"

"This is a trick Kate told me about. She learned it from her friend on the way to Arcata. These older vehicles are easy to steal." Reed turns the knife handle, grinning over his shoulder at me as the RV sputters to life. "A screwdriver or knife in the ignition works just as well as a key. Now buckle up." Reed throws the motorhome into drive. "We've got people to run over and zombies to block."

I pick up the dead guy's weapon and join Reed in the front. From the vantage point of the RV, I spot Kate and Ben in the fray. Kate has a bandage around one arm. She has the tape player out, herding a large group of zombies away from Alvarez's people. Ben backs her up, a gun in each hand. He shoots anything that tries to attack them.

"Mama Bear is clearing out the dead." Reed grins. "Alvarez isn't the only one with badass women at his disposal."

The motor home rolls forward, lurching and sputtering. Reed aims it right at a group of Rosario's men that open fire on a group of Alvarez's people.

I roll down the window, taking aim with my borrowed gun.

"Shit." I fire just as the motorhome hits a pothole. The shot goes wide. "Avoid the potholes if you can."

"You're the sniper. Snipe something and quit complaining."

The RV picks up speed, chewing its way across the hard-packed dirt. I fire again. A man drops. I then take aim again. Another one of Rosario's assholes falls to the ground.

Reed plows right into two remaining goons. One of them hits the windshield and smashes the glass. The other is catapulted through the air and lands on top of a zombie. Before he can recover, the zombie clamps onto him and bites down on his shoulder.

"Four for four," Reed crows.

He maneuvers the RV around a bigger, larger

motorhome. This is a new Winnebago, a sleek gray one with chrome wheels.

The fire has spread to the north side of the fort. The redwood beams crackle with flames. The zombie horde is closing in, no more than two hundred feet away. Reed pulls the vehicle in front of the opening just as a burning timber crashes across the front hood.

"Please wait until the bus has come to a complete stop," Reed says, mimicking the monotone voice of an airplane safety video. Without changing tone, he adds, "Then get your pretty white ass out of the RV before it catches on fire."

I don't have to be told twice. The passenger side door is right next to the fire. I crawl out after Reed, exiting on the driver's side.

The battle is fading. Alvarez's people are gaining ground, chasing after Rosario's men as they flee.

Kate has managed to herd a big group of zombies on the southern side of the fort. Using the alpha zom recording, she drives them toward the opening Alvarez blew in the wall. Ben, as always, has her back.

I spot the tennis player and her teenage sidekick nearby as they beat another man to death with their weapons. The woman's face is spattered with blood and her hand is badly burned, but that doesn't stop her.

A man stands near the well with a pump and a giant fire hose, shouting for help. A knot of people has gathered there. They roll out the hose. Caleb and Ash are among them. Caleb carries the front of the hose, hustling toward the wall.

"Come on," I say, yanking on Reed's shirt. "They need help putting out the fire."

We dodge through the battlefield, taking out a few zombies as we stumble across them. Reed reaches the line before me, grabbing a big section of the hose.

I draw up short as I spot a zombie materialize from behind a tent. It lumbers southward, drawn to the alpha recording. Its trajectory carries it straight toward Ben.

Shit, he's busy fighting off one of Rosario's assholes. They both appear to be out of bullets. That zombie is going to run right into them while they try to punch each other to death.

"Ben!" Kate cries. "Look out!"

Hearing her voice ignites something inside me. Kate already lost one love. I know how much I still hurt over the loss of Lila, and I was only with her for a few months. I refuse to let some undead fuck hurt Kate.

I raise the gun I stole off the body in the RV. Not as good as a rifle, but it will do. I grit my teeth, set my stance, and fire.

"Eric!" Reed's voice pounds at me. "Eric, dude, *look out!*"

The first bullet clips the zombie, sending him sideways.

Fuck. I rack, chamber another round, and fire.

"Eric! Get down, man!"

The second bullet blows straight through the zombie's head. It drops a mere foot away from Ben as the old man stabs Rosario's goon in the chest with what looks like a half-crumpled tin can.

Pain rips through me.

"Eric!"

38
End

KATE

Like a slow-motion film clip, I see the bullet strike Eric in the chest. Blood explodes outward from his body.

He falls.

"No!" I drop the tape player. "Eric!" I sprint across the fort compound. "Eric!"

It's one of Rosario's men. He clawed his way free from a pile of bodies. No one saw him.

And he's just shot Eric.

The tennis player rounds the pile of bodies, lips pulled back in a snarl. She clubs Rosario's sniper in the head with her nail-studded tennis racket. A teenage girl wielding a large piece of wood whacks him from the other side.

Eric doesn't move.

"No!" I close the distance, skidding across the dirt to Eric's side. "Eric, no!"

Not another one. I can't lose another one of my kids. I can't.

I press my hands over his chest. Blood pumps out between my fingers. One lens of his glasses is completely obscured with it.

"Eric," I sob, watching his eye film over. "No-no-no-no-*no!*"

He rests his hand over mine. "It's okay," he whispers.

"Lila says I'm not a con anymore. And she just called me an ass wipe."

"Eric, don't you dare die on me! Don't you *dare*!"

"Worth it," he whispers. "It was worth it. Tom and Lila are here, Mom."

"Tom?" I shriek. "Who the fuck is Tom? Eric, god dammit, stay with me!"

Everyone comes in a rush of color. Ash, Caleb, and Reed—they're all here. The only one not here is Ben, but that's because he's taken up the tape player and is driving back the zombies.

"Do something!" I shout at Ash. "Help him!"

"There's nothing I can do, *Mamita*," she whispers. "It's a chest wound."

"Bullshit," I scream at her. "*Do* something!"

"It's okay," Eric rasps. "It's okay, Mom."

His eyes glaze over. The hand on top of mine falls away, thumping softly to the ground.

I lean over, burying my face in his shoulder as I sob.

Reed drops to the ground beside us. I raise my face to look into his ashen one.

"I was out of bullets," he says numbly. "I was out of bullets, Mama. I couldn't save him." Tears leak down his face. "I was too far away." Reed lets out a long, agonized groan. He pulls at his hair, more tears gushing from his eyes.

Gripping Eric's body in my arms, I watch my other son's heart break open.

39
Angel

JESSIE

I kneel in the dirt, tennis racket still gripped in one hand. The top is dented, misshapen, and coated with gore. Two-thirds of the nails are gone. Most of the strings have been burned away. The tape that wrapped the handle is charred. So is my hand. I feel the pain from a distance.

I rise from the earth, staring down at the body of Shit Stain.

He's the last of the assholes who raped me. With Bella's help, I got them all except for Homer Simpson. Homer would have been mine, but Alvarez got to him first. He stabbed the asshole four times in the chest. I'm okay with that.

My heart beats in my chest. Satisfaction burns in my blood. All those ideologists who preach turning the other cheek can go fuck themselves. This is the best I've felt in months. Revenge is a dish best served. Period.

I scan what's left of Fort Ross. The battle is over. Rosario's people are all dead.

Half of the fence has been destroyed. Men and women work the well, pumping water onto the flames. Four of the motor homes are beyond repair. All that's left of my RV is a blackened pile of smoldering steel. People scurry back and forth with wounded. The zombies are being driven out of the fort by a salt-and-pepper haired man with a tape recorder.

I turn in a slow half circle, my eyes searching, searching . . .

I spot Shaun. He's exactly where he's been for the last twenty-four hours, tied to the laundry pole.

My heart crumples at the sight of his wrecked, dying body.

I stride toward him, surprised to feel tears stinging my eyes. Bella follows in my wake. We stop before him. My pulse kicks up as I take him in, breathing hard.

He's still alive. The sickness of the zombie bite is apparent. The wound is encrusted with maggots, flies, and dried blood. Ugly, grayish-red veins creep up his neck. His irises are covered in a light white film. By the way he blinks up at me, I know he's having trouble seeing.

I scan the nearby bodies, searching for a knife. Bella spots one first. She retrieves it from the body of one of our people. Cleo had been her name.

Bella hands me the knife with the reverence of an acolyte. Her body is coated in blood. Her eyes are wild and fierce.

Thank God I'd gotten to her before it had been too late. I'd been too late for Steph, but at least I'd saved one of them.

I take the knife from Bella. I slice through Shaun's ropes. The knife is dull, forcing me to saw, but I get through them.

Shawn stumbles as the ropes fall away. I catch him in my arms and gently lower him to the ground. Cradling him in my lap, I press a kiss to his forehead.

Bella stands at a respectful distance with the chunk of wood from the wall. Her eyes scan the area, alert for any threat that may come our way. She's protecting my last few moments with Shaun.

This is the end. Shaun's time on earth is over. Our time together is over.

Sadness seeps across me in a slow warmth. I realize with a shock that my anger is gone, snuffed out. I don't know if it's a temporary paralysis that will return once the shock of the battle wears off, or if some part of me is returning back to life.

"I don't want you to go," I whisper.

A strangled sound gargles out of Shaun's throat. His hand comes up to cup mine.

"I'm sorry, Jessie," he slurs. "I'm sorry for everything."

"Me, too." I hunch over at the pain and sorrow that grip me. "I love you."

"You'll always be my angel."

Angel. That's what he used to call me when we were married. *Angel.*

His hand tightens over mine. I stare into his filmy eyes. And even though I know he can't see me clearly, he can see well enough. Our entire life passes between us. I gather the memories close. I gather *him* close.

When I take in the shape of his eyes and brow, I see Claire. His sharp nose and full mouth had been inherited by our other daughter, May.

There's a moment when I feel like the four of us are together again. Me, Shaun, Claire, and May.

The sensation lasts for the span of a heartbeat. The wind shifts around me and blows it away. It's just me and my dying ex-husband.

"Is he . . . ?"

I look up. Alvarez hurries toward us. He's covered in soot and blood. He looks like he just fought his way out of hell, but he's alive.

He drops to the ground on Shaun's other side and squeezes his friend's hand. A spasm flashes across his features as he takes in Shaun's condition.

"We made it, brother," he says, voice thick with emotion. "We beat them. Fort Ross is ours again."

A smile pulls at Shaun's mouth. His eyes shift from me to Alvarez, then back to me again.

"Take care of each other," he says to us.

I choke on a sob and kiss him one last time.

Then I slide the knife into his temple. Shaun slumps, finally released from the prison of his body.

He's gone. Really and truly and completely gone from my life.

I don't even have our children anymore.

Head and shoulders bowed, I bend over his body in silence. I have no tears, but I do feel sorrow. True, genuine sorrow.

It's more than I've felt in the last six months.

40
Hope

JESSICA

I stand naked in the ocean as the sun warms my face.

Half a mile north, I watch the woman named Kate. Using an alpha recording, she drives the last of the zombies toward a one-hundred-foot cliff above the ocean.

Alvarez credits her with his survival during those initial days of the outbreak. He's never shared any of the details of those days with me, but I can well imagine this woman inspiring Alvarez. I saw her sobbing over the body of a young man she lost in the battle. Anyone with that much love in her heart is inspiring. And since she traveled all the way here on foot to help us, she's clearly as tough as shit. I might not know her, but I already like her.

With Kate are the survivors who traveled with her from Arcata. Ben. Caleb. Ash. Reed. Anyone can see they're a tight-knit group. They follow Kate in a loose circle, ready to kill any zombie that gets too close to her.

My body shivers as the cold salt water of the Pacific Ocean buoys me up. It washes away the depraved acts endured by my body. It feels fantastic.

It's the first time I've been alone today. Bella has hardly left my shadow since I rescued her in the battle. But when Alvarez asked for volunteers to help dig the graves for our dead, she stepped up. I'll find her later and check on her.

I tread water, letting the swells of the ocean lift me up and down. When a wave crashes over my head, I don't even care that my eyes sting from the salt.

One by one, I watch the zombies drop over the side of the cliff. It's a sheer drop onto body-shredding boulders. It won't be long now before every last one of them is gone.

The freezing water continues to rush up and down my body with each surge of the ocean. I close my eyes and let it drench me to my core. The cloudy sky turns the skin of my closed eyelids a light pink.

I don't know how long I float there. It feels like forever, and yet not long enough.

Behind me are footsteps on the sand. I hear the soft grind of grains. It's barely a whisper. But even soaking wet in the ocean and with the battle behind us, my senses are still on high alert. I turn.

"Hey." Alvarez stops ten paces away from the water. "It's just me. I was looking for you."

"Looks like you found me." I turn back toward the water. Maybe if I'm not friendly he'll get the hint and go away. I'm not in the mood for company.

He doesn't.

Instead, he sits down in the sand. "How are you holding up?"

I decide not to pretend. Pretending is a waste of time and quite frankly, time feels like a precious commodity today.

I turn around and face him, swimming close enough to shore that my feet touch the ground.

"I was a mess before the apocalypse. Then I lost my kids. I was raped seven times in one day. I lost Shaun. I'm really fucked up, Alvarez."

His gaze is steady. When he looks at me, I feel like he sees all the way down.

"I don't pretend to know what you've been through. But I guarantee you I'm every bit as fucked up as you are." He looks away and sighs. "Why do you think I work so hard for this community? I can at least sleep when I'm exhausted."

"You don't really expect me to believe that you pour your heart and soul into this community just so you can sleep at night?"

A smile curls the corner of his mouth. "You don't believe me?"

"No," I say flatly.

He shrugs. "It feels good to build something in the midst of all the destruction."

Yes. That was the truth of it. His work at the fort feeds his soul. That's something I can understand. I felt the same thing every morning when I cut off the crust from Claire's sandwiches. I felt it when I ironed Shaun's shirts. I felt it when I measured and cut yarn for Claire's Kindergarten class.

Maybe Shaun was right. Maybe Alvarez and I aren't so different.

I exit the water. Alvarez's jaw drops at the sight of my naked body. He scrambles to his feet, trying to figure out where to look. He settles for looking at my pile of clothing, discarded next to a rock. He makes an awkward attempt to hand them to me.

I wave them away. "I'm burning those."

"Oh." He drops them as if the fabric might burn him. "Do you have any other clothes?"

"Back in the fort." I hadn't thought to bring any with me. When I walked out here, the only thing on my mind was getting clean.

I sit on the sand and let the surf wash over my toes and calves, not caring that I'm completely exposed. I've been seen by nothing but dogs and monsters in the last twenty-four hours. It feels good to be seen by someone who is neither of those things.

I feel him fretting over my nakedness. I ignore him. I'm comfortable. A few hours ago, I wasn't sure if I'd ever be comfortable again. No one is going to spoil this feeling for me. Even if I am starting to shiver from the cold.

Something warm drops over my shoulders. Alvarez's blue flannel shirt. I pull it around me, softly inhaling his scent.

"Is that enough? Are you warm? Do you want me to go up to the fort and get anything else for you?"

"No. This is fine. Thank you." I fasten the buttons, wistful to realize that I wouldn't mind wearing Alvarez's shirts on a regular basis. Too bad I'm so much older than him. Among other obstacles.

Still . . . there was that thing Shaun said. I haven't been able to completely forget about it.

Alvarez waits for me to finish securing his shirt before sitting down next to me. He doesn't speak. We sit in easy silence, watching Kate drop zombies over the cliff. The moment is as perfect as I could ever hope for.

"I'm going to light a few bottles of wine on fire and drop them over the cliff when Kate is finished," Alvarez says. "Incinerate the bodies before the tide comes in."

"You should drop Rosario and her assholes over the edge, too."

"I plan to."

I like the ferocity in his voice.

"What did Shaun say to you?" I ask.

"What do you mean?"

"Before he opened the gates to Fort Ross and let Rosario in. What did he say to you?"

It's not that I don't believe Shaun. It's that I want to know for sure if his words really had the effect he claimed they had on Alvarez.

Alvarez picks up a handful of pebbles and tosses them into the ocean, one by one. He doesn't move or even react the first time the surf rushes past his shoes, soaking his feet.

I wait. I'm not letting this go.

Alvarez throws twenty-seven pebbles into the water before he finally makes eye contact with me. "He asked me to look after you."

As the words leave his mouth, I finally see what Shaun saw: the way Alvarez looks at me. Not as just another sheep in his flock. When he looks at me, I feel like I *am* his flock. I can't remember the last time someone looked at me like that.

"I'm going to kiss you." I deliver these words the way a captain tells his crew the ship is sinking. I give Alvarez to the count of three to protest or make a run for it.

He just looks at me, eyes round with surprise. When I get to three and he's still sitting next to me, I grasp the back of his neck and pull him toward me.

The kiss is salty and warm and sweet. I marvel at the feel of it. It's so much more than pure physical sensation. Something deep stirs inside me at the contact. It's been so long since I've felt anything beyond anger that I can't put a name to what it is I'm feeling.

Then a huge wave barrels into us. Stinging water flings us sideways. I'm knocked to the ground and end up with a mouthful of saltwater. Alvarez's weight rolls over me. A large abalone shell grinds into my ribcage.

I sit up, spitting and wiping at my eyes. I peel long strands of hair away from my face.

A sound tickles my ears. It takes me a moment to register it for what it is: laughter.

Alvarez sits up next to me, chuckling as he wipes saltwater from his face. He grins at me.

His mirth and good humor are infectious. I can't find laughter within me—not yet, anyway—but for the first time in a long time, I find myself smiling. He pulls me close and kisses me again. There's sand between our lips this time. I couldn't care less. Maybe Shaun was on to something.

I'm the first to pull away. "You know I'm fucked up. Like, really fucked up. You could not pick a worse woman in the fort."

"Don't care."

"I could have an STD."

"Maybe. Maybe not." He shrugs. "We can deal with it, whatever the case."

"I'm older than you . . . how old *are* you, anyway?"

"Twenty-four."

The air swooshes out of me. "I'm nine years older than you."

"Don't care."

"There are a lot of women in the fort who would be better for you."

This raises both of his eyebrows. I stare at him, willing him to see the truth of everything I've said in the past thirty seconds.

I make up my mind not to be disappointed if he walks away. It would be for the best.

"You forgot to mention you might be pregnant," he says after a long beat. "I don't care about that either, Jessie. I'll love any baby that comes out of you."

My hands move on their own accord. They cover my belly and squeeze.

What I wouldn't give to have another child. *Children.* I always wanted more children.

The notion of having babies with Alvarez sets me on fire. I swallow and look away, not wanting him to know how much his words mean to me.

My voice is hoarse when I at last speak. "I—I don't think any of those assholes got me pregnant. I have an IUD."

"Either way, it doesn't matter." He reaches out one hand and brushes a wet, salt-encrusted strand away from my face. "What happened to you in that RV with those—those *fuckers* doesn't change the way I feel about you. We'll deal with the consequences together." The side of his mouth quirks. "Nice job killing them, by the way. Shaun mentioned you were an animal on the tennis court. Thanks to you, tennis rackets are now on the short list of favorite zombie weapons."

I. Will. *Not*. Smile. I. Will. *Not*—

Against my will, I smile.

"Do you remember that day we cleared out those houses on Mountain House Road?" he asks.

I remember that day. "We found all that flour and sugar in the caterer's house."

Alvarez waves a dismissive hand. "I'm not talking about the food. Remember when Steph went into the barn and nearly got herself bitten by a zom that fell out of the hay loft? You pushed her out of the way."

Steph. Her name invokes pain in the deepest part of me. "I did that because I wanted the zombie to fall on me. I wanted to die."

"Bullshit. It was because you *cared*."

I don't respond, replaying that day over again in my mind. It's impossible for me to forget the way my chest seized when I saw that zom falling from the loft straight for Steph. Just like it had back in the fort when I saw what would happen to her and Bella if I hadn't volunteered.

"When Rosario asked for volunteers, Bella told me you were the only one who raised your hand."

I open my mouth to protest, but Alvarez quiets me with a gentle hand over my lips.

"You are the bravest and most selfless woman I've ever met. I never said anything to you because Shaun was my friend. I considered him a brother. He told me about Richard, but I knew he still cared about you."

"Not in the way you're talking about."

"I didn't know that at the time. I didn't want to risk my friendship with Shaun so I stayed away from you out of respect for him." Sadness flits through his eyes. I know he's missing Shaun.

I'm missing him right now, too.

"I want to see where this goes, Jessie. You and me." Alvarez's index finger points back and forth between us. "We risk our lives just by waking up every day. I don't want to die never knowing if we could have something."

Have something. A fissure breaks open in my chest. Emotion overwhelms me. Tears sting my eyes.

I wipe them away in shock. I haven't cried since the day May and Claire died.

I grab onto Alvarez, pulling myself into him. His arms come up and he holds me while the waves wash over our feet. I cry softly into his shoulder.

I cry for Shaun, for May, for Claire, and for Steph. I cry for everyone we lost in Fort Ross. I cry for myself and the horror of my twenty-four hours in the RV. Hell, I even cry for Richard.

As the tears flow, a new feeling rushes into me. Something I haven't felt in a long time: *hope.*

I hold onto that feeling, never wanting to let it go.

41
The Real Dead

KATE

One day after the battle at Fort Ross, we gather to bury our dead.

The bodies are lined up in two rows beside the well. Eighteen in all, including those who had been partially fed to the zombies before the battle started.

I kneel beside Eric's body, gently wrapping it in a sheet. With me are Ben, Caleb, Ash, and Reed.

We've all been patched up. Ash was shot in the shoulder. The graze I took in the arm turned out to be deeper than I thought. The two of us now sport stitches. She and Ben are covered with bruises and cuts from their beatings. Caleb has a long gash across his thigh and several cuts on his arm. Lucky for us, there's a real doctor in Fort Ross who tended us.

Only Reed escaped the battle without physical wounds, but he's barely spoken since Eric died. My light-hearted, jovial Reed hasn't cracked one joke. It breaks my heart to see him this way.

I finish securing the sheet around Eric.

"I got him, Mama." Reed scoops up the body of his brother and carries him out of the fort. I follow with Ben, Caleb, and Ash.

Alvarez leads the residents of Fort Ross. The stronger

men and women carry the bodies of the dead, all of them wrapped in blankets and sheets like Eric.

We drift in a long procession through the broken wall on the southern side of the fort, heading toward an old graveyard for the original Fort Ross residents.

Ben takes my hand as we walk, squeezing my fingers. He walks with a limp, his right leg badly swollen and bruised from the beating he took from Rosario.

We enter the graveyard. Russian Orthodox crosses, each one crafted from wood, spread out around us. At one time those crosses had been in straight rows. Time has shifted them. Now they rise up from different directions. Some have fallen over completely.

Eighteen gravesites have been freshly dug. Reed selects one on the end and sets Eric's body inside. I put my arm around Reed and kiss his cheek. He stands stiff beside me, unresponsive. I hug him anyway.

Across the graveyard, I watch Alvarez. With him is the tennis player. Jessica is her name. She and Alvarez have never been far from one another since the battle.

I heard rumor of what she endured in the twenty-four hours that it took us to get to Fort Ross. Of what she volunteered for to protect her people. The memory of her beating a man to death with a tennis racket is forever burned into my brain. It's impossible not to admire her. I can see why Alvarez likes her.

Not far behind Alvarez and Jessica is the dark-haired teenage girl. Bella is her name. I dimly recall Johnny talking with someone named Bella on the ham. This is likely the same girl. She dogs Jessica's heels like a little sister.

One by one, bodies are placed in the graves. Silence descends on the tiny hillside cemetery. The ocean hums in the distance. I inhale the salty air, wishing it could flush out the grief I carry in my heart.

Alvarez makes his way to one side of the graveyard. He stands on top of an old tree trunk, looking out over his people. Jessica stands a few paces behind him.

"Today we lay to rest our fallen." His voice, ripe with emotion, washes over me.

Eric. I squeeze my eyes shut at the sudden surge of emotion. I don't fight the tears. Ben puts his arm around me and kisses the top of my head.

"There are a lot of ways to live in this new world," Alvarez continues. "Some chose to live like Rosario. They find security in breaking things. That's not how we do things at Fort Ross. We have chosen to live differently."

His dark gaze sweeps the gathered crowd. It makes me proud to see the leader Alvarez has become. There isn't a dry eye among us. Even Ben knuckles his eyes.

"We find security in building rather than destroying," Alvarez says. "We find security in each other. In friendships and family. That's how we do things in Fort Ross. Our friends died honoring the way we've chosen to live. Never forget that. We all do our part to hold back the darkness. Whether that means fighting zombies in our backyard or protecting the community we've built, we've all chosen to make a stand against the darkness. Always remember those who sacrificed everything so that we may have a future that's built on community and family. Never forget that we *are* a family. Every last one of us. We are brothers and sisters of the apocalypse. We are strong. Together."

A sound emerges from Reed's throat. This time, when I pull him in for a hug, he doesn't fight me. He hugs me back and sobs into my shoulder.

"I'm so sorry," I whisper to him.

He says nothing, just hangs onto me like I'm the only thing keeping him from blowing away in the breeze.

42
Strong

KATE

"Have a little more." Alvarez fills my cup with another splash of wine.

"Thanks." I take a long swallow and pass the cup to Ben, who sits beside me.

His injured leg is propped up on a rock. "I forget this is considered wine country."

"We're on the fringe of wine country," I reply. "The town where Carter and I lived before the apocalypse is true wine country. Vineyards everywhere." I take the cup as Ben hands it back to me. It's been a long time since I've enjoyed wine. I sip the zinfandel, savoring the flavor.

We sit around one of several large bonfires. Large kettles of stew sit over the fires, filled with rehydrated meat scavenged early in the apocalypse. Alvarez pulled out all the stops for the wake. He insisted on it, even if it plundered half of their supplies.

"We can scavenge tomorrow," he firmly told a woman who protested. "Tonight, we celebrate being alive and honor those who are no longer with us."

Alvarez even authorized the use of an iPod and a small portable solar charger. Music plays near the well. People dance and laugh.

Ash and Caleb are with them. I watch their silhouettes,

arms entwined. They haven't left one another's side since the battle. I like seeing them happy together. The barrier that sat between them for all these months has finally been broken.

Even more amazing than the food, music, and wine are the showers. Alvarez has no less than six solar showers in Fort Ross. I made sure I had my turn under the warm water. It's nice to have grime-free hair and a body free of blood splatter. All of us are officially the cleanest we've been since we left Creekside.

Ben helps himself to another portion of stew. "We really need to get some cows at Creekside. We need to eat real meat once in a while."

"Right. Cows. Check." I wrinkle my nose at him. "We have *so* much excess pastureland. We should try to find a whole herd."

Ben takes my sarcasm in stride. "Then we have to find some chickens. That needs to be a priority when we get back." He plops back into his chair and digs into the stew. He offers me a spoonful, which I gladly take.

"Speaking of returning to Creekside, when do you guys plan to leave?" Alvarez asks.

I'm careful not to look at Ben. His limp is still pronounced, though he never complains.

It's not just Ben's leg. Ash doesn't complain, either, but I can tell how much it hurts to lift her arm after being shot. My own arm aches and itches like crazy.

"In a few days," I say. "We'll stick around to help you guys refortify the fort." I push up the arm of my shirt. "It'll give time for this wound to heal."

"That's a baby wound," Ben says. "Show them your scar from the other gunshot wound."

Alvarez spits out his wine as I roll my sleeve all the way up. "Fuck," he says. "Is that where Frederico shot you?"

"Yep."

"Some asshole gave you some serious Frankenstein stitches." He winks at me. "Sucks to be you, Kate. It's amazing you managed to get yourself a boyfriend with that thing."

I roll my eyes.

Jessica purses her lips as she studies my arm. "Are you the one who stitched her up?"

Alvarez pours himself more wine. "Maybe."

"*You* did that?" Bella gapes at my arm. "Were your eyes closed?"

"They were definitely *not* closed," I say.

"Where did you learn how to sew?" Jessica asks.

"He learned by watching his grandma sew patches onto his jeans," I offer, taking another drink.

"No wonder it looks like shit," Bella says.

Alvarez waves a hand in protest. "Don't hate a man for being shitty at women's work. At least she didn't bleed to death."

Jessica raises an eyebrow at Alvarez. He ignores her and takes a long gulp from his cup.

I chuckle, settling back into my chair. "You're definitely much better at leading Fort Ross than you are at stitching people up."

"You can stay here with us," Jessica says abruptly. Even in a fuzzy sweater, she sits with an edgy alertness I don't think will ever go away. She looks like she could go from docile to wrathful tennis player in less than three seconds. She's even taken to carrying the dented tennis racket on her belt, much the way I carry my zom bat.

"You'll always have a home here at Fort Ross," Alvarez agrees.

I shake my head. "Our home is in Arcata."

"Besides," Ben says, "who's going to come rescue your asses the next time you get in trouble? We can't do that if we stay here."

"I think the old guy just made a joke." Reed stabs a finger in Ben's direction. He's been a bit more talkative since the burial this morning, though I have a sad feeling it will be a while before the old Reed fully returns to us. If he ever does.

"Don't worry," Ben replies around a mouthful of stew. "That will be my last one for at least six months."

"Thank God." I raise my brow at him. "I didn't sign up for a funny boyfriend. Stoic and reliable. That's what I signed up for."

"Don't forget badass motherfucker," Ben replies.

I burst out laughing.

"That wasn't six months," Reed points out. "That was, like, barely six seconds. Someone is frisky tonight."

It might be the firelight, but I swear I see a flush creep up Ben's neck. It's hard to tell with all his attention on his stew. He stops chewing only long enough to take another swig of wine from my cup.

"Have you thought about how you're going to get back?" Bella asks. "I mean, are you really going to run all the way home? I played soccer before the apocalypse. I'm good at running."

Alvarez tugs on the long braid that hangs down her back. "Are you auditioning for Creekside or something?"

Bella huffs and bats his hand away. "I'm just saying I was a good runner before the world ended."

"We'll take a few of the bikes and ride back to Braggs," I say. There's a pile of them left behind by Rosario.

"We should take *Wild Thing*." Reed gestures toward the semi, which has been parked in front of the hole in the south wall of the fort.

I shake my head. "*Wild Thing* is where he needs to be. Bikes will serve our purpose. Once we get through Braggs, we'll make our way back to Westport to get our friend. I'm hoping we can negotiate with Medieval John for a boat ride back to Arcata."

"That asshole will want all our guns," Ben says. "You can't give him our guns."

"I'm not going to give him our guns."

"So what are you going to offer?"

"I'm working on a few ideas. I'll let you know when I

figure it out."

Ben snorts and takes another sip of his wine.

"You think you can trust that guy?" Alvarez frowns at me.

"You were the one who once told me we need friends more than we need enemies."

"That sounds like something Alvarez would say." Jessica's eyes soften as she looks at him.

"Ideal to a fault?" he asks her.

She shakes her head. "No such thing."

We remain before the fire, talking and laughing. At one point, I even notice Reed and Bella move to the far side of the fire. They appear to be having a cozy chat. That's nice.

I'm having such a good time that I lose track of hours. It isn't until I start yawning that I realize it must be near midnight.

"You done here?" As usual, Ben reads me like a book.

"Yeah, I'm ready to turn in."

"Let's go. I'll show you where we're sleeping. The Creekside Crew has graduated from that tent we had last night."

I won't say no to a real building to sleep in. I froze my ass off last night, even though I'd been sandwiched between Ben and Reed in the tent.

We say goodnight and rise from the fire. I cross my arms across my chest for warmth. When Ben puts his arm around me, I lean into his solid strength.

As we near one of the old wooden buildings in the fort, Caleb comes out the front door. A grin splits his face when he sees us.

"Hey, old man," he calls. "Got something for you. Found it in the supplies." He tosses a small Ziplock through the air.

Ben catches it with one hand. I assume it's a bag of pot or something else drug related. When I lean forward to peer into Ben's hand, I see three square plastic wrappers. I do a double take when I realize what they are. Color creeps up Ben's neck, obvious even in the dark.

"Good thing you're finally making your move." Caleb saunters by us, a smug grin on his face. "I was gonna make a move on Mama Bear if you didn't get off your ass. I like older women." He winks at me.

Ben finally finds his voice. "Fuck off, you little shit."

"Uh-huh." Caleb never breaks stride. "I'm pretty sure I'm not the one you want to be fucking." Chortling, he saunters away.

I stare at the condoms in Ben's hand, pieces clicking together in my head. Caleb's words. Ben's odd behavior earlier tonight. Reed's use of the word *frisky*. My mouth goes dry. Equal parts nervousness and excitement course through me.

Ben, scowling at Caleb's retreating form, shoves the baggie into his pocket.

"Little shit," he growls.

My voice completely fails me.

We enter the old building, closing the thick door against the coastal chill. The solar panels on the roof power lights in the inner hall and second-floor landing.

"The room is upstairs."

I look sideways at him, wondering what he means by *the room*. When he first offered to take me to the sleeping area, I'd assumed we'd be sharing a space with everyone else from Creekside like we had last night. Now I'm not so sure. Anticipation prickles across my back and neck.

I follow him up to the second-floor landing. He pushes open a thick wooden door and lights a candle inside the room.

A single air mattress sits in the far corner.

On the floor at the foot of the mattress are two running packs: mine, and Ben's. There are no other belongings in the room.

Air whooshes out of my lungs. I'm suddenly back on the bridge in Braggs. I see Ben almost die all over again. I taste my own helplessness. The old terror boils up, making my chest tight.

I turn to him and meet his eyes, but can't bring myself to close the space I've abruptly put between us. All my fears sit between us like a wrecking ball.

He opens his mouth, closes it, then opens it again.

"I'm going to try and say the right thing." His voice is husky. "I asked Alvarez if we could have a room. I—" He swallows, then tries again. "We can just sleep, Kate. Just tell me what you want."

I want him. More than anything, I want him.

Remembered pain freezes my feet and eats up my words. The pressure in my chest mounts, making me feel like I might burst open. I don't know how to put my feelings into words.

"I . . ." Sucking in a deep breath, I try again. "I've only ever been with one man."

"Your husband." He nods, his expression folding in on itself. "You miss him."

"No. I mean, of course. I'll always love Kyle. But I said my goodbye to him on my trip to Arcata." I squeeze my eyes shut as a wave of emotion breaks over me. I feel the pain of unbearable loss all over again. It was a pain so unspeakable it had me holed up in a dark room for days until Carter and Frederico dragged me into the sun. The idea of going to that dark place again terrifies me.

"I wasn't the same person before the apocalypse. I wasn't strong. Losing Kyle almost broke me." I open my eyes, searching Ben's bruised face and willing him to understand. "I don't think I can survive another breaking, Ben. I don't want to be that broken person ever again." Tears sting the back of my eyes.

Compassion softens his features. The awkwardness between us dissipates. He pulls me against his chest, holding me tight. His arms feel so good, so safe. His heart, strong and steady, beats against my cheek.

"Nothing breaks our Mama Bear," he murmurs. "You're the strongest person I know, Kate."

A bitter laugh passes my lips. "You didn't see me. You don't know how far I descended into darkness." I don't like to think of those days.

"But you found your way out. That makes you stronger than all of us who've never fallen into the dark hole. You're a mama bear, Kate. Those kids didn't give you that name to make you feel good."

"But even mama bears can die." I think of the bear we killed back on the Lost Coast.

"Yes. Mama bears can die. But that's not the same thing as breaking."

He's right. The tension in my chest loosens, like icebergs cracking apart under the summer sun. His words release the fear I've carried around ever since the day he nearly died on that bridge in Braggs.

I wrap my arms around his neck, squeezing him tight. "How do you always know how to say the right thing when I feel shitty?"

"It's a gift, I guess."

"If you applied those superpowers to the rest of the day, you'd be a lot more popular."

Ben leans back and looks into my face. "There's only one person I want to be popular with. It's the only reason I try so hard. I don't give a shit what anyone else thinks."

Despite everything, a soft laugh escapes me. Blunt to a fault.

I lean into him, softly kissing his lips. He returns the kiss, cradling me in his arms. It makes me feel precious.

The kiss deepens. Our bodies meld as he presses me up against the wall. Fire fills me from head to toe, thundering beneath my skin. I'm so desperate for Ben I can hardly breathe.

He breaks the kiss, pressing his forehead to mine. "I want you, Kate," he rumbles. "I want you right fucking now. Can I have you?"

In answer, I kick shut the door to our room, sealing us away from the world.

43
Goodbye, Hello

KATE

Five days later, we leave Fort Ross before dawn.

Our running packs are stocked with water, food, and extra clothes. The bicycles stand in a neat row outside the fort, waiting for us. Alvarez and Jessica are there to see us off.

The only one not here is Bella. She's never far from Alvarez and Jessica, but maybe she decided to sleep in today. That's what normal people do in the pre-dawn hours.

"Radio us when you get back to Creekside," Alvarez says. "I need to know you're safe."

"Of course she'll radio you," Jessica says. "You guys have standing bi-weekly phone dates."

"Just be safe, okay?" Alvarez squeezes my forearm. "I'm going to worry until I hear from you again."

"Don't worry," Caleb replies. "If shit goes south, Mama Bear will figure out a way to get us out of the trenches."

"She always does." Ash leans her cheek against Caleb's shoulder.

I give Alvarez a long hug. "Be safe. Kill anyone who tries to take over the fort." I glance at Jessica. "Take care of him, will you?"

She answers by lacing her fingers with Alvarez. Her free hand fingers the handle of her tennis racket. Yeah, Alvarez is in good hands.

"Let's move out," Ben says. "We're burning daylight."

Ash snorts. "It's not even dawn."

Ben ignores her, grabbing one of the bikes.

The rest of us follow suit. I wave to Alvarez one last time before pedaling up the hard-packed dirt road that leads back to the highway. My arm is still sore from the partial bullet wound, but it's minor compared to the other pains I've suffered on this trip.

As soon as we hit the open road, we pick up the pace. It feels weird to be riding rather than running, but since we drew just about every zombie between here and Mendocino, I feel the roads are relatively safe and clear.

"Mama."

I slow, waiting for Reed to catch up with me. The others pedal ahead of us.

His once-dancing eyes are somber as he pedals up beside me and stops. "I'm not going back to Creekside, Mama."

I stare at Reed in confusion, sure I misunderstood him. "What?"

"I'm not going back to Creekside."

"What do you mean you're not going back to Creekside? That's your home."

Reed looks away. "I know. I just . . . I just need to be alone for a while. I don't want to make a big deal about it. Tell the others I'll see them later."

"See them later? What the fuck does that mean?"

"I'm going to strike out on my own for a while."

"Reed." I can barely comprehend this conversation. "We're your family. You can't go."

"Don't worry. I found you a replacement."

"A *replacement?*" My voice goes up serval octaves. "What the hell are you talking about?"

Movement on the east side of the road. Bella emerges

from behind a cluster of bushes, pushing a bike.

"I want to go back to Arcata with you," she says. "I . . . I can't stay at Fort Ross."

"Will you take her back to Creekside, Mama?"

"I'll take you both back to Creekside. Reed, you have to come home."

The look he gives me is anguished. He throws his arms around me in a brief hug. "I love you, Mama. I'll see you soon."

Without another word, he turns his bike around and pedals away from me as fast as he can.

"Reed!" I scream, not caring if I alert every undead between here and Hawaii. "*Reed!* Come back!" I spin around, glaring at Bella. Emotion crowds my chest. "What the fuck just happened?"

"He blames himself for Eric's death," Bella says softly.

"That's bullshit." I drop the bike and cup my hands over my mouth. "Reed! Reed! Please come back!"

He keeps pedaling, never turning around at my call. I stare after him, feeling like I've been drop-kicked.

"Reed," I whisper.

"What's going on?" Ben pedals up beside me, closely followed by Caleb and Ash. He takes in the scene, looking from me, to Bella, to Reed's retreating form.

"Reed isn't coming home with us." My voice is strained. "He blames himself for Eric's death."

"He told me he and Eric were side by side for the entire fort battle, except at the very end," Bella says. "That's when Eric was killed."

Ben sighs and gives me a sad look. "You have to let him go, Kate."

"This is bullshit, Ben. We're his family. He belongs with us."

"He has to do this, Kate."

"He wasn't like this when we lost Jesus. They were even closer than he and Eric were."

"Doesn't matter. That was a different situation. He's

processing guilt and grief in his own way. That's his right."

"God dammit." I pound my fist on the bike seat in frustration. "I miss Eric, too! You don't see me riding off into the sunrise by myself."

"Didn't you tell me a story about a death that almost broke you?" Ben says softly.

I feel like I've been slapped. I spin around to face him, unsure if I want to scream or cry.

"You have to let him go, Kate."

My shoulders sag. Ben folds me into a hug. I cling to him, my heart constricting with grief. *Reed.*

"Reed is smart," Ash says. "He'll be okay."

"And when he gets bored, he'll come back home," Caleb adds.

I don't reply. They're just trying to make me feel better. For all they know, we may never see Reed again.

I push away from Ben and turn to Bella. I think back to the night of the wake when I saw her and Reed talking together on the other side of the fire. Here I thought they'd been having a cozy chat. I know for certain that's when they'd hatched the plan that's unfolding right now.

"Do Alvarez and Jessica know?" I ask her.

"I left them a note. They'll try to talk me into staying if I tell them in person."

Ben studies her. "You're looking for a fresh start. A place away from the memories here."

Bella nods.

I recall her friendship over the ham radio with Johnny. Maybe she has a future in Creekside. I can't deny it to her if it's really what she wants.

"You're welcome in Creekside," I tell her. "But are you sure this is what you want? It could be a permanent decision, Bella. It's not like we can just hop in the car and drive you back here if you change your mind."

Bella doesn't hesitate. "I'm sure. I love Jessica and Alvarez, but I need to start over."

I look one more time down Highway 1. Reed has

completely disappeared from sight. It makes my heart heavy.

I let out a long sigh. Ben is right. I need to let him go. I can only hope his journey into grief isn't as dark as mine had been. Regardless, I have to let him have his journey.

Just as I need to let Bella have hers. "Welcome to the Creekside Crew," I tell her.

44
Neighbors

KATE

A day later, the town of Westport comes into view. In the time that has passed since we were last here, the wood and corrugated metal wall has more than doubled in size. They've even installed an impressive gate made of the same material.

The cages with Rosario's dead still hang from the telephone poles at the entrance to the town. They don't even bother me anymore. After all that Rosario and her people did, I wouldn't care if the lot of them were strung up in cages.

We jog in a tight cluster up Highway 101. The sun is out. A cool breeze slides in from the ocean, chilling my lips, the top of my nose, and my fingertips.

We've been on foot ever since we crossed through the town of Braggs a second time. Our pace is a moderate, easy lope. Every ten minutes, I give the group a walking break. Mostly for Bella's benefit, but in truth, we're all still exhausted and beat-up from our ordeal. Bella's cheeks are ruddy with the effort. I can tell by the look in her eyes that she's determined not to complain. She'll be a good addition to Creekside.

"You ran your first half marathon today," I tell Bella.

She blinks at me in surprise. "Really?"

"It's fifteen miles from Braggs to Westport. A half marathon is thirteen-point-one miles."

"You logged a few more miles getting through Braggs," Caleb adds. "You're probably at twenty miles or so."

A satisfied smile pulls at Bella's lips. It doesn't touch her eyes. Even so, it's more expression than she's shown in the last day with us.

"Don't get too excited," Ben says. "You won't be able to walk for a week."

I poke him in the arm. "Killjoy."

"Someone has to tell her the truth." His voice is flat, but I see the twinkle in his eye. He's messing with me.

"He's joking," I tell Bella.

"No, he isn't. But it's pretty cool to say you ran your first ultra." Caleb grins up at the sky.

The friendly banter makes me miss Reed and Eric more than ever. The two of them would be in the thick of this conversation.

I try not to think too hard about where Reed might be right now and what dangers he might be facing. He made his choice. There's nothing I can do. I can only hope he'll come back to us one day.

As for Eric . . .

My heart tightens. I breathe through the sadness.

"Just be glad you didn't have to fight a bear." Ash gives Ben a sly wink. "That's what the old man had to do on his first ultra."

"Your hypothermia was pretty shitty," Ben replies. "I'd take an angry bear over that any day."

Bella soaks in our words without comment. All her focus appears to be in putting one foot in front of the other.

Smart girl.

Distant shouting from Westport draws my attention. A figure slips out from behind the new gate.

"Kate!" Susan waves her arm in the air as she races

down the blacktop in our direction. "Kate!"

A grin splits my face. I pick up the pace, racing toward Susan. We collide in a hug, grabbing onto one another like our lives depend on it.

"I knew you'd be back." Susan dabs at tears that run down her cheeks. "No one believed me. But I knew Mama Bear would be back."

I lean back to study Susan. "Are you okay? Did John keep his promise?"

Susan nods. "He's not a bad guy." She wrinkles her nose. "He's kind of scary, but so are you." She throws her arms around me for another hug. "God, I'm glad you're back. I want to go home."

Home. I want to go home, too.

"Well, well. I have to admit, I never thought I'd see any of you again." Medieval John saunters down the road in our direction. Fanning out behind him are half a dozen armed men and women.

"I *told* you she'd be back," Susan says, hands on her hips.

"Indeed, you did."

"We're not that easy to kill," I reply.

John grins at me. "Apparently not. Did you kill Rosario?"

"Yep."

"Everyone at Fort Ross is okay?" Susan asks. "They . . ." Her voice trails off at the look on my face.

"Eric didn't make it," I tell her. "Reed . . . Reed decided not to come home. Fort Ross lost people, too."

Grief flashes across Susan's face. "Eric and Reed are gone?"

I nod.

"But Fort Ross is free of Rosario?"

I nod again.

"No one was gonna get out of that fight for free." Medieval John slaps me on the shoulder. "You did good, Kate. This calls for a feast."

My mouth waters at the thought of food, but I'm careful not to let my eagerness show. "Are you offering a trade?"

His smile is disarming. "Everything is a trade, Kate. But I'll make this one easy for you. All I want in exchange is every gory detail of how that bitch died."

Susan leans over to whisper in my ear. "That's a good trade. They just brought in a big haul from a root cellar in a nearby house. The people have enough canned fruits and tomato sauce to stock a small convenience store. They're making spaghetti tonight."

John watches this exchange with a wry twist to his lips. "Loose lips sink ships, Susan."

She rolls her eyes. "Not when you have a ship captain on hand."

The last thing I want is a long, drawn-out affair in Westport. But I'd be an idiot to blow off a hearty meal. Besides, as eager as everyone is to get back to Creekside, we're all hungry and tired.

And so it is that I find myself sitting at a large table in an elementary school cafeteria, shoveling food into my mouth while my companions and I relate the story of Fort Ross.

With us at the table are John and a handful of his scarier looking people. Most of them look like they could crush rocks with their bare hands. These were probably the people who helped him keep his pot business secure before the world went to hell.

More people from Westport crowd around us, many of them standing while they eat, eager for the story. It's nice to see that John welcomes them all.

I wish Reed were here. He was the best storyteller among us. Ash, Ben, and Caleb do their best to help me as I recount the story, but none of us has Reed's charisma.

Bella doesn't say a word during the whole ordeal. The young woman sits at the far end of the table, inhaling food like she hasn't eaten in a week. I don't miss the stiff way she moves, even while sitting. No doubt she hurts from head to toe after our journey here from Fort Ross.

"Tell that one part again." John waves a hand at me, dabbing sauce off his mustache.

"Which one?"

"The part about the woman with the tennis racket."

The audience cheers when I recount the way Jessica bashed in heads with her tennis racket. They hush with awe when I tell them why she killed with such a vengeance. Bella seems to fold in on herself as I tell the story again. I make it a point to leave her out of it, even though she'd been the avenging angel's sidekick.

"Did you say she's married to the leader of the fort?" John asks when I finish.

"Basically." I don't want John thinking he might have a shot with Jessica. She's with Alvarez.

John sighs dramatically. "Too bad. She sounds like a fine woman." He takes that moment to look me up a down. "There is a shortage of fine women out there."

Ben scoots close to me, giving John a pointed stare. "All the good ones are taken. Sucks to be you."

I elbow him in the ribs while John roars with laughter. Ben just glares and snugs an arm around my waist.

"So." John takes a sip of the clear liquid in a shot glass before him. Apparently, there's moonshine production taking place in Westport. "What's your next move, Mama Bear."

I put my fork down. I've been waiting for this. By the look on John's face, so has he.

No reason to beat around the bush. "We want to go home to Arcata. As quickly as possible. I want one of your boats."

John's expression is that of a very satisfied cat who's found himself a plump mouse. "You'd like one of my boats."

"Yes." Without a boat, there's no fast way back to Arcata. We'll have to go miles and miles out of our way.

Medieval John knows this.

"I rather liked that cannabis salve you gave me on your last trip through here. I'd like the recipe."

"I've got something better." I push my empty bowl aside, resting my elbows on the table.

"What might that be?"

The table has fallen quiet. The people of Westport lean forward, eagerly watching the open negotiation. The only one who appears uninterested in the whole affair is Ben, who helps himself to another generous portion of pasta.

"I'll give you alpha zom recordings." During the entirety of my tale, I noticed John made no comment about them. That alone was enough for me to gauge his interest. He wants them.

But he's not about to come out and admit that. "That might be of interest."

God, he's such a bullshitter. "I'll give you all three of them, plus the next two commands my people uncover in the future."

"How do you know they'll uncover more in the future?"

It's my turn to give him a flat stare. "You wouldn't ask that if you knew the guys on the job."

"One of whom happens to be my husband," Susan adds.

"Trust me when I say they'll uncover more commands. Do you have a ham radio?"

"Not here. But I know of a few places where I might acquire one."

"We have a working one in Arcata. Dial us up when you get one and we'll pass on the commands when we have them."

The alpha recordings could be the difference between life and death. It's a good fucking deal. John knows it.

But that doesn't mean he isn't going to try and get more. "Let's talk some more about the cannabis salve."

For some reason, this rankles. No fucking way will I

give him Lila's recipe. It feels too much like giving a piece away of her. I won't do it. Besides, it could be a precious Creekside commodity in the future. I would be an idiot to give John everything of value in our first serious trade negotiation.

"Let's talk about the alpha recordings instead," I reply. "Those are the only things on the table. We both know five of them are worth more than one boat, but that's all I'm asking for."

"But you're only giving me three. You don't have the other two yet. A bird in the hand is worth two in the bush, you know."

He's not going to make this easy. We spend the next fifteen minutes arguing the point. John keeps pushing for the salve. I keep refusing.

Just when my temper starts to steam, Ben interrupts us.

"I got something to sweeten the deal." He pushes away his empty spaghetti bowl.

Medieval John raises an eyebrow. "Something sweeter than a cannabis salve recipe?"

"Yep." Ben downs the shot of moonshine on the table in front of him. "It's something you don't know about Rosario."

"What's that?

"She'd died thinking Medieval John was the reason for her undoing."

The crowd had been silent up until now. Or at least, I thought it was silent. The moment Ben speaks, a hush falls over the entire cafeteria.

John's eyebrows climb up his forehead. "Did she, now?"

"Yep. When she captured me and beat the shit out of me and tied me to a pole so that I could be eaten alive by zombies, I told her I was sent by Medieval John. She died without ever finding out it was complete bullshit."

"You told Rosario that *I* sent you to Fort Ross?"

"Yep." Ben helps himself to another shot of moonshine. No one stops him.

"He did," Ash confirms. "They beat the shit out of both of us when he told her that." She rubs at the bruises still darkening her face.

"Let's say I believe you," John says. "Why would you tell her that?"

Ben gives John a flat stare. "I was hoping that if I gave her the answer she wanted to hear, she wouldn't try to beat the answer out of us." He shrugs. "She beat us anyway. Basically, I got the shit kicked out of me in your name. And Rosario died thinking you were her undoing. If that's not worth a ride home, I don't know what is."

Medieval John throws back his head and roars with laughter. He laughs so hard tears stream down his face. The tough guys at our table guffaw with him, slapping one another on the back as though they've all just heard the best joke of the century.

I study Ben's face, trying to discern if he's bullshitting. One look in his eyes and I know he's not.

"My friends," Medieval John says at last, "you got yourselves a deal. One boat in exchange for five alpha recordings and the sweet, sweet knowledge that Rosario died thinking I was the one responsible for fucking up her grand plan." He slams both fists on the table so hard, all the bowls and silverware rattle. "Damn, I like you guys. I foresee a hearty trade between our communities in the future. Now, tell me all the details. I want to know everything."

"Sure." Ben pours himself another shot of moonshine. He downs it, pours himself one more, then launches into the story. There's a flush to his cheeks and his eyes are bright.

I can't help but laugh as John makes him tell the story not once, not twice, but *three* times. Each telling is accompanied by another few shots, so that by the time Ben gets to the third re-telling the bottle on the table is empty.

He doesn't even slur. I guess my boyfriend can hold his liquor.

His story becomes more lurid and detailed. He has everyone in the cafeteria hanging on his every word. They *ooh* and *ahh* and wince at all the right places. They cheer every time when he retells the part about Alvarez putting a bullet in Rosario's head, skillfully driving home the point that she died thinking John had come to take the fort from her.

Who knew Ben could spin a good story? I guess hidden talents come out when a person has moonshine. Lots of it. It's practically a miracle drug.

Under the table, Ben squeezes my knee. I give him a grateful smile and return the squeeze.

We've done it. With his help, we've closed the deal with Medieval John.

We're finally going home.

Epilogue
Right Here, Right Now

KATE

"What are you doing?"

Two days after our return to Creekside, I stand in the doorway to my dorm room watching Ben wrestle a second bed into the tiny space.

He grunts, kicking aside a pair of shoes that are in his way. "What does it look like I'm doing?"

"It looks like you're moving a second bed into a room only designed to hold one bed."

He raises an eyebrow at me. "Is that what it looks like? I thought it looked like I'm moving in with you."

I lean against the doorframe, refusing to help him. The leg of the second bed gets stuck in a pile of dirty clothes I left on the floor. Ben scowls in my direction as he levers the pile to one side with his foot.

"You're going to have to learn how to use a laundry basket." He opens the closet, glowering as he comes face to face with the previous owner's clothing. "And we're getting rid of this guy's clothes. The only man's clothes that are going to be in this room will be mine."

I fold my arms over my chest. "Is that so?"

"Yes."

I suppress a smile. This playful side of Ben has been coming out more and more lately. I like it that he lets his guard down enough to banter with me. Caleb said it had something to do with him getting laid, but I pretended not to hear that.

"Were you going to ask me about any of this before you decided to move in?" I ask.

"I thought about it." He gives the bed a shove, grunting in satisfaction as it slides into place.

"You thought about it and . . . what? Decided not to bother asking?"

He slides around the bed and comes to stand in front of me. My blood heats as he looks down at me. He presses me up against the doorframe and kisses me until my knees are weak.

"I decided I was moving in regardless of what you said."

I huff as he breaks away. He turns around to tackle the closet, yanking out armloads of things that belonged to the previous occupant.

"I told you I wasn't dropping this thing between us." He flings out baggy jeans and T-shirts with pithy slogans on them. "This is me not dropping it."

I decide to quit pretending that I'm mad. I like that he's making space for himself in my life. Even if that leaves us a mere eleven inches between the bed and the closet. Walkways are overrated anyway.

"Hey, Ben."

"What?"

"I'd take a bullet for you."

He extracts his head from the closet. His eyes crinkle around the edges as he gazes at me. "I'd take a bullet for you, too. Any day of the week, Kate. Don't ever forget it."

He returns to his task of emptying the closet.

"I'm still throwing my dirty clothes on the floor," I tell him, just to see what his reaction will be.

"You think so?" Three pairs of dirty sneakers are ejected out of the closet.

They land by my feet. Damn, they smell awful. Maybe

that's part of the reason this room always had a rancid scent. And here I thought it had been me and my stinky running clothes.

"Yep." I kick the rank shoes out in the hallway one at a time. I suppose I should have cleaned out this closet months ago. If not for Ben, the room wouldn't look as good as it does. He covered every inch of wall and ceiling with pictures of nature for my birthday a while back.

When I straighten up, Ben is standing in front of me. "I'm the only one who will be throwing your dirty clothes on the floor."

I squawk when he scoops me up and kicks the door closed. He tosses me onto the bed and lowers himself on top of me. I melt into him as he kisses me. One hand slips under my shirt to grip my waist. I unfasten the top button of his fatigue shirt, ready to do my part in adding dirty clothes to the floor.

"Dude, I could have gone my whole life without seeing that," says a voice.

Ben and I jump apart like two kids caught making out in the janitor's closet.

"What the fuck?" Ben yanks at his fatigues, fingers automatically flying to the top button.

Caleb stands in the doorway, thumbs hooked in the pockets of his pants. He raises amused eyebrows at us. "You guys really have to get into the habit of shutting the door. No one wants to see old people going at it."

"Who are you calling old?" I ask.

"The door *was* shut," Ben growls.

"The door was definitely *not* shut," Caleb replies. "It was *mostly* shut. I wouldn't have been stupid enough to open it without knocking if it had been *completely* shut."

"What do you want, Caleb?" My voice might be a tad squeaky.

He grins at me. "Gary sent me to get you guys. The welcome-home dinner is ready. For what it's worth, I *may* have kept walking if Gary hadn't spent the last six hours preparing the meal. It's not legal to miss out on food someone worked so hard to prepare." He saunters away, leaving me and Ben to collect ourselves.

"The door was shut," Ben snarls. "That little fucker just wanted to fuck with us."

I kiss his cheek before climbing off the bed. "Come on. There's a feast waiting for us." I pause, looking down at him. "I'm glad you moved in. I like having you here."

His eyes soften. He takes my hand and kisses my knuckles. Hand in hand, we head into the main common room.

In the days we've been gone, a lot has changed. Carter got it into his head that we needed to "open up" the main dorm suite. He enlisted Margie, the kids, and Christian to help knock out the walls to the bedrooms. The result is jagged sheetrock and exposed beams, but the suite actually feels like an open common room now. Christian and Carter even brought in more tables and sofas from other rooms. For the first time, there's a seat for everyone.

"About time, lovebirds," Jenna says as we enter the room. "Gary, can we eat now?"

"Hold up." Gary waves a spatula to ward off Kristy and Evan. The two kids dart back and forth, eyeing the four casserole dishes sitting on the counter.

"I just want to say a few words before we dig in." Gary has graduated from his wheelchair to a walker. His leg will never completely heal from the shark attack, but it's good to see him mobile. "First off, Kate, congratulations on a successful mission to Fort Ross. From everything I've heard, you guys did a hell of a job crashing Rosario's party." He salutes me with his spatula. "May we all have semi-trucks and zombie armies at our backs when things go south."

Chuckles run around the room. I laugh and return Gary's mock salute.

"Let's take a moment and acknowledge those of us who didn't make it back from the mission to Fort Ross,"

Gary continues. "Eric and Leo, we salute you, brothers. You will be remembered."

Gary picks up two rocks from the kitchen table. They've been brightly painted with flowers. The names *Leo* and *Eric* adorn each of the rocks. Without a doubt, they are Jenna's handiwork.

"Will you do the honors?" Gary holds the rocks out in my direction.

I place them on the shrine erected by Jesus that still sits in the common room. It's a plastic tub spray painted red. Inside is Jesus's St. Roch medallion and a vase with plastic flowers. Though the shrine was built to honor St. Roch, it's become a way for us to remember the family members we lost. Eric and Leo's rocks now sit next to the ones made for Lila and Jesus.

I face my Creekside family, recalling Alvarez's words at the burial. "We'll honor their sacrifices and their memories by living our lives to the fullest. They died in the name of friends and family. We'll never forget them."

Murmurs of agreements run around the room.

I bow my head. Leo. And Eric. I'll carry both of them with me. Always.

And Reed. I can only hope he'll come back to Creekside someday.

"Okay." Gary bangs his spatula on the countertop. "Let's eat!"

I step aside as people bustle into line, eager to dig into Gary's casseroles.

I take in our small community. Laughter and happy chatter washes over me. The kids zip around the room, playing tag while adults shout for them to slow down.

So many are missing from Creekside. Jesus. Lila. Eric. Reed. Of the original Creekside crew, it's just me, Jenna, Carter, and Johnny.

But since those early days, we've added new family members. There's Ash, Caleb, Ben, Susan, and Gary. There are those from Leo's group, too: Todd, Christian,

Margie, Stacy, and the kids, Kristy and Evan. And our newest addition, Bella from Fort Ross.

I don't know what the future holds for us. Creekside might get new family members. We may lose others. All I know for sure is that I plan to enjoy this moment.

Right here, right now.

Acknowledgments

To all the ultra rock stars in my life who help me bring these books to life: THANK YOU!

Linda Bellmore
Lan Chan
Victoria deLuis
Joe Dulworth
Jayson Fowler
Chris Picott
Andy Salas
Jon Theisen

Printed in Poland
by Amazon Fulfillment
Poland Sp. z o.o., Wrocław

64147626R00171